I0573944

The Heat Cure

Addison James

To everyone who spends every day in pain. May we all find a love as supportive as Mickey.

Contents

Content Notes

This book contains:

*Depictions of chronic illness, including high levels of pain, light and sound sensitivity, nausea (including vomiting), fatigue, and brain fog

*Depictions of chronic pain related to the American healthcare system and medical gaslighting

*Discussions of past bullying (non specific)

*Discussions of neglectful parenting

*An emotionally manipulative ex-boyfriend who makes ableist comments

*Discussions of past domestic abuse, emotional and physical (non-graphic)

*Discussions of pregnancy, birth control, and abortions (the FMC is not actually pregnant)

*Alpha/omega dynamics, including consensual heat sex with the slightly dubious power dynamics associated with heat

*Multiple sexual scenes

*18+ language

Please put your mental health first. If you'd like any further clarification on any of these topics, please don't hesitate to reach out to me on my socials or via email at addyjames@addyjameswriter.com.

Before You Read

Paige, the main character of this novel, is one of my favorite characters I've ever written. Authors shouldn't have favorites, but Paige is a character who ended up taking on a lot of me.

Paige has a chronic pain condition called New Daily Persistent Headache, or NDPH. NDPH is characterized by the patient developing a headache one day that isn't explained by other causes, and the headache just never goes away. It is constant pain. For many, Paige included, the pain fluctuates between tolerable and full-on migraines.

I've had NDPH since I was a child, so a lot of Paige's experience with the condition is personal. The way her pain and the sensory needs caused by her condition interact with her sensory needs as an autistic woman, and the way she navigates a healthcare system steeped in gender bias, is all very real.

While omegas are fictional, I've always found the dynamic of alphas and omegas an interesting lens for exploring gender. Paige's health insurance company making decisions about her body based on her gender is something unfortunately rooted in a reality that woman and marginalized groups frequently face.

Nalcodin, the medication Paige is fighting for, is made up, although it is based on a real class of drugs. No drugs currently exist that specifically target NDPH.

In this story, the goal isn't being cured. Stories where chronic illnesses are "cured" by unrealistic means erase our very real struggles of building lives around and within our medical conditions. Rather, the point of this story is the love, support, and deep understanding we can receive along the way. Mickey might be a fantasy, but real people like him do exist.

If you see yourself in Paige, I see you too—and I hope you find your person the same way she does.

CHAPTER 1

Paige

"**Y**ou have got to be kidding me." Emma throws her hands up as she stands and starts pacing her brother's living room. "They *can't* do that to you."

"They can," I say calmly. I've already got the big feelings out, in the privacy of my own home, tucked away in my nest, just like I always do. Watching me melt down is no one's idea of a good time.

Emma gives me a cutting look, which is fair. Since we practically shared a nest during our teen years and then shared a college dorm room for four years after that, it's not like she hasn't seen me having big feelings before. She knows full well what I'm trying to hide.

But if there's one thing I've learned, it's that big feelings get you nowhere. At best, it earns me the *poor little omega; the world is too big and bad for a delicate creature like you* look, which is pretty intolerable. And anyway, it won't change anything. "They can do any-fucking-thing they want," I remind her. "That's kind of how the system works. If I want this new drug, *and I do*, then yeah. This is the cost."

I'm lucky, I tell myself again. Lucky that I live now and not fifty years ago. And that's for a lot of reasons, but right now that's mainly because the drugs they're coming out with to treat migraines seem to actually be working for people.

And okay, migraines aren't exactly my problem, most of the time. But they're close enough that neurologists keep trying to medicate me like it is. And just because it hasn't worked yet doesn't mean it won't start working.

Nalcodin is brand new, just hit the market, and is an injectable that's supposed to be the miracle anti-migraine maintenance drug. And more than that, this drug is supposed to have some success with my issues, too.

New Daily Persistent Headache is the ugly stepchild of the headache world. Caught somewhere between *what's that, again?* And *it's just a headache, how bad can it be?* NDPH doesn't get drugs targeted specifically at this condition. At best, they treat me with migraine drugs. At worst, they ignore me.

That's been my experience for twenty-two years now. I've been in pain every moment of every day, but the rest of the world seems to barely care. It had been teachers who found out I was sick before my parents, which, looking back, isn't surprising in the least. There'd been two schools of thought among the teachers and other staff: Paige is having sensory issues and freaking out at lights and sounds and she's probably autistic, and Paige is having sensory issues and there's something wrong causing her actual pain. Turns out, two things can be true simultaneously.

So at six years old, my school nurse advocated for my mother to take me to the doctors, which she did, presumably because it would look bad if she didn't. They ran all the tests. Eight years later, I had a diagnosis. A diagnosis, but no treatment.

For twenty-two years, I've dealt with this pain. I've lived it and done all the grieving and learned to process that it's part of my life. I plan around good days and bad days, and got good at advocating for the accommodations I need. And I've come to accept that medical science doesn't consider me a priority.

Except Nalcodin actually *has* been used in a study specifically targeted at patients like me, and there's some proof that it *works*. It's not a cure, but it can make the pain more manageable. I want it, and my neurologist wants to give it to me.

But it'll cost about fourteen thousand dollars a year if my insurance doesn't cover it—and they absolutely refuse until I exhaust every option.

I thought twenty-two years of pain, suffering, and trying drugs over and over again was exhausting my options. I've done acupuncture, tried stupid diets, and been hospitalized four times for adverse reactions to different drugs. I've suffered with fucking miserable headaches since I was six. But that's not enough for them.

"And you called, right? You escalated it? You know you have to push these things, the rules are meant to stop you, but if you speak up a lot of times you get what you want and—"

"Of course I called. It didn't help." Emma means well, because there was a time when I wouldn't have known to speak up. But I'm not fourteen anymore. I got myself to college and law school. I'm a trained lawyer and I know exactly how to fight for myself. I've spent my entire life advocating for my own accommodations.

But in this case, it didn't matter. I'd spent an hour scripting out exactly what I would say. I'd even taken the legal angle, preparing to talk about lawsuits. But the phone call had gone the same as when my doctor called: no heat, no drugs.

"What did the doctor say?" Emma asks after a moment.

I grimace, remembering the conversation. "She was sympathetic." And Dr. James had been. She's been the neurologist I like the most, mostly because she's optimistic without over-promising. And she's never implied that my pain is something related to being an omega or my other sensory issues, and she'd been apologetic about what the insurance company is demanding. "She had her nurse look up heat clinics for me. My insurance will cover *that*."

And hadn't *that* been a slap to the face?

There's a clanging sound from the kitchen, and I wince. I hadn't exactly forgotten that Emma's brother is in the next room—we're in his damn apartment, after all—but he's kept

4

quiet, and I'd managed not to think about him listening to my medical woes. Which wouldn't be that bad; I don't usually blurt out my medical information, but Mickey knows enough that it's not exactly a secret. He was there for most steps of my childhood, and as a result has seen me in super embarrassing, compromising positions. I don't have many secrets from Mickey. I wouldn't mind him knowing, up until I'd dropped this bomb.

A fucking heat. I can barely talk to Emma about this, and Emma has heats willingly. She's gone off suppressants by choice and has had three heats with her little pack and is desperately trying to conceive a baby, and I figure if she can tell me that, then I can tell her this, even if it still feels embarrassing.

Emma was there the first time I got my period. Emma and I started our suppressants around the same time and used to help each other keep track of taking them when they were new. I heard every one of her dating stories when she started making her pack. I know way more about Avery, Philip, and Jackson—her alphas—than I really want to. Emma is a safe person to talk to about this, if I have to talk to anyone.

Mickey? That's just embarrassing. Not that he's not *safe*, because Mickey is undoubtedly one of the safest people I know. But there are some things you don't tell anyone who's not your best friend in the entire world.

"So, are you researching the heat clinics?" she asks. "When are you going to do this? I know you like to take your time and do your research, but—"

"I'm not going to a heat clinic," I hiss, feeling the visceral disgust just thinking about the idea.

She looks at me. "They're perfectly respectable, Paige. Don't say it like that, like they're sketchy. Plenty of people who can't or won't use suppressants use heat clinics. If we stigmatize them, then we stigmatize omegas' health."

"I know that. You think I don't know that? I care about omegas' health and heat clinics are great. I write letters to my congressperson about omegas' health laws and sign petitions and donate money and all that. But I'm *me*. I won't have strangers touching me," I say adamantly. "I'll go out of my fucking mind."

I've had sex with exactly one person and come to the conclusion that it sucks. Or maybe I suck at it, I'm not sure. The idea isn't unappealing, but this seems like a time that reality didn't match what's in my head. I'm not trying it again for the first time with a group of strangers.

Emma's hand drifts up to one of the bite marks on her neck. She does that sometimes when she's thinking about them, without even noticing she's doing it. "When you're in heat, it's all different. You probably won't feel the same—"

I school my face into neutrality, which isn't that hard even when my brain is screaming. Right. A heat will make me not *me*. Paige and her quirks, Paige who hates being touched wrong, and all that. But not if I give into those omega instincts and have a heat.

Because being an omega in heat is so *wonderful* and *natural*, and how do I know I'm not in pain because I'm suppressing that side of me, hm? How do I know if I don't let myself be a *normal* omega, I won't miraculously feel better? That's the insurance company's gamble, anyway. Make sure nature won't magically fix me before they shell out the cash for the drugs.

Fuck them.

"I won't," I tell Emma resolutely.

Emma comes to a stop and sits beside me. She leans close, closer than I like most people getting who aren't her, and frowns. "Then what's your next option?"

I shrug. "Ride out a heat. Plenty of sex toys. You know. The basics." When I'd been less than enthused about the heat centers, the nurse had reluctantly offered some sex toy brands that simulate "almost life-like" knots. *That* had been a fun conversation.

Emma sucks in a breath. "That's dangerous, Paige. Omegas end up in the hospital for that."

Honestly, I'm kind of hoping I do. And that it costs the insurance company thousands. I need to prove that just giving me my doctor-prescribed medication would be the better choice.

But no. They'll probably somehow weasel out of the bill.

There's another clang in the kitchen. What is Mickey doing in there? I know there's a stereotype that alphas can't cook, but the man lives alone. Surely he's figured it out by now.

Emma looks over toward the kitchen and rolls her eyes. "Mickey, is the chicken beating you up?" she calls out to him. She doesn't raise her volume much, and his near immediate response makes me cringe, because yup, that's proof he heard me talking about everything, including *sex toys*.

Mickey's going to think I'm a loser. That's an irrational thought, because if Mickey was going to think I'm a loser, he'd have thought it a long time ago. Mickey's seen me crying in pain and having complete shutdowns and hiding in his sister's nest. Mickey beat up the kids who bullied me when I was in middle school. He's had plenty of opportunities to think I'm a loser.

Maybe he already does. Maybe he's thought it for ages and just never said it. Maybe everyone knows it but me—I'm not great at figuring those things out if people don't say them out loud.

But that feels wrong. For one, Emma wouldn't let me be around someone who thought of me that way without saying something. And for another, Mickey used to bring me ice packs when I practically lived with them as a teenager. He'd bring them to me in his sister's nest, where we both slept, and never touch a single thing in there, never step a toe out of line. He's a good guy.

He's too good a guy to think badly about me for something like this.

"Fuck you, Em," Mickey says. Only Mickey can say that and not sound at all threatening. Mickey is a big guy. Not like those fitness model alphas who look like they could bench press cars and like they live off of protein powder, but like a guy who looks like a bear. Tall, broad, strong with a layer of softness, and now with the lumberjack beard to match, Mickey doesn't look like someone who could sound soft, but I've never known him to be anything else.

He steps into the wide open archway between his kitchen and living room, leaning against the buttercup-yellow wall. "If you want dinner done a certain way, then come do it yourself."

Emma sniffs. "I'll have you know I don't cook in my home."

"Spoiled," he taunts, but it has no bite, and Emma grins.

"Happily and completely. And I expect the same service here."

"You're in town two weeks and it feels like ten years," he grouses, but we all know he doesn't mean it.

When Emma left town two years ago because Avery accepted a job out of state, we were all sad to see her go. Video calls aren't the same. So having her back for their parents' anniversary celebration has been great.

Her alphas came for the anniversary and left, but Emma stayed, getting a little more time with us before she goes back home.

I like Emma's alphas. She met Avery our first weekend in college, when they'd shown the two of us how to get back to our dorm when we got hopelessly lost. It's like the first time the two of them met, it was all over. Emma and Avery had heart eyes from day one, and I'd adjusted to having them in our life. The other two had fallen into place over the next three years. Jackson was in Emma's computer science classes, and Philip was Jackson's oldest friend turned lover. The four of them are thick as thieves, bonded for life, and seem happy for it.

I miss her when she's gone, but I'm happy for her. Just because it's not the life for me doesn't mean that I can't see how happy Emma is with it.

When Mickey leaves us alone, Emma turns back to me, our prior conversation apparently not forgotten. "Paige. Sex toys are *not* enough."

"Well, I haven't decided yet," I hedge.

Her face lights up. "So you're considering the heat clinic?"

She looks so relieved; how do I tell her I'm deciding if the new medication is worth it? Dr. James seems optimistic about this one, and I trust her judgment more than most, but every doctor is convinced every drug will be *the cure*. Twenty-two years in, and I'm still in pain.

"We'll see," I tell her, because what else can I say?

CHAPTER 2

Mickey

I take out some aggression with my knife-work when cubing the chicken.

I try my absolute hardest not to be seen as a particularly *aggressive* alpha, but I think it's justified here. Paige is sitting in the next room, describing the current fuckery of her life, and I want to stab something more substantial than chicken breast.

I've always wanted to fight the myriad of demons that haunt Paige. Bullies I could fight, and she's found her own ways to fight people who say shit about how her brain works over time. She developed a cutting tongue sometime in her teens that I'm still proud of today. I've wanted to fight her parents, too, but they've remained tragically out of my reach. And her nervous system, sadly, isn't something I can fight.

But I'm beginning to think I'd like to go a few rounds with some insurance executives.

For what, my brain whispers, mean-spirited but not wrong, *for making her uncomfortable and being fuckwads, or practically forcing her to have a heat with someone who isn't you?* My knife stabs into the cutting board hard enough that there'll be a permanent mark there.

Heat clinics are perfectly respectable and, as the name suggests, clinical. They're professional spaces and do a great service for omegas. Omega's health initiatives are critical and heat clinics are a cornerstone of that. I've never said a word against them and I never will. But I don't want Paige there.

It's not just because I am apparently becoming a selfish asshole, either. I know Paige won't like being touched like that. It'll be too much for her. All it would take is one wrong touch, one careless move, and she'd no longer feel good.

I've never been such a haphazard cook in my life, but I eventually get multiple plates made and set them on my small table. "Ladies! Dinner's up."

"Oh," I hear Paige say, "I should go, I—"

"I made food for you," I interrupt her, frowning even though she can't see me. Doesn't she know she's always welcome at my table?

Paige walks into my kitchen, wearing her signature leggings and a pink t-shirt, her hair piled into a bun that I rarely see her without. Her sweet lavender and woody scent follows her, and I know my house will smell like her for days. It's the sweetest torture. She takes a seat next to Emma, and I breathe a sigh of relief. But it's not until we're all sitting together that I realize I have no idea what to say.

Hey, I heard you mentioning the heat your doctor is forcing you to have. Yeah, no thanks. That's half a step from sexual harassment.

Emma's the one who breaks the silence, because of course she is. My sister, who couldn't keep her big mouth shut if her life depended on it, and I've never been more grateful for it. "Bill and Mom sent me pictures earlier."

"Yeah?" I ask. "Why didn't I get pictures?"

"Because, you heathen, you don't know how to reach out first. Want to see?"

Do I want to see our mom and Bill on their silly cross-country road trip to celebrate being married for fifteen years? Fuck yeah.

So we all look at the series of pictures, laughing at how Bill still can't take a selfie, and dinner passes quickly enough.

Paige glances unsubtly at the clock behind me. "Well, I think it's time for me to get home," she announces, and I hide my smile. Same old Paige.

Emma walks her to the door while I get the dishes, but I can hear them still. My apartment isn't that big.

"I'll miss you," Paige tells her, her voice slightly muffled. Probably in one of those bone-crushingly firm hugs that, as far as I know, only Emma is allowed to give her.

"Hey, we'll call."

"I know, but who the fuck said you were allowed to move?"

"I married a rocket scientist, and Avery had to go where the rockets are. It's not my fault they're brilliant."

"Not a good excuse. Work from home is popular now."

"You building rocket pads in your backyard?" Emma laughs. "They have a habit of literally blowing things up at work. I'm sorry, but Avery is not a *work from home* type of person. It's just not happening."

I don't hear whatever Paige says next, too muffled, but Emma laughs slightly. "I'll call you on Saturday, you goof. Have I ever missed one?"

"No," Paige admits.

"Mhm. And I want to hear about your decision, alright? Don't think I forgot."

Paige grumbles and then leaves. Once the door clicks shut, Emma makes her way back into the kitchen, pressing one hip against the counter to watch me wash up.

"She going to be okay?" I ask, because it's useless to pretend I didn't hear any of it.

Emma frowns. "I don't know," she admits. "They're really fucking her over."

"Will it hurt her?" I can't help but ask, which is stupid. I know it will.

"Probably not if she goes to a heat clinic," Emma hedges, but I know Paige won't. I know she'll try to stick it out on her own.

But I don't tell Emma that. If I do, Emma won't leave to-morrow, will tie herself into knots and stay here, even though she can't exactly help Paige with this problem and she has her own family to handle.

But I don't. And it might be greatly overstepping, and it might be rude as fuck, bordering on harassment, but I know I have to find a way to help Paige.

⌒꙳⌒

"Let me get this straight: you want advice on how to fuck your sister's best friend?" Andre asks me, and I can hear the suppressed chuckle.

"Shh!" I hiss while looking over his shoulder to make sure we're still alone. We're technically in the break room, but it doesn't actually have a real door, and I know from experience little ears are everywhere.

"Sorry, sorry," Andre mutters, but he's still laughing, the asshole. "Listen, I don't know if you think this is some sort of omega hive mind thing, but I can't actually tell you how to seduce her. We aren't all the same, and I've barely met her."

"I know that," I mutter. *Dickwad.* I bite my tongue so I don't say that last part out loud. I know there's not a magic *get an omega to fall for me* button, alright? "And I'm not looking to fuck her." It sounds weak even to my ears.

I've wanted to fuck Paige for a long, long time, but it's way more than that and, more to the point, completely not something that can happen. I'm only letting myself entertain this because Paige needs me, and she's going to hurt herself.

15

Andre rolls his eyes, leaning back in his chair. His sandwich is long since forgotten on the table, but I'm irritated enough that I'm not going to remind him. There's only five minutes left on his break, but if he has to go face the after school teen rush on anime club day without proper nutrition because he was too busy laughing at me, then that's his problem.

"Hey, April!" he calls, alerting everyone in the world that something interesting is going on here. April's desk in reference is right outside the breakroom, and we both hear her ancient squeaky chair push back before she sticks her head in. "Mickey here is looking to seduce an omega."

She raises an eyebrow and then steps back out. I think for a fleeting moment that she's decided this is beneath her, that she doesn't need to deal with us, but nope—she comes back. So she's put the annoying little *back in a minute!* sign on her desk and walked away then, because my suffering is entertaining to these two assholes.

April and Andre are some of my favorite two people in the world outside of my family, but there are days where I have no earthly idea why.

"Alright, I'll bite," she says, coming to sit down. "Who?"

"No one—" I start, but Andre is all too willing to shout, "Paige!"

And of course, Fatima, the library's nineteen-year-old page, sticks her head in. "Yeah?"

I make a mental note to tell the kid that she should *not* jump to answer people who yell her job title, but Andre is already waving her away. "Not you, hon. Paige. Like a name. You know, the woman who comes in twice a week that Mickey is obsessed with."

Her eyes get wide and I glare at Andre, because he is *not* going to tell kids about my love life, or lack of one.

"Alright, I'll—I'll go shelve downstairs. Yeah."

When the poor kid walks away, I turn on Andre. "Don't go starting rumors."

I worry about getting angry. I don't ever want to be the angry alpha, especially toward an omega, and I look too much like my father already. But Andre doesn't seem to actually react to people getting angry. Maybe it's working with teenagers, or maybe I don't scare him.

Case in point, he chuckles.

April rolls her eyes. "Your sister's friend, Paige? The one who keeps our circulation numbers up in adult fantasy almost exclusively on her own?"

I nod morosely. No sense in denying it.

"Fuck, I thought you two were already dating," April says, which hits like a punch to the gut.

I don't talk about Paige that often, do I? I mean, she stops in twice a week to pick up her holds, and every once in a while she'll come up to the children's room to say hi. And my mother hasn't suspended family dinners on the second Sunday of the month even though Emma moved away, and Paige has always been invited. But surely I don't talk about her *that* much.

Andre snorts.

"But you suddenly decided now is the time to seduce her?" April asks, continuing to be skeptical. It's what makes her good at her job, helping people sort through piles of information. It's what makes her a difficult person to have inspecting your life sometimes.

"No." I'm not encouraging this comedy of errors. "She has some medical problems, and there's a new drug that might help her, but the insurance says she has to have a heat before they'll cover it. Some sort of fucked up, has to prove she tried every natural option first thing."

Even Andre looks serious now. "I didn't realize that's where this started. I thought you finally got your head out of your ass." He shakes his head. "That's fucked up, but not surprising. It's how they missed my tumor for six years. Just kept telling me the pain was anxiety and to lose weight. Actually, now that I think of it, there was definitely one specialist who assured me it was a hormonal issue and if I had a heat, it'd all go away. At least I had a pack that I trusted if they ended up *making* me do it, though."

Fuck, I hate that for him. Andre is doing well now, but he'd been laid up for months around his surgery. The teens had nearly rioted without him, and I'd been one of the staff members who'd brought him the hundreds of get-well cards they'd made.

I've never gone to the doctor with Paige or anything, but I know this is sadly all too normal. Whether it's doctors pushing back against teenage Emma's birth control—because what if it messes with her ability to give alphas she didn't even have at the time babies—or my mom being looked down on for being a single omega with two kids, or Paige being dicked around for over two decades now, I know the system comes down worse on omegas.

"So you're, what? Going to offer your dick out of the kindness of your heart?" April asks.

I look at the doorway. "Can we not talk about my dick in the workplace?"

April is unperturbed. "Tell her to sign up for a heat clinic. That's what they're for."

"Paige is..." I hesitate. I'm already giving them way too much personal information about Paige, although they've both met her and probably made some assumptions. But Paige is the one who gets to choose how and when she discloses her specific health problems or her autism. "Paige doesn't always like people touching her," I settle for.

"And you think you're different?" Andre asks, eyebrow raised. "What, she doesn't like alphas touching her, but you're an exception?"

I mean, maybe? Not to sound conceited, but I've known Paige since she was eight. I'm not going to pretend that I'm a Paige expert or anything, but I know her. And I'll listen to her.

Would a heat clinic listen to her? Probably; that's their job. But what if she needs something they don't provide? What if someone there thinks they know best, and they freak her out? What if she changes her mind halfway through? Paige deserves not to have to make any compromises.

"Holy shit," Andre says, watching me like I'm a reality TV program. "You are so serious about this."

"I don't want her to be sick—"

"Cut the shit, you want it to be *you*," Andre interrupts.

I can't say anything for a minute. Because yes; he's not wrong. And not just for this heat, but that's something we're not getting into here.

"Have you ever been with an omega in heat?" April asks me, astute as always. I shake my head. I've been with more than a handful of omegas, but they'd always been on suppressants and those had always been short-term relationships, anyway. "Set boundaries in advance, plenty of water, and—I'm assuming if she's so picky, she's not going to tag in a second alpha?"

I practically see red. Some omegas like the pack thing, and I know Emma is happy at the center of the pack she built, but I've long since known that's not for me. I can't imagine anyone else's hands on Paige and not lose my mind. I don't share well, never have, and it's a big part of the reason why, up until now, I've kept my distance from Paige.

"Right, so—remember this," April advises. She and her omega are also monogamous, although I didn't know Chelsey had heats. Frankly, I could have gone my whole life without that fact. But this is crucial information, so I listen like there'll be a test. "Toys are your friend. Don't be afraid to tap out and give them a chance to shine."

Right. I doubt I've ever blushed harder in my life—and my mother had to give me the *your first knot* talk, so that's saying something—and I'm grateful that the beard hides some of it.

"And," Andre drawls, and somehow this is even worse, "get to know her first. Ask what she likes. I wasn't kidding when I said we're not a hive mind, alright? She's going to have unique things, which you seem to already know. Don't be afraid to ask about them."

Fatima pokes her head back in. "Uh, Mr. Richards?"

Andre turns to her. "Yeah, hon?"

"All the kids are downstairs. They said you're supposed to start now?"

Andre glances at the clock on the wall. "Shit," he mutters, and I should tell him off for cursing in front of the kid, but he's already in motion. "Alright, alright. Anime club waits for no man. Seriously, Mickey, this is good advice—you should take it." And he runs out the door.

So I'm left with April, who has her arms crossed over her chest as she studies me like I'm a bug under a microscope. I try not to fidget. "I should get back—" But fuck, I have ten more minutes on my break. *April* should get back. She's not even on break.

"Talk to the poor woman," April tells me, standing suddenly. "And be honest with her. She deserves that much."

I still have no idea if this is even a good idea. Offering to help her with her heat feels sleazy at this point. Everything between us has been fragile for years, ever since the day I realized she was an adult and a woman that I wanted more than anything, and I've been balancing on the knife's edge of wanting her and knowing I'm not good for her. This could ruin whatever we have between us forever, and I don't know if I'm ready to give that up.

CHAPTER 3

Paige

My life works best when it's run off a neat, orderly to-do list, so I start my mornings by making one and check items off as I go. Clean the bathrooms and vacuum the second floor, check. Run laundry, check. Order sex toys, an embarrassing and awkward moment that had me back-clicking four times before I finally did it, check. Send an annoying email to a client using small words to make my point crystal clear, check. And then finally, dinner at Emma's parents' house.

Bill and Sherry Condor have returned from their little anniversary road trip, and Sherry texted me to tell me in no uncertain terms that dinner was happening tonight. She didn't need to tell me; even if I somehow miraculously forgot, I have a recurring alarm in my phone calendar for the second Sunday of every month and have for years now. Besides work, which doesn't count, and the four Discords I sometimes hang out in to talk about books, this is usually the most social event on my calendar.

I arrive right on time, bottle of wine in hand. I don't drink wine, but when I first started getting invited to these as an adult post-college, I knew I was no longer the little kid who could get away with mooching off the Condors. So I looked up what the rule was, and all good etiquette books said wine. I've found a red that everyone seems to like, and I buy a bottle once a month.

Sherry smiles and gives me an air kiss, which she's done for years. She thinks it doesn't count as touching me, but I don't have the heart to tell her that it's too close and almost tickles. I scrunch up my face; I can't help it, but she's too close to see it, so she never knows.

Sherry Condor is the reason I'm a functioning human being. She's also the epitome of the "omegas are affectionate" stereotype. An air kiss is a low price to pay for all she's given me.

"Come in, come in," she smiles. "Tell me all about how you've been." She takes the wine in one hand and leads me to the kitchen, waiting for me to tell her some sort of story.

My life is boring, though, and I'm definitely not going to share what I did with my afternoon, or any of my medical woes. And no one wants to hear the ins and outs of intellectual property law, even though I could talk about it for hours.

"I want to see pictures of your trip," I tell her. People like to talk about themselves, I've learned, and this has the added bonus of being true. I love that Sherry met Bill shortly after she met me, and they have a love story for the ages. He treats her well and they're happy and take road trips to celebrate their anniversary after leaving a party their kids threw for them.

That kind of relationship seems to take a lot of work, but I've always admired it. Sherry showed me that love is real when I never saw it in the house I grew up in. My parents barely tolerate each other and like me even less. My Uncle Gavin seems to have a happy pack, but he hates my father. He wasn't around much, and when he was, he just seemed to cause trouble in my family, so he didn't serve as a great role model.

Sherry's showing me the tenth picture of farm animals they drove past, cooing over cute cows, Bill setting the table and chiming in occasionally, when the front door bangs open. "Sorry I'm late!"

It's Mickey. I never react badly to seeing Mickey, and it's not like I didn't know he'd be here tonight, considering this is his mother's house. But he heard that whole conversation the other day. He doesn't know what I did this afternoon, but he knows more than he should.

It's only just now occurring to me that I should feel more than awkward about this. I should feel *bad*. I definitely made a social faux pas there, discussing things like that in his home when I knew he could hear. Mickey's never been anything but kind to me. He's Emma's brother, and I'm sure he never planned on thinking of either of us like that.

I'm not apologizing to him in front of his *mom*, though. Should I apologize, or awkwardly pretend it never happened? Which one is the least damaging choice?

Mickey walks into the kitchen, shoes off and hair a windswept mess. He has dark hair that curls slightly, so different from Emma and their mother's pin straight light-brown hair. It must have come from his father, but that's definitely something we don't talk about.

His dark eyes take in the room as he walks over to his mother, wrapping an arm around her and kissing her cheek. "You left a candle burning, Ma," he tells her when he pulls away. "In the front room. I blew it out for you."

Her hand flies to her mouth. "Oh, Paige, I'm sorry! You should have said something." Because Mickey and Sherry aren't worried about fire safety and unattended candles. They're worried about the scent aggravating my headache.

My own mother wouldn't burn anything as plebeian as a candle most definitely purchased at a supermarket, but even if she did, she'd never blow it out on my behalf. Meanwhile, Sherry looks heartbroken that she forgot.

"It's fine," I tell her. "We're all the way in here."

Mickey frowns, looking at me in a way that makes me avert my eyes. "Scents like that bother you."

He's not wrong. It being in the other room would have made no difference, and while there are some scents I can tolerate better than others, most burning candles and strong perfumes make the pounding in my head worse. At least right now, the simmering sauce on the stove is drowning out most everything else.

"It's fine," I tell him again, because he's not going to make his amazing mother feel bad over a mistake.

He opens his mouth again, but Bill cuts him off. "Everything okay? You're not usually late."

Mickey rakes a hand through his hair, making it look even more disheveled. "Mike offered to donate cardboard to me for craft time this week, and the store gets deliveries on Sunday, so my car is filled with crushed cardboard boxes."

That's cute. I love that Mickey loves the kids he works with so much. It hadn't surprised me as much as it did everyone else when he told people he was going for a masters in Library Science, and focusing on Children's Literature. People think a big alpha can't be good with kids, but all I know is that this guy has perfected the voices for story time, has a box of hand puppets he regularly trots out when kids need cheering up, and spends his day off rescuing cardboard from supermarket dumpsters for whatever craft he's planned.

I can't always go into the children's room when I'm at the library, because it can get loud and chaotic, but I try to stop in when I can to say hi. And I've never seen Mickey being anything less than a perfect librarian for those kids.

"They're making surfboards," he adds, like that somehow explains everything. "So tomorrow my intern and I are going to trace out forty surfboards and hope it's enough cardboard."

Fuck, is he a good guy.

"Well, that's lovely," Sherry decrees. "And you're just in time for dinner, so no worries. Go wash your hands, and then it'll be ready."

Dinner is delicious, but when it's done and we've cleaned up, Mickey looks at me in a way I can't quite understand. "Let me get you home," he says.

I squirm, because I don't know what that look means, but I do know he has no reason to look at me weird other than what he overheard the other day. "I'm fine; I'm not—"

"That far, I know," he interrupts. "It's dark. Humor me." It's not even fully dark yet; the days are getting longer and longer, and the sun is barely beginning to set. And I could walk most of this town blindfolded and be fine, anyway. But Mickey stares at me, waiting for me to say *yes*.

From someone else, I might bristle. Poor little omega can't walk home alone after dark, even if I live in the condos four streets over. There are even street lights here. And I want to put up some protest, but it's not the same with Mickey. I've spent too long around him to actually think he believes I can't walk home alone.

People never say what they mean. Mickey wants to talk, and I have to decide if I want to kick up a fuss and risk him explaining why, or let him have this one.

I nod, knowing when I'm beat, and let Sherry air-kiss my cheek goodbye before waving to Bill and heading out.

There's cardboard in the front seat, but Mickey shoves it into the pile in the back, squishing it all smaller. When we're finally seated in the car, Mickey can't properly see out the back.

I fidget, unsure if I should say something. Maybe now is the time to apologize? Just when I resolve to try, Mickey speaks up, "Let's go out for dessert."

I swallow. "I'm not—"

"Please?" he implores, taking his eyes off the road to look at me for a minute. "We need to talk, Paige."

"I'm sorry," I blurt out. "I shouldn't have had that conversation in your home; that was inappropriate and—"

"No," he interrupts again. "There's nothing wrong with you talking about anything in my home. You're welcome wherever I am, Paige, and if you have problems, I want to know about them."

"Not that problem."

"Yes, that problem. All problems." He looks at me again before turning left, and I know he's taking me to Molly's. I didn't say yes, but he also knows I won't turn down a hot fudge sundae from Molly's ice cream stand. Damn him. "How bad is your pain?"

"Right now?" I ask.

"Right now. In general. Both."

"Right now, it's like a four?" I guess, even though I hate those out-of-ten pain scales. How am I supposed to know what other people consider debilitating? "Three to six is pretty normal. I've had three flair-ups with migraines this month." That's pretty normal too. So many of the drugs I've tried have promised to help control the migraines at least, with some success. I haven't gone to the emergency room with a migraine in over three years, so that's a victory.

His lips thin. I don't think he liked that answer much. "And you think this new medication will help you?"

I shrug, but I've done hours of research. The day before I told Emma about it, I read every report I could get my hands on, and Dr. James had given me all the literature she had to read through, too. I know everything there is to know about every study on this drug. "It might. There are trials with people like me. It's mostly anecdotal data at this point, but it could mean something." I shut my mouth before I explain any further and drag us both down this rabbit hole.

"Like what?" he asks. "What's the best possible outcome?"

"Best possible outcome? I'm somehow cured. No more pain." That's a dream that I gave up on a long time ago, though.

And I have to respect Dr. James for being the first doctor to not pretend that they miraculously know how to do that.

"Most realistic outcome?" Mickey asks.

"Assuming it works at all, then more days where the pain is barely an annoyance. Maybe even periods of time where it breaks for a little while. I'm already on something that helps control the migraines a bit, but if it could help minimize those too, I'm for it."

"So it sounds important."

I shrug. Every medicine has sounded important; almost all of them have let me down.

And I have to wonder where this is all going. Mickey probably doesn't suddenly want a crash-course on my medical issues.

He drives in silence, then parks at Molly's. I go to unbuckle my seatbelt and leave, but he hasn't turned off the car, still gripping the steering wheel. I let my seatbelt go and sit back.

"I'd like to help you."

"Help... me?" I ask, sounding the words out like I've never heard them before.

He nods. "With the heat part." When I don't reply right away, he starts speaking faster, words tumbling out of his mouth. "I know it's awful, but I thought that since you trust me, or I think you do, and I know you told Emma you won't go to a heat clinic, and I know most of your boundaries—or not, you know, about sex, I'm not spying on you or anything. Just about *touching* and stuff. And I can tell when you're in pain but

31

a heat clinic officer might miss it. And I was thinking, I could probably help? If you'd be comfortable with that."

Good god. I sit there, perfectly still, trying to process all of that, trying to absorb all the information he just dumped on me. I cannot have heard him correctly. Mickey Condor cannot have offered to fuck me.

No, Mickey offered to fuck me in order to get my insurance to pay for my medication. That's somehow worse.

Is this pity? Does he pity me, and is that why he asked about my pain and the drug? Or, somehow even worse, is this some sort of big brotherly duty? Having sex with me isn't the same as turning down the music when it was too loud, or giving me the blanket that doesn't scratch during movie night though. This is too much to ask.

Mickey clears his throat. "You don't have to answer right now," he says, his voice a little rough. "I know it's a lot. Probably not what you expected. So you can think about it. *Should* think about it."

"Mickey," I say, my voice barely coming out as more than a whisper. "This is..." What is it? Kind? Awkward? Self-sacrificing to the extreme? All of that and more. Mickey never expressed any interest in me before, never crossed that line of seeing me as more than his little sister's friend, and now he's here, throwing himself into this like a sacrificial object. I don't want to be one more thing he has to sacrifice for. "You don't have to fix everyone's problems," I tell him. I heard Emma tell him that once, when they were on the phone when Emma and I were in undergrad. He'd offered to drive over a hundred miles because she was sad—I think she and Avery had their first fight. Avery fixed it the next day when they showed up with flowers and a heartfelt apology, but Mikey had still called to check in every night for a week until Emma told him off.

He flinches a little. "Just think about it." Before I can decide what to do—ask or turn him down outright or, bizarrely, *accept*—Mickey turns off the car and opens his door. "Let's get you your ice cream," he mutters, and then I'm left staring after him as he climbs out of the car.

CHAPTER 4
Mickey

The drive to her home is the most uncomfortable ten minutes of my life. Thank god she has her ice cream, so at least it seems like we're not talking because she's eating.

Vanilla hot fudge sundae, extra peanuts, but no cherry. It's been the same order at least since she was nine or ten, and she looks like it's the best thing ever every single time.

I park in front of her condo, turning to look at her and not knowing what to say. She opens her mouth, then closes it, then opens it again. Just when I think we're going to have a real conversation, she blurts out, "Goodnight," then unbuckles her seatbelt, grabs her ice cream, and runs out of my car like her ass is on fire, leaving me and my melting cup of salted caramel ice cream in my cup holder staring after her.

I drive home, throw away the melted ice cream I no longer want, and wait for a call from my sister to chew me out. I'm sure Paige called her, because I know Emma is who she goes to when she's unsure.

The call doesn't come.

Fuck, what was I thinking, propositioning her like that? I basically told Paige to sleep with me for her health. I had her stuck in a car with me when I said it. Just thinking about it makes me feel gross, and I immediately go to shower.

It's the longest, hottest shower of my life, trying to scour myself clean, but when I finally exit, I still don't have a phone call. No Emma chewing me out. No Emma threatening me for hurting her best friend. Nothing.

I go to bed, wake up, and still not even an angry text.

Did Paige not call her? Somehow, that's even worse. Paige and Emma tell each other everything, and if Paige didn't call Emma—well, why? Did she feel like she couldn't?

"You look like shit," Andre tells me when I get to work.

"Bite me." I'm hauling in cardboard, my arms absolutely full. Craft time is at two this afternoon, and I still have twice this much in my car. "Come help me."

He heaves a theatrical sigh, but follows me outside. "So, why do you look like shit?"

I glance around the parking lot, but thankfully I don't see any patrons. It's still early, and we're not open for another twenty minutes. Still, you can never be too careful. Old people seem to think there's a race to get here first, and there's always someone using the outdoor book drop.

"I offered to help Paige last night," I say evasively.

"And that made you look like shit?"

"I made her uncomfortable."

He grabs the cardboard I hand him, but doesn't start moving. "Tell me what happened then. Explain it to me."

That's what I like about Andre. He'll tease me and anyone else all day long, he loves a good joke, and he takes so little seriously. But he's also the least judgmental person I know. It's why the teens love him, and something I'm taking shameless advantage of now.

So I tell him about the conversation in the car last night. He listens, but he just shrugs. "So she's thinking about it. No need to freak out."

I stop. "You don't think I made her uncomfortable?"

"I don't think you did anything wrong," he says. "You made her an offer and told her to think about it. You didn't pressure her or do anything overtly sexual or weird. Ball's in her court, right? She can take you up on it or not. That's up to her. The question really is, why do you care so much?" he asks slyly.

Because it's Paige. "Because I don't want to go around being a giant predator?" I suggest.

He rolls his eyes. "Look, I don't know what to tell you. You made an offer, and she'll either take you up on it or not. That's her choice. But it doesn't mean you did something wrong."

And I guess I can trust Andre on this. I mean, he's my friend, so he's more biased to see me in a good light, but he's also an omega like Paige, so hopefully he sees things from her perspective. So I take a deep breath, nod, and carry the stack of cardboard inside.

The surfboard craft is cute and goes well. With summer break right around the corner, I spend the end of my shift organizing things for summer reading. We have some prizes left from last year, but we're going to need to order a boatload more, and it's always work to try to turn the budget into enough prizes. Meanwhile, signs and posters need to be finalized, and the event schedule needs to be published soon.

I try not to take work home with me, but I end up designing posters on my couch. I know most people who know what I do don't believe I can take work home—they believe my job is all shelving books and reading stories and cleaning up the kid's toys. But libraries are a science, and I don't joke about kids' literacy. What we can do for them now sets the foundation for the rest of their lives. Plus, so many parents rely on us during the summer to not only provide activities, but to help keep their child's education from sliding backward.

It's a tough job, but an important one.

Libraries save lives. I know that's dramatic as hell, but it'd been part of my application when I applied for my masters, and I still mean it now.

When Mom left my useless biological father, she was a single young omega with two kids. She had to move in with her sister, despite Jessica having a one-bedroom apartment, and she was incredibly lucky to get the receptionist job that funded our lives after that. Mrs. Smith at the veterinarian's office had felt bad for my mother, this being a small town and all, so she'd hired her even though Mom had no job experience to speak of, but the position had only been part-time at first. Library books had been our entertainment while she worked, and free library programs had been a crucial part of our childhood, often the only fun things we had to look forward to. I was old enough to watch Emma so Mom could have ten minutes to herself in the library, getting to be an adult with a magazine and a free cup of coffee. This library saved our family.

It's also where we met Paige, although even at eight she'd been hiding in the adult stacks, the children's room a little too over-stimulating for her. Her experiences are what encouraged me to turn the never-used children's study room into a quiet space, filled with a beanbag, soft rugs, low lighting, and noise-canceling headphones. This place saved me twenty years ago, but I want it to be there for all kids today.

So yeah, I'll take work home when I need to. The local elementary school needs to have summer reading flyers to hand out to families by the end of the year, and if I can get those out of the way tonight, then I can focus on next week's craft time tomorrow, and perhaps have some time to spend on the absolutely disastrous bins of legos no one sorted after the last lego club meeting.

And if it keeps me from thinking about Paige? Well, then I'm killing two birds with one stone, and I'll take that.

I successfully distract myself with work all the way until four o'clock the next day. I've made it through story time, three requests for dinosaur books, a quest for pirate books but only about the specific pirate the child was interested in, and an impassioned speech from Ms. Markle's second grade class for a children's room pet. They're voting for a snake, an iguana, or a parakeet. I promised to consider a hamster.

So it's been a busy day, and I have a meeting with the library director about the summer budget tomorrow, and I've spent every spare minute preparing for it. And when I finally get a moment to breathe, Paige is standing at the doorway that leads into the children's room.

She looks wrecked—dark circles under her eyes and her skin pale and drawn. Has she lost sleep over what I said? Is she finally here to cuss me out?

When I make eye-contact with her, she sets her shoulders and grips the strap of her old purse tighter, walking over to my desk. "Hey," I say in a voice I barely recognize as my own.

"Hey, I—" She swallows like she has to search for the words. "I, uh—"

"Are you here for your holds?" I ask her, because it is her regular day to come pick up her books. Paige is addicted to fantasy novels, and gets two or three a week through the library. Sometimes she stops in to say hi to me, but something tells me today isn't quite normal.

"We need to talk," she says slowly, and I nod, bracing myself for whatever she's going to say.

CHAPTER 5

Paige

It's been an awful two days since Mickey dropped me off at my house.

That first night I try to distract myself, but I can only get into so many pedantic discussions online about hard magic systems and the importance of good quality maps in books. All our discussions in this forum just retread old ground, but I honestly think we're just too stubborn to come up with anything new. I guess that's what you get when you willingly join a Discord with other autistic fantasy lovers: complete obsession with the genre and everyone's niche special interest on full display.

It's not distracting enough to shift my thoughts from Mickey, so my brain just starts turning over everything he told me again and again and again. Mickey is offering to *fuck* me out of the kindness of his heart.

Mickey is treating my heat the same way he treated scraped knees from being pushed down by bullies when I was twelve: something a good big brother just deals with, and I *hate* that thought. I don't want to be a duty to him, one more obligation on his plate.

I can't sleep for shit, my brain buzzing too fast. When I sleep badly, my headache gets worse. It's practically inevitable, and so I sit in my home office the next day preparing paperwork for a client with the lights as low as I could possibly get them and still see, then going to bed as soon as my work was done.

Where I, once again, sleep badly.

I need to talk to someone, but there's not a lot of options. Our Discord server does *not* have a "help, my best friend's brother offered to fuck me" channel. It does have a few channels for personal discussions, and I've definitely used them before, but this feels too personal. We talk about graduations and long days and small wins and the shit neurotypicals do there. Definitely not sex; there are minors in here, after all. Other than that, my options are people at work or Emma, both of which seem to be out for obvious reasons.

The only thing to do seems to be to talk to Mickey. And then maybe take him up on his offer. I'm not going to pretend this drug will magically fix me, but it might've made the last two days more tolerable.

I can't keep doing this. If there's a treatment out there, then I owe it to myself to get it. No matter what hoops I have to jump through. No matter how awkward it might make things with Mickey.

Do I invite him out to dinner to discuss this? Ask him to my house? We clearly can't have this conversation in the library, but stalking him outside his apartment seems inappropriate, so I had to come here. But maybe that's invading his space at work. So I should've, what, called him? I don't know the rules. I wish I just knew the rules.

But it's too late. He's here, he's seen me, and I can't turn back now.

"You look like you're hurting," Mickey says slowly, looking me over like he can see through my skin and into my broken brain.

"I took something."

He frowns but doesn't push me, and I do appreciate that. I don't want to sit and argue about how I look like crap; I'm well aware already.

"Did you come here for me?" he asks.

I hesitate a moment, but then nod. No use in lying, and it's too late to back out.

He looks at his watch, a clunky silver thing his mother gave him when he graduated high school. "I need twenty more minutes, and then we can go wherever you want. How about you get your holds, and then we go?"

I do like that he knows I'll have holds. It's ridiculous; he's known me for years, and he works here. Of course he knows that I order and read three or four books a week. But it still feels like being *known*.

So I nod, and go to get my books, already wondering how bad this conversation is going to be.

I only have one book on the hold shelf, so I check it out and flip through the first few pages while I wait. I usually devour books like this. That's been my preferred free time activity for my whole life. A good fantasy book is always where I want to be, but right now I couldn't tell you a single detail of what I read.

Mickey finds me exactly twenty minutes later, a messenger bag over his shoulder and a sort of frantic look about him. Despite that, he's calm when he talks to me. "My place?" he suggests. "Or not, if you don't want to—"

"That sounds good." His place sounds like we won't have listening ears, and I can leave if things get too awkward. Perfect.

"Did you walk here?"

"Yeah." At a little over a mile, the library isn't a short walk. But I need to get more steps in my day, and anytime I don't have to drive is a win for me.

"Alright then. I'll drive. You okay with that?"

He's talking to me like I'm delicate, like I'm fragile, and this conversation is about to break me. Mickey's never talked to me like that before. Other people assume I'm broken, that anything and everything can make me fall apart. But Mickey's never done that until today.

"Mickey. We won't be able to have this conversation if you're freaking out at me even being in your car."

He runs a hand through his hair. "You're right. You're always right. I'm calm. I just—I don't want to hurt you."

"I'm not breakable, Mickey."

He just looks at me for a long moment, but then nods and leads the way to his car.

The drive is absolutely silent except for the radio, even though we're alone now. And maybe Mickey doesn't want to start this conversation while he's driving, but the waiting is killing me.

He pulls into his driveway and turns off the engine, then sits there for a moment.

His apartment is actually a converted in-law apartment off of Mrs. Delaney's old house. Mrs. Delaney died five years ago, and the main house is now occupied by her nephew and his pack, but they still let Mickey rent the in-law apartment. At least it has its own entrance. Will he want to have my heat here? It's a nice enough place, but it's not *my* place. The suppressants dull my omega sense of smell, but I know going off them will make me overly sensitive. I'll want my stuff, my scents. My nest. But some alphas are so territorial, considering their homes a castle that they single-handedly protect.

Fuck it. I'm asking for a favor. I'm asking him to help me in a really intimate, personal way. If he wants it to be at his house, then I can't quibble about it. I'll just have to bring some of my blankets or something.

He opens his car door and I jump to follow him out. He holds his front door open for me, and I leave my bag and book on the end table by the door.

Once my shoes are off, we sit on the couch with so much space between us that his entire family could sit down and there'd still be room left over. I curl my legs up under me, needing to pull everything close and secure.

"Why'd you want to see me today, Paige?" he asks, seemingly calm even while my pulse is racing.

"I'm... I..." I'm stuttering and I know it, but how do you say, *please fuck me when delirious and begging for it*? You don't ask someone that. The presence I had at the library is slipping away, and I desperately need it back.

I take a deep breath. It sounds ridiculous. This is all ridiculous, but it's my life right now. "I really want that medication," I tell him. "And I need my insurance to cover it."

He nods. "So, the heat."

"The heat." How can two little words say so much?

"I already told you, I'm happy to help. We can make this work." It's like he agreed to help me move or something, and I'm struck with the whiplash. Are we having two completely different conversations?

"So. What should I know if we're going to do this?" he asks.

"I've never had a heat before." I've actively avoided them my whole life, and now I'm staring one down and we're talking about it like it's *normal*.

"But you have had sex—right?"

"Yes, I've had sex." Four times, all with Samuel, all off-putting, and the last time enough to convince me I was happier alone than I was with him.

"Right, then you can tell me a bit about what you like and what you don't. If you're in heat, you might not be in the best position to tell me, and I don't want to hurt you or scare you or for this to wreck our friendship. So, I need to know, the sooner the better."

"I always say what I mean and mean what I say," I tell him. "So if I say something, I'm not being a *bratty omega*. Don't call me that." Even saying the words myself makes me want to cringe. They're like nails on a chalkboard down my spine, leaving the worst taste in my mouth. My father called me a brat whenever he bothered to acknowledge me. Samuel had called me a brat when I'd ever so much as disagreed with him, and now I can't fucking forget it. "I'm not saying it to argue or question you or be difficult. I just might need clarification. Please don't call me that."

"Never," he promises immediately. "What else?"

I look away, because there's no way I can even fake eye contact while saying this. "Look, I've seen porn, alright? And it's a type of porn I try hard to avoid but—" Good *lord*, I need to stop talking about porn. "Anyway, I know there's this idea that you can do anything to an omega during heat and they'll take it all gladly. And that omegas probably don't even remember most of their heat, and—" I have to take a deep breath. I knew this would be awkward, but I had no idea we'd get here today. That I'd have to dig up some of my worst fears.

There are reasons I've never had a heat before.

"Just don't film it," I tell him. "I won't be one of those omegas who sees the most uncomfortable moment of their lives, sees someone who isn't even them anymore, on the internet."

"Fucking hell," Mickey says, and then he's sliding across the couch to me. He leaves a few inches between us, but now he's close enough that his radiated warmth sinks right into me.

He doesn't touch me, doesn't make me look at him. But he does crowd into my space a bit, and I don't know if he knows how that calms my omega instincts—I love small spaces, love tight pressure, love feeling surrounded—or if he got a lucky guess, but my heart rate slows.

"Abso-fucking-lutely none of that will happen," he promises, voice low and insistent. "I won't film anything, certainly not without your explicit consent—and I mean real consent, not consent given in the middle of a heat—and none of that other stuff. If you're with me, Paige, then I'm going to make sure to fucking worship you. Your heat is meant for your alpha to show you you're a queen, and shame on any alpha who doesn't treat their omega that way."

My cheeks are flaming red—I've made this weird, haven't I? I've said too much, said the wrong thing, and now—

"Take a deep breath for me, Paige."

48

I didn't even realize I'd started hyperventilating. I try, and it's a half-assed try at best.

But Mickey acts like I did well. "That's it," he murmurs. "You're doing so good for me, Paige. Thank you. Thank you."

He keeps saying nonsense like that, and it shouldn't mean anything. But it does. And suddenly, I can breathe.

CHAPTER 6
Mickey

S he's starting to breathe, but I don't stop with the gentle prattle. It's practically automatic, which is good because I am so far in my head.

I ask Paige what she likes in bed and she tells me not to call her a brat and not to film her when she's vulnerable. Fucking *shit*.

Has Paige ever had a sexual encounter that she's enjoyed? I can read between the lines. Paige is willing to do this with me because she wants the medication. She's not so sure that it'll actually be good, which I'm trying to take as a statement about a general distrust of alphas or even of sex, and not a statement about me. I know Paige trusts me. I'm pretty positive she does.

Paige isn't into demeaning things. And it concerns me that she can't think of things she *likes* before she thinks of things she hates, but I'll do some interpretation here. Paige needs me to prove that this can be gentle and good. Never mind not filming her, she needs to be shown that her heat isn't an opportunity to

50

demean and embarrass her. It's supposed to be a time to worship her.

She's breathing normally again, and I back up, but to my immense shock, Paige reaches out and grabs my wrist. I freeze. Her touch feels like fire. She's branding me, I'm sure of it, and I'm more desperate for it than I am for oxygen.

"Stay," she murmurs.

I don't move a muscle. "I'm not too close?"

She shakes her head. "I like—tight. Small spaces. Close."

"Alright." And then, because my mouth and brain have completely disconnected, I say, "I could hold you? Squeeze you like Emma does?"

She nods immediately and leans into me. I wrap my arms around her, keeping the pressure firm, and she sighs, melting into me like she's boneless.

I thought only Emma got to hold her like this, that she was special. But judging by how soft and relaxed Paige is against me right now, she wants a lot more of this. No, she probably needs it. Most omegas crave touch, and I think we all treat Paige like her sensory issues make her the exception, but she's not. She just needs me to touch her a certain way.

I give her an experimental little squeeze, and Paige lets out a little squeak that goes straight to my cock.

Fuck. I need to get it under control; Paige can't know. I know it's stupid, because we are going to end up fucking, but I can't scare Paige off with how much I feel for her.

But even so, I need to make her make that noise again. I can't stop imagining it in her nest, with us both naked. I've never appreciated my big build so much as right now, knowing it can give Paige the surrounded feeling she craves. I'll be able to surround her completely while fucking her into the mattress, can put her in a mating press, legs up by her chest and press down and it'll be perfect fucking pressure, and she'll—

No. *Bad Mickey*. Stop fantasizing about the poor woman.

"Are you in pain right now?" I ask her, experimentally rubbing my hand along her back in firm strokes.

She squirms, and not quite in the same way she was a minute ago. "I'm always in pain, Mickey. That's kind of the point."

My brain is completely divorced from my body, because that's the only way to explain why my free hand cups the back of her head and then starts stroking through her hair. "And what do I do to help you?"

"Nothing."

"Paige. If we're going to do this, then you're going to be in pain and maybe not lucid enough to advocate for yourself. So I need whatever you can tell me now." And this is what I worried about at the heat clinics, that they wouldn't bother to do this work and Paige would be left in pain with no ability to get help. Just because it's not all I worried about doesn't mean that it wasn't an active worry.

"I doubt I'll feel it during my heat," she mutters into my shoulder. "I read that omegas can handle a lot of pain while in heat."

I have no desire to know where she read that, or in what context. Paige seems to have a propensity for worst-case scenarios about this. "Can handle and can't feel are two different things, honey."

Fuck, I shouldn't have called her that, but she doesn't react. I file that away for later.

"Darkness is the best thing," she tells me after a long minute. "Bright lights hurt." I already knew that. I also know that strong smells are a no-go, and that is the reason why I never wear cologne. "Cold compresses over my eyes sometimes helps soothe the pain. But a hot pad on my neck can too. And quiet. I can't get dehydrated, and I know that's difficult during heats, but I have to try to stay hydrated."

"And how about your meds? You take them for the pain sometimes too, right?"

She tenses right back up in my hold. "I need to take my meds. And I don't know if I'll be able to remember to take them—"

No, she probably won't. I rub her back again, keeping my touch firm like she seems to need. "Alright. You'll write me some directions? And I'll make it happen."

"That's a big ask, Mickey. Are you sure—"

I squeeze her, and she squeaks again. "I'm so sure, Paige," I promise. I'm trying to find a delicate balance here, needing her to know I'm serious without giving away how obsessed with her I am. "You are not a difficult person to be around, alright? I promise you, helping you is not a difficult ask." If only she knew how much I want to help her.

"Your family are the only people who think that," she mutters into my shoulder.

And I hate that fact. I can't dispute it, because unfortunately I know all about her parents.

"You're not difficult," I tell her again, because she clearly needs to hear it. "You're not, Paige. I promise."

She shakes against me, and I keep rubbing her back in firm strokes until she stops, then keep going for another minute just because I can.

"So, what happens now?" Paige asks, her voice quiet but otherwise normal.

"Have you gone off your suppressants yet?"

"I didn't take them this morning. If you had changed your mind, I'd decided I was going to go through with this alone. So, you can still change your mind. Me being off my suppressants doesn't lock you into this or anything."

"I'm not changing my mind." If only she knew how well my mind was made up. I don't need an excuse to leave; I'm frantically searching for every excuse to stay. "Do you want me to change my mind?"

Paige will get whatever she wants, but I desperately don't want her to do this alone. Emma was right when she said it could fuck Paige up. I don't know the exact statistics, but there's a reason insurance companies are forced to cover heat clinics for patients who need them.

"No," she says shortly. "I want to do this. And I trust you, Mickey."

I feel ten feet tall when she says that. "Thank you." I hope my voice doesn't sound as hoarse to her as it does to me. "If you went off them this morning, how long...?"

She shrugs. "From what I understand, it could be tomorrow, or two weeks from now. Somewhere in there."

"Okay. So I'll put in for heat leave, then. And I'll be ready whenever you tell me it's time. You'll call me, right? Even if it's the middle of the night."

"I'll call you," she agrees. "Should I come here, or...?"

"Don't you want your nest?" My mother and sister obsess over their nests. Nests are important to omegas, the place they feel safest and most grounded. I doubt it's any different for Paige.

"Yeah," she agrees after a moment. "You don't mind?"

"Hon, the only thing I care about is your comfort. That's all," I promise her.

"Then, yes. My nest. Please."

I rub her back. "Sounds like a plan." I think this is the most honest and vulnerable conversation I've ever had with Paige—maybe with anyone. Her face is still buried in my shoulder, and I keep brushing my cheek on the top of her head, and I've never felt so connected to another person.

So, in other words, I'm fucked. If I ever thought I could hide what I feel for Paige, if I convinced myself that time and distance would dull my obsession, then I've been more than proven wrong.

CHAPTER 7
Paige

Mickey drives me home, because he's such a gentleman that he won't let me walk. Most of my exercise comes from walking pretty much everywhere in town, and I'm going to end up out of shape if Mickey keeps insisting on being chivalrous.

"Call me," he insists.

"Yeah, I will," I promise before walking into my house, my brain absolutely overwhelmed by the past couple of hours. I need quiet desperately.

I can't believe I went to his work and asked him for this today. I can't believe I looked at my best friend's big brother, the guy who's always seen me as one more person to take care of, and asked him to fuck me through my heat.

What's worse is I'm going to have to tell Emma, and soon. I'd love to never talk about this with anyone but Mickey, but Emma and I tell each other practically everything. I know about her heats and how high her hopes are for this baby, how they've tried three times now and it hasn't happened yet and she's starting to worry even if she wants to tell people she isn't. I know every relationship issue she ever had with her alphas. I've been her sounding board for everything for the last twenty years, and she's been mine. I can't keep something this big from her.

Will she be mad? Will she think I pressured her big brother into this, that I made the alpha who's such a giver take care of me? Will she hate me?

Should I wait until Saturday? That's when we usually call, but does this warrant a special call? Will she be mad if I wait?

The stress turns the pain from earlier in the day into a full-fledged migraine. The spearing pain in my left temple grows worse by the minute, until I can't even see out of that eye clearly, and I know I have no hope of deciding anything tonight. I take a pill and go upstairs to my dark, quiet nest, the nest I carefully built with all the right fabrics, all the best textures. It took months, and sometimes I'm still not satisfied with it.

The overhead light in my room only gets turned on when I'm deep cleaning and need to see every corner. I have fairy lights and one gentle lamp, but I leave them all off, fall into bed, and don't move for twelve hours.

The pain is more manageable in the morning. I go through my morning ritual, making my to-do list for the day before I wander into my home office and boot up my computer.

It's still too early for my workday, but Mickey had the right idea when he said he'd put in for heat leave.

Heat leave is federally protected, so I know it's not going to be denied. Still, I summon all my law school training to type up the blandest, most factual email I possibly can.

Because what's worse than having to notify your boss you're going on heat leave? Having to notify your uncle.

He doesn't read his own emails, I remind myself. He has Janice for that, and if I'm lucky at all, she'll update the calendar with vague terms without saying a word to Uncle Gavin.

I doubt I'll be that lucky, though.

Sure enough, Gavin calls me after lunch. I stare at my phone like it's a snake poised to bite, but the caller ID says *Uncle Gavin*, and I know better than to ignore the boss. He knows I don't like unscheduled calls, though, and that I like to know what the call is about well in advance. He's usually pretty good about making sure he gives me that heads-up. Whatever else you can say about Gavin—and I can say a lot, considering I've been a part of his and my father's emotional tug-of-war for years—the man cares about ensuring his employees have reasonable accommodations.

But maybe I'm supposed to be able to guess what this one is about.

"Hello?"

The line is silent for a moment. "Heat leave?"

Fuck. Not even a *hello, how are you today, Paige?* Just straight to the point. "I'm legally entitled to the time."

"Are you and Samuel—?" The words are sharp, cutting, and I don't like it.

"No. Never again." Not that he's entitled to ask about my relationship, but I can't have anyone thinking I'd still be with someone like Samuel.

"Good. You know I always thought he was a tool." And yes, I do. Gavin never tried to hide that; another thing that can be said about him is that he never beats around the bush, so I never have to try to play guessing games with what he means.

He's right, too; Samuel is a tool. I hope I never see his face again.

"Then who?" Gavin presses. "I didn't know you were serious with anyone."

Gavin can try to play the concerned uncle all he wants, but I never would have thought to tell him who I was seeing, even if I was dating someone. Gavin might have hired me when my father refused to, but I know I'm nothing more than another piece in their rivalry with each other. I'm sure Gavin only hates Samuel because my father loves him.

"Is my right to a heat leave being unlawfully denied?" I ask, drawing on all my law school training to sound like I'm about to sue if the answer is wrong. It's a great skill that's served me well over the years with doctors, insurance agents, and my former landlord who didn't think fixing leaking faucets was a priority.

"Paige, I think we should talk. Outside of work, I mean. This is a big step, and it feels like you're rushing into things. Let's talk it out. At least let me meet the guy. Come to dinner?"

I can literally think of nothing worse than sitting with my uncle and his pack and discussing my sex life over dinner. "Pass. This really isn't up for debate. I'm not asking you; I'm telling you I'm going out on leave."

Gavin makes a disgusted noise that might be a growl. "It's on the calendar. Make sure to notify Janice when it becomes official and hand off your work before then." Then he hangs up, apparently not here for goodbyes.

After work, there's an uncomfortable surprise on my doorstep. My package arrived. And while I order a lot of things to my home to avoid going out into crowds, I've only ordered one thing recently.

It's a giant, knotted dildo.

I take the package inside like my neighbors will somehow see through the cardboard and realize what it is. Then I unwrap it like it might be a bomb, looking the thing over.

It's off-puttingly huge, something I would never want anywhere near my vagina. I read the dimensions online, but this seems even bigger than I imagined. But according to the internet, when I'm in heat, that'll look like a good option. No, that'll look like the best option.

I shouldn't need it, unless Mickey changes his mind. Which he's obviously still entitled to do. Did I make that clear enough to him yesterday? I don't want to coerce him into anything, and what if hanging my medical treatment on this makes him feel like he can't back out without hurting me?

I need to call Emma. She's the only person I'd want to ask about this, even if it's super awkward. Even if I'll have to confess what I've somehow tricked her brother into.

I dial her number before I can talk myself out of it. It only takes two rings for her to pick up, breathing heavily and voice frantic. "Paige? What's wrong?"

Am I such a mess that she automatically assumes that something's wrong when I call without warning her first? "Nothing's *wrong*," I hedge.

"Bullshit. When have you ever called without texting me first?"

Pretty much never, but I didn't know how to put this in writing. "I might have done something," I tell her. "And I think you might hate me for it."

"I could never hate you," Emma says without even hesitating. She's way too forgiving.

"Is that Paige?" I hear, half-muffled in the background. "Tell her I said hi!"

"Hi Jackson," I mutter back automatically. Jackson is fun. He's a total sweetheart and loves board games and tabletop games and is always welcoming when I'm around. Even so, I really, *really* don't want him in this conversation.

"Go away. Girl time," Emma commands, but then I hear her moving, then a door closing. "Paige, what's wrong? I could never hate you."

"Mickey is going to spend my heat with me," I confess all at once. I need to tell her right now before I talk myself out of it.

She's silent for too long. "Start at the beginning."

So I do. I tell her about the offer he made me after dinner that night and how I wasn't going to take him up on it, but I gave in because I'm selfish and want this medication, and how worried I am that I've somehow manipulated him into this.

"He offered first, Paige."

"But he's Mickey. He's, you know, him. Always taking care of people." Emma herself has said it a thousand times about her brother. Surely she gets it.

"So let him take care of you," she says.

"It's not that easy, Em. This is more than letting him tell your mom to blow out her candles while I'm around. This is a heat. It's a big ask."

She's quiet for a moment. "He wouldn't have offered it if he didn't want to, Paige," she promises, although I'm still not convinced she's right about that. Mickey would offer someone the shirt off his back. I don't want to take advantage of that. "You don't have to act like you're allergic to accepting help."

"I accept help from you."

"Barely."

I bite my lip. "You don't get it. If I accept help, then people assume I can't handle it on my own. And I *can*. I *have*. But people don't see that."

"That's not how Mickey sees you."

"I don't want to be one more thing he worries about. I won't be his obligation."

"Then tell him that. And he might surprise you. I don't think Mickey got into this because he has a savior complex or whatever. I always thought my brother had a thing for you."

I choke on my own spit, gasping for air for a moment before I manage to ask, "What?!"

"Mickey is obsessed with you. He thinks about you way more than a big brother should. There's three years between us, so I thought he'd ask you out when you graduated high school. And then maybe after college. I know Mickey always thought he was like fifty years older than us—I don't remember my father that much, but Mickey absolutely does and that always made him older—so I thought maybe he thought the age gap was too big. So maybe after college. But he hasn't; he just watches you."

"I don't need him watching over me."

"Neither do I. For one thing, I'm a grown ass adult, and for another, I chose my people to watch over me when I do need it, and they let me watch over them when they need it. But I've had that conversation with Mickey, Paige. Like ten times, because he's got a thick head. I had to make him understand what he can and can't do for me. Maybe you need to have that conversation."

"I don't think I can handle another emotionally fraught conversation with your brother."

Emma laughs. "Sorry, babe. But it do be like that sometimes. If you want the results, you need to put in the work." She pauses for a long moment. "You make it sound like he's just convenient to you. And that's fine if that's how you feel, as long as you're clear with him. But do you want my brother too?"

"I don't know. I've never thought about it," I mutter. It's not a lie. But it's maybe not true either.

Mickey was the first alpha I knew who I liked. Mickey's always been safe in a way I didn't know I needed until he was there, and he never makes me feel bad for anything about me. And Mickey never looked at me like that, and he was obviously out of my league. I was socially awkward in high school, but not unobservant. I know full well Mickey dated people far prettier and more stable than me.

"You haven't?" Emma asks.

"What? You think I've been weighing the merits of every alpha I come across? I'm not that desperate for a partner, Em. I know what I am, and I know I'm probably better off alone." I don't want to be alone, not necessarily, but dating Samuel taught me one thing: there are way worse things than being alone. I know my worth, and being alone is far preferable to someone looking down on me all the time.

"We'll come back to that," Emma says after a pause. "But first, Paige, I thought you might be interested in my brother just a little. You let him help you sometimes. And you went to him with this—you let him in. You trust him."

"This is just an arrangement, Em." Why does that sound weak to my ears?

Emma is silent again, and I've known her long enough to know that means I'm missing something she considers obvious, but also not something she knows how to explain to me. "I'm not mad at you for sleeping with my brother, Paige," she says at last. "And I won't be mad if you do two things for me, alright?"

"Okay." Two things? Anything to ease my guilt, to make this so it won't be awkward between Emma and I. Even with her halfway across the country now, I still need her more than anyone else. She is my rock and has been since I was eight. I need to make sure I fix things.

"First, think about what I said. I don't care what conclusion you come to, Paige; that's entirely your choice and I have no skin in the game. But think about it."

I swallow. I wish she asked for something easier, but whatever she wants. I will think about Mickey Condor like he's someone I could ever possibly have a chance with.

"And two: don't just spend your heat with him. A heat *is* a vulnerable experience, Paige, and I know that scares you. But it can be good if you know them. Trust them."

"Mickey isn't my alpha. It's not like you and your alphas," I protest.

"I'm not asking for you to commit to him forever, Paige. You don't have to ask him to bite you. But get to know him a little better. As adults, I mean. As people who are going to do this together."

"What are you saying, Em?"

"You should date him, Paige. You need to get comfortable with him for this to be in any way a tolerable experience. Go out with him a couple times. Get to know each other."

It's like someone pulled the plug on my brain and all processing stops. Emma wants me to *date* her brother?

This is not how I expected this call to go.

"Think about it, alright?" Emma murmurs. "And remember Paige, whatever could happen between the two of you, I could never hate you."

"I love you," I tell her impulsively. I know I don't say it often enough, but it's true and I need her to know it right now.

"Love you too, Paige. Always, right?"

I know when she first moved away that she was worried I'd take it hard. I know she delayed making the decision best for her family because of me. I know she worries about me. I don't want her to, though. I know she loves me wherever she is, and I love her, and nothing in the universe can change that.

And as soon as I think that, everything inside me gets lighter. I don't know why this thing with Mickey ever made me believe that Emma could stop loving me.

"Think about what I said," she insists. "Both parts of it. Then you make the decision that's best for you, alright?"

And that's what I love about Emma. She could pressure me. She could try to steer me where she wants me to go. It probably wouldn't be that hard to do. But she doesn't. She doesn't think I need to react a certain way to be right.

"Love you," I say again, a little choked up now and not wanting her to hear it, so I end the call.

Chapter 8

Mickey

It's been two days since Paige agreed to let me help with her heat. I've kept my phone inches from my hand the entire time and even turned the ringer on for the first time in years, terrified of missing her call. So far, nothing.

But, barring her calling in the next ten minutes, I have something I need to get done today.

Bill looks up at me from under the hood of his car, grinning. The garage is his domain, and it looks the same as it always does: neatly organized tools and his ancient convertible with the hood up, receiving yet another tune-up. "Hey, Mick. You just missed your mom."

I know; I purposefully came right after she left for the book club she's in. This conversation with Bill will be awkward enough, and I don't need to drag my mom into it.

"I know. I came to see you."

Bill looks appropriately shocked at hearing that, and I should maybe feel bad about that.

Bill Condor is a good guy. I'm glad he married my mother, and I was happy to get his name and shed at least the name of my biological father. I know Emma looks up to this man like he hung the moon, and my mother loves him with her whole heart. I'm glad they have that kind of relationship.

Bill and I have always been a little different. It's hard to give into that whole-hearted love for someone when you saw the last man in your house punch your mother unconscious when she didn't cater to his whims fast enough. Vigilance had been beaten into me, and Bill stopped trying to win me over a few months after he met me. Oddly enough, that had helped. It felt like there were fewer pretenses between us; his job was to make my mom happy, and my job was to make sure no one ever hurt us like my father had again.

So I don't come to visit Bill just to chat. I've never called him *dad* like Emma often does. We co-exist, and we get along, but we're not friends. And he's probably confused as hell right now.

"You and I are going to have an awkward conversation," I tell him. "And after we're done, we're going to pretend it never happened and never have it again."

Bill sets his tools aside. "Alright. I'm listening."

"You're a beta who married an omega."

"Yeah, I am. What about it?" His tone sharpens and his shoulders tighten, and I take a moment to think about this man who has probably heard for the last fifteen plus years that he can't properly satisfy his wife because society is full of a bunch of ignorant assholes who love to shove people in little boxes.

But as much as I don't want to think about it, I know Bill satisfies his wife. It's why I'm here.

"I know Mom's had heats." Only three or four as far as I know, but I wouldn't bet on that being entirely accurate. I know we'd gone to visit my Aunt Jessica a few times when I was a teenager for that reason, although mom definitely hadn't told us that's what it was about. I know she and Bill had wanted more kids, and heat was always the most likely time for an omega to conceive. They'd never had any more, and as far as I know, the heats had stopped when that failed, although I don't want to know if that's true or not.

"Mhm."

I sigh. "I know an omega who's about to go through a heat. She needs help, and I want to know how to help her."

He raises an eyebrow at me. "At the risk of stating the obvious, you *are* an alpha, Mickey. You have all the right equipment for that task."

"It's Paige," I admit, because that's the only way to explain what I'm thinking. Bill's eyebrow shoots ever higher, but I don't stop to let him ask questions about how that's come about. "And I'm not sure she's going to want that. Be comfortable like that. So I'm looking for alternative options." Do I want to knot Paige? More desperately than is right to admit, even to myself. But I'm not convinced Paige has ever had a positive

71

sexual experience, and I didn't offer to help her just so I can get laid. If Paige needs me to make sure she takes her meds and be the guy who holds the sex toys and gets her water, then that's who I'll be.

Bill is silent for a long moment. "If you're under the impression that betas don't fuck their omegas during the heat, then—"

"Stop." I'd like to say I sound firm and not like I'm begging, but I really, really don't want to hear that. "I'm mostly talking about simulated knots. In case she doesn't want mine."

"Are you going to have that kind of self control?"

I bristle at that. "Of course I will." Like I'd ever hurt Paige. Like I'd ever hurt any omega, but especially not Paige.

I've slept with my fair share of people, and a good number were omegas. I never lost control in my adult life, and it'll be doubly important I don't with Paige. I'm up for the task.

"Don't *of course* me. That's a lot of hormones and pheromones flying around."

"I'll be fine." I'll have to be. I absolutely won't entertain anything else.

Bill moves around the car so there's nothing between us. I wish he wouldn't; this conversation was so much easier with a barrier separating us. "What exactly do you want from me, Mick?" he asks, stepping closer. "Because if you're genuinely here to ask for sex toy recommendations, I'm going to tell you you're thinking about it wrong."

"I am?" I ask, my voice barely coming out as a croak.

"You ever been with an omega in heat before?" he asks me.

"No." I'd never wanted to.

"It's not about the sex toy. First of all, the omega chooses what goes inside them, and there's absolutely no guarantee she'd like whatever I told you to get. Let her choose what she wants and work with that. Second, a heat probably would be hard on Paige, but I think you'd be good for her."

I try to dismiss that, because that's irrelevant, and Paige doesn't have a ton of options, but Bill stares me down, forcing an uncomfortable eye contact. "A heat is about trust, Mick. It doesn't work if there's no trust. And I think you're one of the only people she trusts. Talk to her, listen to her, and it'll all be fine."

I take that in for a moment. "Paige trusts me to take care of her," I repeat, almost numb at the thought.

Bill doesn't find that as terrifying as I do and gives me a half smile. "Yeah, she does. When will this happen, anyway? I didn't know she was planning to do that. When?"

"Could be any day now. She went off her suppressants already. She'll call me when it starts."

But Bill is already shaking his head before I finish. "Mickey: you care about Paige. Right?"

"Of course I do."

"And you want this to be good for her? You want her to enjoy this?"

73

I hesitate a second. "Paige isn't doing this entirely by choice. It's more of an obligation."

He stares straight through my soul. "Whether this is something she has to do or something she wants to do, if she chose you to help her, then *help* her. And I'm telling you, in this very awkward conversation that we will never acknowledge again, that it doesn't matter what equipment you bring to this. It's all about the feelings. A heat is a vulnerable time and I can only imagine how awful it would be without trust." His face goes dark, and I'm forced once more to remember that Bill sleeps with my mother, a woman who probably had multiple heats with my father, considering she conceived two kids with him. I wonder how much she's told him about that. "Your whole goal should be to ensure that Paige trusts you and feels safe with you. That she really knows you and you know her."

I get it. I was stupid to ask about sex toys like that would somehow solve all of Paige's problems; this is about so much more than that.

"So, no waiting for her call. Go to her and make sure she's comfortable. Date her, Mick. Take care of her."

Date her sounds uncomfortably too close to a dream I can't acknowledge that I've had, but the rest of the advice is sound. "Alright," I agree, turning to leave, but I stop by the door. "Bill—thanks. For everything." I hope he knows I mean this, but also everything else. For giving that type of trust and safety to my mother. For being the father Emma needed. For never making any of my fears come true.

He's already back behind the hood of his car and looks up at me. "I'm forgetting this conversation as soon as you leave this room."

I smirk, there and gone. "Fair enough," I agree, and turn to go make a plan.

I'm wondering if it would be appropriate to go to Paige's house and what I should even say to her when my phone rings.

I nearly knock it off my end table in the rush to pick it up. It's Paige, and I hit the accept call button so fast I jam my finger.

"Hello?" I ask, bracing for her to tell me it's time. My breath comes in shorter. I can't get what Bill said out of my head. What if she doesn't trust me? What if the difference between her having a tolerable heat and not is a date or two, but I didn't get to give her those?

"Mickey?"

I don't know why she asks; she's the one who called me. "I'm here, Paige. What's up? Is it time?"

"Not yet," she says, and it's like a physical weight lifts off my shoulders. "I was wondering—do you want to have dinner?"

Paige has never asked me for that before. Paige sees me at the library, at dinners with my mother, and when Emma is in town.

She never asks to hang out. But fuck, I'm glad she is. "Yes. Let's do that. Do you have a place you want to go?"

"I've been cooking," she says. "Want to come over? Or we can go somewhere else if you don't want that, and I'll eat this tomorrow, and—"

"Your place sounds great." It's a good sign if she invites me into her place, right? It's one step away from being invited into her nest. "Can I bring anything?"

"No, just come over." She sounds unsure as she says it, but I don't think it's hesitation to have me there. Maybe I'm projecting that, though. I don't want her to be hesitant about having me over.

"I'll be there. Thirty minutes?"

"See you then."

I stare at my phone after she hangs up. I can do this. I can *date* Paige. I can make her feel safe.

CHAPTER 9

Paige

I'm breathing like I ran a marathon when I hang up with Mickey.

I can't believe I invited him here to eat my mediocre cooking. But if the alternative is a restaurant, then that's not happening tonight. I've had the lights as low as possible in my house all day, trying to minimize the pulsing pain in my right temple.

What if he doesn't like my cooking? What if I embarrass myself?

If he doesn't like it, then he'll pretend to, I sternly remind myself. That's what people do, and Mickey is polite enough to pretend.

But I don't want him to pretend. I don't want to make this awkward or make him not like being here.

Too soon, there's a knock on my door, and I barely have the table set with my nicest dishware—still not that nice, but at least not chipped—when I have to go let him in.

As soon as the door closes behind him, Mickey pulls me into a firm, deep hug. I squeak at first, not expecting it at all, but

Mickey learned fast exactly what type of touch I like; the hug squishes me in all the best ways. He rests his head on mine and I melt into his arms.

Emma's voice won't get out of my head. She says Mickey likes me, that he wants this to be more. Is this a sign of that? He's never hugged me before the other day.

Do I want this to be more? I'm still a little stuck on why Mickey would want *me.* I'm a hot mess at all times, and while Emma would say *emphasis on the hot*, I know I can be a lot to handle. I don't understand people half the time, I miss social cues, I get overwhelmed easily when a lot is going on. I'm great at detail work, but not so much the big picture, or anything requiring human interaction. I don't drive because there's way too much stimulation involved and cars terrify me. I'm in pain all the time and that sometimes makes my life quiet and boring by necessity. I couldn't guess how to flirt and I bet he'll think I'm needy before long.

And that's *fine*. I accepted who I am. I accepted that it means I'll probably be alone, at least romantically. I have Emma and her alphas and the rest of the Condors as my family, and that's enough.

Except I can't get Emma's words to leave me alone.

"It's good to see you," Mickey murmurs into my hair. I shiver, but not in the bad way when something too light tickles along my skin. No, this is good. Soothing, like warm water.

"I made meatballs," I say, then wince, because even I know that's an inappropriate response.

But Mickey just chuckles, squeezing me extra hard for a moment before letting me go. "How are you feeling, Paige?"

That's a loaded question. I know he's asking about my heat, though, so I try to keep my answers relevant to that. "I think I might be nesting? I moved furniture earlier in my office and re-made my nest three times. And I cleaned after work." Which probably explains the splitting headache. Most cleaning chemicals don't agree with me.

"Sounds productive. Did you work earlier?"

"Mhm. Busy morning."

"Would you be upset if I told you that I don't understand your job?" he asks. "I know you went to law school and are good at what you do, but I could not tell you the day to day goings on to save my life."

"Why would you? It's not an exciting job. Lots of paperwork and reading fine print and research. I send a lot of emails. Do video calls too. It's all very boring."

He smiles at me in a way that's so blinding I stop breathing for a second. "But you're great at it."

When I remember how to breathe, I ask him, "How do you know? You don't understand what I do."

"I know you, Paige. You're talented at whatever you put your mind to."

That is so patently untrue it's not even funny. I was certainly not talented at the soccer team I tried to join with Emma in middle school, my one and only attempt at organized team sports. I was never talented in the way my parents wanted me to be, graceful and charming and the type of omega who seduces a rich husband.

But Mickey sounds so sincere when he says it that I can't help but smile. It's like he pulls it right out of me.

"Should we eat?" I manage to ask, because we're standing in my entryway and I'm probably being a bad host.

Mickey looks around, nodding slightly as he does. "I haven't been here since you moved in."

Emma, Avery, Philip, Jackson, Bill, Sherry, and Mickey had helped me do a lot of the moving when I'd bought this place. I hadn't owned much at the time, so it hadn't been too bad. Bill had rented a truck, and we'd all loaded my limited furniture and then wrestled it into the house. Now it looks like a real home, lived-in and full. It's like my nest, every piece properly placed and exactly how I want it.

I hope Mickey likes it too. Not that it matters; he's going to spend my heat here and then leave, and it'll probably be years before he's back again.

Unless that's not true. Unless Emma is right, and Mickey wants more with me, and this would become something.

Emma is so often right about anything that has to do with people, but I can't see how she could be right about this one.

Mickey had already made it to my table, smiling and turning to look back at me. "What can I do to help?"

I shake my head. "Nothing—have a seat. I've got it."

"I can pour drinks?" he offers, like he didn't hear me tell him to sit.

"I don't have any alcohol here. Sorry. Did you want something? I should have reminded you before—"

He cuts me off by stepping toward me again. "Paige, don't worry about it. I'm well aware you wouldn't have any, and I don't want any. Whatever you have is more than fine."

My mouth is suddenly dry. "Glasses are next to the sink," I manage to say. "I'll have water. There's some soda in the fridge and orange juice too."

"Got it. Two waters, coming up."

Mickey steps into my kitchen like he belongs here. I plate up the food and Mickey moves deftly around me, like we've been doing this dance for years.

Samuel had never stepped foot in my kitchen. He saw the kitchen as something beneath him as an alpha. He certainly didn't know that I didn't drink and would have been offended that I didn't have wine ready for him.

But Mickey is different. He's always been different.

I plate up spaghetti and spicy Italian sausage meatballs. "Here you go." I look at the plate as I go to set it in front of him. "You're okay with spicy food, right? I should have asked."

He takes the plate from my hands, and I don't think it's my imagination that his fingers brush along mine. "I'm all good, Paige. Thank you for making dinner."

I grab my own plate to hide my reaction to that. Why does him saying *thank you* make me feel like this?

As soon as I'm sitting opposite him, my brain dries up of things to say. That's not unusual, but it doesn't usually happen with Mickey. I start eating, like shoving food in my mouth will fix the problem.

"This is delicious, Paige," he says after a long moment.

"What do you like to eat? So I can have it here, for when... you know..." I shouldn't be having a heat if I can't even talk about it, but it's so goddamn awkward. Mickey and I have arranged to have sex when I likely won't be a good partner, and we set it all up like he's doing me a favor, like when he helped me move or something. It's uncomfortable, to say the least.

"Yeah, I know," he promises. "And whatever you have will be fine, Paige. I read that fruit is a good option? Pre-cut. And someone else online mentioned cheese cubes."

Something inside me warms. "You read about heats?"

"Of course. I do my research, Paige." He seems to hesitate for a second, then admits, "And I talked to a few friends as well. Not specifics about you, just asking them for advice. Since they've done this before."

I'm oddly touched by that. Anyone would think it's fairly obvious and straightforward; insert tab A into slot B and repeat until my fever goes down. But not Mickey. Mickey did research.

It's because Mickey, like always, is too worried about taking care of others. He's somehow decided my health and my heat are his problem, and I worry that he'll give too much of himself to helping me.

I watch him eat out of the corner of my eye, darting looks at him like I'll get in trouble if he catches me. Mickey eats with precise, careful moves, which shouldn't be a surprise. I've never noticed how another person eats before, but all I can think is that Mickey's big hand on my small fork perfectly encapsulates who he is. And then I marvel at how he manages to eat and keep his beard so clean. I suppose it shouldn't be a surprise—it's not like I smear food all around my mouth every time I eat—but a beard seems like a recipe for catching crumbs and making a mess, but Mickey doesn't have a hair out of place.

"Do you want dessert?" Mickey says as soon as we finish our food. "I'll drive us to Molly's."

I shake my head before he even finishes. "I can't go out," I tell him. "The sun's still out and it's too bright."

His head turns so fast I'm worried he's going to injure his neck before his eyes lock onto me. "Have you been in pain this whole time?"

"I'm always in pain, Mickey."

"You know what I mean. More than usual pain. An intolerable amount." He frowns like he doesn't like something he said, shaking his head. "All pain is an intolerable amount. You shouldn't have to be in pain."

"Well, I am. Always. And yes, it's more than usual right now."

"Why didn't you say anything? I didn't have to come over."

"I wanted you to come over. And I'm used to making decisions like this, Mickey. I know people don't think this way, but I do. It's about trade offs, and I was willing to trade this to have you here."

His whole face goes soft. "Thank you, Paige," he murmurs, sounding a little choked up. "I'm happy to be here. Would the ice cream make you feel better? Or at least not worse?"

"Ice cream isn't going to make me worse, but if I go out to get it, it'll be bad," I explain, but he's already shaking his head.

"No, I'll go. You rest. And don't clean up—I'll do that when I get back."

"Mickey, you don't have to—"

"I want to," he interrupts. "I hate that you're hurting, Paige. And I know this is small, but I can do this much."

"You're doing a lot," I mutter. He's doing way more than most, and that's before I remember that he volunteered to help me through my heat.

"What will help you right now? Meds? More water? Going to bed?"

If Mickey is going to leave and come back, then I'm not going to my nest. I'll wait on the couch. "I should teach you about my meds," I say, already thinking through the process. "For, you know. My heat."

"Next time I'm here," he says, warming my heart when he so easily talks about a next time. "You get yourself some meds and lie down. Let me take care of you for a minute."

"All you've done lately is take care of me," I protest.

Mickey steps toward me, but then stops suddenly. I watch him, head tilted and curious, wondering what he wanted to do but decided against. "Taking care of you isn't as hard as you think," he murmurs, stepping back. "Ice cream. I'll be right back."

Ice cream isn't going to magically make me better, but I appreciate the gesture for what it is. Mickey wants to make sure I don't miss out on the experience just because my body betrays me sometimes.

As soon as he's gone, I lie down on the couch and close my eyes. There's the brief rebound pain, the throbbing headache that hadn't seemed so bad when I was ignoring it and distracted a minute ago, but now is all I can think about. I try not to tense under the pain, knowing that only makes things worse, and ride it out.

By the time Mickey returns, the darkness and ease of closing my eyes is making things slightly more manageable. You usually have to get worse to get better, I learned a long time ago, and I always remind myself of that when riding out the worst of the pain.

"Ice cream now, or should I stick it in the freezer?" Mickey whispers. I fight opening my eyes, knowing I'm safe with him and he won't be offended.

"In a few minutes?" I whisper back.

I listen to his footsteps moving away, then the freezer door opening. I hear water running, and I should tell him not to worry about the dishes. But then the footsteps are coming toward me again, and then a blessedly cool compress is laid over my eyes.

I have a washcloth I prefer for this and this one definitely isn't it, but I know it's the gesture that counts. It's so cool and soothing, somehow even better than when I make them myself.

Then I hear him moving away again, and he starts washing the dishes from dinner, and I know right then that Emma was probably right. Whatever this is between Mickey and I, I want more of it. I want it to be real.

Chapter 10
Mickey

I'm acting like ice cream is somehow a cure-all for Paige's pain, but I have to do *something* to help her. I drive a little faster, a little more intently, even though Molly's isn't that far and I'm just getting Paige's sundae.

She invited me over for dinner. She cooked for me, fed me, and talked to me, all the while she was in pain. I need to know how to do better for her, and I don't think she's going to tell me easily.

I understand on an intellectual level what she said, about always being in pain and making decisions about what she's willing to endure. I can understand it and still hate it. I hate feeling helpless, and right now I'm grappling with the idea that I just have to sit and watch as Paige has to make those choices. I'd take it from her if I could.

Well, if Paige won't tell me how to do better for her, I know one person who knows more about Paige than anyone else on the planet. I dial my sister's number before I even consciously think it through.

"I was wondering when I'd finally hear from you," Emma says. "Paige called me yesterday, you know. You're slow on the game."

I didn't know Paige called Emma, although I probably should have guessed it. I don't particularly want to talk to my sister about sex, but I have to work under the assumption that Paige told Emma everything happening between us.

"Hello to you too, Em."

"Don't bullshit me, Mickey. You finally manned up and made a move on Paige?"

"Don't know what you're talking about. I'm doing her a favor—"

"You're doing yourself a favor. You've wanted Paige for years," she corrects.

Only my sister could read me for filth like this. Not my friends, not my mother—there's just something about siblings.

"It doesn't work like that, Em," I tell her. "I'm not what Paige needs. She trusts me, though, and I can help her."

"So could a heat clinic. Notice you didn't spend any time trying to convince her to go to one of those."

I bristle at the thought. "She doesn't like the idea of it. And I'm available."

"Have you seen her at all recently?"

"Yeah, I just left her house. I'm going to get us ice cream. I called you because she's in a fair amount of pain right now, and she's not giving me enough about how to help her, so I thought I'd ask you."

"What kind of pain?"

"A headache?"

"I know that, dumbass. What caused it? Is she photo-sensitive or sensitive to sound? Did her neck do that thing where it locks up? Is she seeing an aura, or nauseous? Is it a full-on migraine, or still a headache? Is it localized to one side or the other?"

I don't have any of those answers. "She didn't want to go out because she said it'd be too bright," I say slowly, because that's truly all I know. I didn't know to look out for those things. I've known Paige for years, seen her in pain more times than I ever could count, and I still don't know enough to be helpful. "Would she tell me any of that if I asked?"

"Probably not," Emma huffs. "You're listening to two decades of wheedling this information out of her."

"I need to learn this. I need to help her."

"Okay, two things," Emma says. "One, no one cares this much about someone they're just doing a favor for. You care about Paige; why won't you admit it?"

"Of course I care about Paige." I *adore* Paige, and not like an extra family member like my mother and sister do. I know I want to be the person she relies on when she's in pain, and I want to eat dinners with her and wash the dishes after. I want to have ice

89

cream sundaes together. I want all of it, every second I can get from her.

And that's the problem. I don't know any way to love that's not greedy like that. If Paige is ever truly mine, I worry I won't know how to let go, and I won't do that to her.

"Paige is going to find someone fantastic for her some day," I tell my sister, and then pretend this doesn't hurt to think about. "There will be someone for her a thousand times better than me."

She's quiet for a moment. "Part of Paige's autism is that she sees things in black and white," she says quietly. "It's common; Philip is the same way, too. Basically, there's not a lot of shades of gray in their perception. But for Paige, it means she can't read between the lines on this. Whatever she experiences is just the way it is, in her mind. If you make her feel special and important and then reject her, she's going to assume it means she was never worthy of feeling special and important. Mickey, if you give her mixed signals and do that to her, I'm not sure I'll forgive you. Don't do that to her. If you care about her, you won't."

"It's just her heat," I tell her, pretending it doesn't hurt like I'm pulling out my own heart. "That's all we've agreed to. Just that."

"There's no *just* when it comes to a heat. Trust me. Be careful, Mickey. Please."

"I will be. Help me help her feel better tonight."

Emma sighs but gives me some tips, and I store it all away, priceless information that it is.

When I get back to her house, I put her ice cream away and get her a cold compress, then wash the dishes. I worry for a second that even this will be too loud, but I'm not going to cross the line by bringing up her nest first. She gets to decide when I enter that space.

I haven't been in her house since she moved in. It's a nice townhome-style condo, with two floors and a back deck. It's a swanky place, and I can tell Paige clears good money by looking around. But what this place is not is well set up for a heat. The kitchen is down here, and her nest is all the way upstairs. I need to convince her to stay hydrated, take her meds, and eat when possible. I'm not sure how well that's going to work when I'll have to leave her for extended periods to get those things.

This is why packs exist, why historically a group would build around the omega. Omegas were the social and emotional center of the pack, and everyone else would join in. Group dynamics had a lot of benefits, including the sharing of resources, communal child rearing, and having more people to support the omega's needs while in heat. The last reason is the strongest surviving need, although having four or more people to split a mortgage with is also a big selling point these days.

If only I had it in me to share. But the idea of anyone else being present whenever Paige goes into heat has me gripping the water glass so tight under the soapy water that I'm almost afraid it'll shatter.

When at last her kitchen is spotless and the dishes are drying in the rack, I go back over to her with another fresh cool cloth. I swap out the one on her face, barely resisting the urge to bend over and kiss her forehead.

"Anything I can do for you before I head out?" I ask.

"I'm so sorry about tonight," she whispers instead of answering.

I can't resist it any longer. I press a kiss to her forehead, trying to keep my touch firm to see if she'll like that as much as she does a firm hug. She doesn't pull away. "I'm not sorry. I'm sorry you're hurting, but I'm never sorry we get to spend time together. But you should rest. We'll do this again soon? Maybe tomorrow or the next day?"

"We never hang out that much," she murmurs.

"Well, I think it's about time. But only if you want it."

She gives me a tired, pained smile that's so heartbreakingly sweet I almost kiss her again. "I'd like that. Want to go for a walk?"

Her and her walking. I squeeze her shoulder. "Sure thing. Want to meet me at the library?" Tomorrow should be her day to pick up her holds, so that'll kill two birds with one stone.

She nods, and I take that as my excuse to slip away, but not before looking back at her on the couch one last time, jealously hoarding glimpses of her.

CHAPTER 11
Paige

I drag myself upstairs about two hours after Mickey leaves. The medication I took while he was out and the little nap I managed have helped stabilize me, even if I still feel like a ghost. Those pain-induced naps can leave me waking up and wondering what year it is sometimes.

I long for my nest, but it's only nine, and I promised Gavin I'd finish handing off my work before my heat. Without knowing when it'll start, it'll be best to get this out of the way sooner rather than later.

So I wander into my home office, plopping into my oversize desk chair—the big kind that lets me sit cross-legged when I want—and boot up my laptop. Work emails are boring, but also easily manageable. A good spreadsheet can manage most projects, and I spend forty minutes or so updating mine so someone else can understand exactly where I am if needed.

Once my spreadsheets are color-coded and my comments are meticulously detailed, I flip over to Discord to see what people are talking about tonight. I know I should get off the computer—being on here too long is just going to bring my headache back—but right now, I just want a normal interaction that makes sense to me, and the best way to get that is to argue over whether or not glossaries are necessary in books.

After emphatically stating all the reasons they definitely *are*, with a curated list of examples I pull off my shelves, I flip through the channels, landing on the personal channel for life updates. A twenty-one-year-old kid is contemplating grad school, but says they're worried about how they come across on paper. I know that feeling, so I offer to workshop their essays whenever they get there. Someone got married yesterday and posted a picture of what looks like a tiny little ceremony and a beaming couple. After posting my congratulations, I look at the clock and decide it's long past time for bed.

I'll feel better in the morning hopefully. I think I promised to go out with Mickey again, and there's a tiny, fluttery feeling in my belly at the thought. Maybe Emma was right. If this was just a favor, then he could just wait for me to call and be done with it, right? If he wants to see me more, there has to be a reason for it. Mickey wants *something*.

Maybe I'll find out tomorrow. I close my eyes and begin to drift off, letting sleep ease my pain so I can have a good day tomorrow.

⌀

I wake up early, take my meds, and then make my to-do list before work. It's remarkably short for today—a few work-related tasks, a reminder to clean up the kitchen, but the last item just says *meet Mickey*. I have no idea what's going to happen when we meet, so I can't plan for it. I don't like a lack of specificity and not knowing what's coming. But what usually leaves me completely out of sorts now just puts that fluttery feeling back in my belly. I don't like not knowing, but this is probably what people mean when they talk about taking a leap of faith, and I think I'm willing to take one.

I have ice cream for breakfast, digging the sundae out of my freezer and eating it while watching my backyard out the window. *Backyard* is a bit of a misnomer, considering it's just a five-foot strip of grass and then trees, and I don't own the land, anyway. But I can usually watch birds and squirrels and sometimes even deer and foxes out my window, so I'll take my mediocre little yard. Today there're just squirrels, and I watch them run around until the ice cream is gone.

A part of me wants to text Emma and ask her what the ice cream means, but another part of me already knows. Or guesses, at any rate.

I set an alarm on my phone before heading back upstairs. I can't be late seeing Mickey this afternoon, after all.

CHAPTER 12
Mickey

Paige shows up at the children's room about fifteen minutes before we close for the evening. She hesitates by the door, clutching the worn strap of her bag and looking around. "C'mon over, Paige," I call. "You can wait in the office if you want." It's technically my office, and I use it when I'm completing paperwork or writing emails, but I'm rarely in it otherwise.

"I know I'm early," she mutters as she draws closer.

"That's okay, Paige. Happy to have you whenever." I hope she knows how much I mean that. If she wants to hang out here all day, every day, then I'd be thrilled. "Only need a few more minutes."

Paige opens her mouth to respond, but then a patron cuts her off. "Excuse me," a woman says, her voice high and nasally. "But where in the world is the librarian?"

I look over at her, irrationally annoyed she's interrupting my conversation with Paige, but patrons do have to come first. She's clutching the hand of Timmy, a four-year-old who comes in to play with the train set and pick out a few picture books while his sister is in the Girl Scout meeting in the function room downstairs. He never comes in with this woman, though; usually he's with the nanny, a sweet omega who tries to use the time to study for the business classes she's been taking.

This must be the mother. She's holding Timmy's hand like he's a wild animal who might run off, and Timmy's eyes keep darting toward where he knows the trains are. "I'm the librarian," I tell her.

She scoffs. "No, the *children's* librarian. Oh, there you are. I didn't see you behind him." And then she turns to Paige.

Paige, who always looks amazing but definitely isn't dressed for work, what with her leggings and too-big t-shirt. Paige, who can't help making a disgusted face when the woman steps closer with the child in hand.

"No," she says, shaking her head and stepping back.

The woman gets closer. "Excuse me?"

I step in front of Paige, shielding her from this woman and her cutting stare. "I am the children's librarian, ma'am. She is a patron. What can I do for you?"

She looks me up and down like she can't believe what she sees. "You? A big alpha with the little kids? What could you possibly want with them?"

"To do my job, ma'am," I tell her, trying not to sound completely exhausted. I should have expected this. She thinks alphas have nothing to do with child-rearing, and omegas are natural little nurturers. Never mind that I actually enjoy spending time with the kids and Paige looks like the idea might give her hives.

She turns to Paige again. "The train set is germy and needs to be wiped down."

The train set is perpetually germy, and while I clean it every day, we have toddlers in here all day long. It kind of comes with the territory of having small children. I debate offering her the wipes to do it herself, but something tells me that won't go over well, so I take a deep breath. "I am the children's librarian," I reiterate. "Let me grab some anti-bacterial wipes."

"You're *not* the children's librarian."

What the fuck does she think I am? I'm standing by the children's room desk, I'm wearing a name tag that literally reads *Mickey Condor, Children's Librarian*, and there's even a plaque on the desk that says my name. I have a Thomas the Tank Engine pin on my lanyard. Who else would I be?

"I am," I assure her.

She grips Timmy's hand even tighter. "That's not natural. I think I should talk to the director. What kind of role model are you for Timmy?"

Paige flinches out of the corner of my eye, and my muscles in my neck lock. I'm used to this, but not the hot flush of humiliation that comes from having Paige watch it.

She can speak to the director. I'm qualified for my job, and it's not like the director hasn't heard it all before.

"Mickey is great with kids," Paige says, her voice no-nonsense and firm, the way it gets when she digs into something. She takes a step closer, stepping between the angry mother and me. Paige is maybe five two, and while the bun piled high on her head gives her a little more height, she could never hope to block me from sight.

I'm torn between being warm inside that she'd want to defend me, and being angry that she'd ever put herself in the potential line of fire for me. I'm left unnaturally warm and unable to speak while watching this all play out.

"And who are you, then? If you don't actually work here?" she sneers, and I nearly find my voice again, because she's not going to talk to Paige like that.

But Paige doesn't need me to defend her, and she hasn't in a long time. She tilts up her chin, staring this woman down, and says, "Mickey has been a critical part of this library and a tireless advocate for the kids. And more than that, he's a great role model for the kids, showing them what it means to be literate, kind, and knowledgeable."

"What does an *alpha* want with kids?" she bites out, whip-fast and just as brutal.

"To promote childhood literacy?" Paige asks, voice dripping in sarcasm. "He's got a masters degree in it."

The woman scoffs. "And what, are you his bodyguard?"

Paige holds her ground and says, "His girlfriend, actually," and I think I've lost my damn mind.

CHAPTER 13
Paige

I recognize this type of person. The woman is a beta, but the type of beta who *loves* a system that favors alphas. She probably pays an omega to watch her kids because they're more *nurturing*, and loves alphas when they're doctors or politicians or cops or whatever, but thinks it's not showing proper alpha pride when they dare to look after kids or clean or do anything even remotely associated with an omega.

It's like looking at my mother twenty-some-odd years ago, and I refuse. I put up with that once, when I was too young to do anything else. I'm a grown ass adult now, and I'm fueled by rage and pain. I won't let this woman get away with being an ass, especially not to Mickey.

So I step in, and then I say the dumbest thing I can possibly say.

Now, I stick my foot in my mouth sometimes. I've said things that get me in trouble more than my fair share of times. I try hard not to; I am the queen of thinking before I speak, and I've tried to learn from my social faux pas in the past. I'm not perfect, but I do try.

And I know as soon as I say *girlfriend* that I've fucked up.

I'm thinking about the heat. I shouldn't be—that should have no bearing on this—but I'm thinking about the elephant in the room between us. I'm thinking about what Emma told me, and I'm thinking about how Mickey stepped in front of me when this woman started being rude.

I'm also thinking that betas like this trust a family man a little more than a lone alpha, and if she's going to practically accuse Mickey of being a predator, then I should do whatever I can to dissuade her of that.

So my stupid comments spew out of my mouth, and now it's too late. I can't take it back.

Mickey inhales so sharply I think he might be hyperventilating, but I keep staring this woman down. I want her to leave. I don't want her to say another word to Mickey. Only when I've accomplished that much will I deal with the mess I've made.

I try to salvage this. "You look at me because I'm an omega and think I'm good with kids, but I promise you, you don't want to leave your kid with me. But Mickey is literally an expert in kids and childhood literacy and all of that stuff. He has a masters degree. He is a good role model for kids, way better than I ever could be. Your own prejudice is stopping you from doing what's best for your son. You're hurting him in the long run, and I think that's sad."

The room is dead silent, and the only thing I can hear is my pounding heart. She blinks at me, then seems to come back to life and sputters, "Well, I've never—come on, Timmy. We're going."

"Twain," the boy says stubbornly, trying to tug out of her grip.

"I *said*, we're going."

"Twain!"

Mickey steps around me and crouches down to the little boy's level. "I promise, the train will be here when you come back in a few days, buddy, alright? It'll be waiting."

The mother tugs her son back like Mickey might be diseased, but Timmy doesn't move.

I study Mickey and the kid. I've never wanted one of those—they're loud, and demanding, and I don't think I can give them what they need—but I can already see that Mickey has this boy's interest in a way I couldn't hope to duplicate.

Fuck the people who say omegas are nurturing. This man knows exactly what to do. Mickey sticks out his hand. "Pinky-promise."

The little boy solemnly makes the promise and finally allows his mother to tug him away. Mickey straightens up, smiling like this woman didn't call him a bad role model for daring to do his job. He even smiles like this is some ordinary interaction.

I'll never understand people's ability to fake shit like that.

Mickey watches them for a minute before turning to me. "Are you okay, Paige?"

Am *I* okay? I'm not the one who was publicly insulted just because I don't fall into what this woman thinks alphas should behave like. I should be checking on him, should make sure he's okay after that nonsense—but then I realize I'm nearly hyperventilating.

"Sorry," I manage to gasp out, but Mickey is already moving, wrapping me in his arms and squeezing tight, the perfect pressure, and fuck, how did we go so many years without touching when he's so good at it?

"You're okay," he murmurs into my hair. He keeps doing this, keeps holding me and burying his face in my hair. Does he like this too? Or is it just another thing Mickey does to take care of others?

"I'm sorry," I say again. He squeezes tighter.

"Let's go into the office," he says, and yeah, that's a good idea. There are children here, and their parents, and I hope most of those people are way nicer to Mickey than that woman was, but they probably won't be if they think Mickey is letting an unstable omega melt down in front of their children. I nod, expecting him to let me go.

Instead, he keeps me wrapped in his arms, keeps the pressure perfect, and walks us both backward into the office. I peek out from where I'm hiding my face in his shirt, and there are big windows by the office door, so we don't have that much privacy, but at least we can shut the door.

"Can you tell me what's going on in your head?" he asks gently.

No, I can't. What's going on in my head is static, a recursive loop of noise I can't possibly hope to sort through. I shake my head against him rapidly, like I can somehow shake my thoughts loose.

"Alright, alright," he murmurs. "You're okay, Paige."

"Sorry," I mutter again. If it's the only thing I can manage to say, at least it's something important. I don't know what I'm apologizing for—for this, or for what I said, or for everything else, how awkward I've made things between us recently—but the apology seems more than warranted.

"Do you want to sit down?"

I shake my head again. I don't want him to stop holding me, even though I'm sure I should want it, because I'm probably making things incredibly inconvenient for him.

"Alright, that's fine. We can stay here for as long as you need, but I need you to take some deep breaths for me, alright?" When I don't immediately succeed, he continues. "Together, okay? In for three—" He takes an exaggerated breath—"and exhale for three. Alright, again."

It takes a few repetitions for me to get my breath to match his, but eventually I do, and the static in my brain slowly turns quieter. I can hear my own thoughts and begin to process through them.

Mickey shouldn't be treated like that. Dynamic essentialist bullshit has no place in our world, and what that woman said was crap. But even so, what I said was so out of line. Poor Mickey. Whatever Emma said about us, I know you don't gain boyfriends by claiming them against their will. And I did it in his workplace. I was so furious when Samuel came into my workplace and dragged my personal business in front of everyone.

"Tell me five things you can see," Mickey murmurs.

I squeeze my eyes shut. "This isn't a panic attack, Mickey."

"I know. But you're so far in your head, and I think this will help you be here. Can you try it for me?"

I reluctantly force my eyes open. "Your shirt," I mutter, staring directly at his chest. "Red and gray checks. Your lanyard. I don't know that character."

"Thomas the Tank Engine," he supplies quietly.

"Him." I force myself to pull back, but only slightly. "Your computer. That thing is ancient. Books. And this ugly carpet."

"Thank you. How about hear?"

"You. My heartbeat. The lights are buzzing. The computer hums."

"You can hear all that?"

"Mhm." Electricity never stops buzzing, and it's a special kind of annoying sometimes.

"Okay. Touch?"

"Your shirt is soft. Your beard tickles on my head." I wiggle my toes. "My socks."

"Thank you, Paige. How're you doing?"

I force myself to take another deep breath. "Okay. Sorry."

"No need to be sorry. Do you want to talk about it?"

"Did I ruin things for you here? I shouldn't have said that. If you need me to apologize to your boss, I can. If you need me to stop coming around here, I will."

"No," he says firmly. "None of that is at all necessary. Besides, my boss would kill me if I was ever crazy enough to tell you to not come around. I think you single-handedly keep our fantasy circulation numbers up."

That's *a little* funny, considering the two new fantasy books I shoved into my purse when I first got here. I manage to giggle, and Mickey smiles at me. "You were not the one in the wrong, Paige. She said something inappropriate, and I wish she wouldn't say shit like that in front of her son. That boy is an alpha and I wish she'd let him have role models that don't perpetuate every toxic stereotype. But if she chooses not to come back, that's on her, not either of us. You didn't do anything wrong."

"I shouldn't have said we were dating," I mutter. "People heard that." Mickey's never dated anyone for long, as far as I know. I don't think he exactly picks up dates at his place of business, but me telling people he's my boyfriend can't be convenient for him. It's a small town; word gets around.

"You said it to protect me. And I don't mind. Trust me."

Is he hinting at what Emma told me? Mickey should know better than to think I can understand hints. I need him to come out and say it, or dispute it, or literally do anything but leave me here guessing.

But he doesn't give me a chance to ask. "Let's go for our walk, if you're still up for it."

"I'm up for it." I love a good long walk, although I don't know if it'll be as relaxing with someone else along with me. But with Mickey, I'll try it.

"Alright, great. Let's go."

I glance at the clock to find the last fifteen minutes have indeed ticked down. "Do you need to do anything before we go? Considering everything?" Considering *me*, and the mess I made.

"Nope," he says. "We're out of here. You need anything else?"

I shake my head, still waiting for the other shoe to drop, and follow him out the door.

CHAPTER 14
Mickey

A ndre is standing on the stairs by the main circulation desk as we go to leave, eyes wide as he stares at me, and I know one of his teenage spies must have overheard what happened. Andre gets the gossip faster than anyone else I know. The teenage pages can't seem to keep their mouths shut around him.

I widen my eyes and shake my head, hoping he has the brains to not say anything. But all he does is nod and smile. I'm sure I'll get a text later, but I'm so damn thankful he didn't say anything in front of Paige, who is still barely containing her freakout.

That said, I need him to go make sure the children's room gets emptied out properly. I tilt my head in that direction and he nods, and I know I owe him a favor or two. He's a damn good friend.

"So, where are we walking today? Back to your house?" Her house seems like a good option. I don't know how much of being in public she's up for, and at least if we walk to her house I'll know she makes it home safely.

But she shakes her head. "There's a path out behind the library, connecting to the old rail trail. If you're up for it?"

I'm still wearing my work clothes, khaki slacks and a checkered shirt. At least I have real sneakers on, and I can shed the checkered shirt and leave myself in an undershirt, and that'll be good enough.

"Sounds great; let's go."

It's quieter out here once the trees swallow us up. Not that we live in an especially loud town—there's enough sidewalk and few enough cars that I don't truly worry about Paige's habit of walking anywhere she can—but there's something peaceful about this, and I get why Paige likes it so much.

"I'm sorry I embarrassed you at work," she says matter-of-factly, looking straight ahead.

"A beautiful, intelligent woman with a great job, her own house, and a voracious love of books claiming to be my girlfriend isn't *embarrassing*, Paige."

No, I'd liked it too damn much. I hadn't had time to revel in it because she'd started panicking, and that had to take priority. But there's still some sort of vicious, possessive thrill inside me. Paige claimed me in public. It sent my brain into overdrive, thinking of her making that statement with a kiss, or wearing my clothes, or having my ring or my bite on her neck.

The alpha instincts drive me to *possess*. The fact that I can't hear her say something like *girlfriend* without wanting to lock her down forever isn't great; I've been told before I'm too intense, move too fast, and I know that's one step away from my worst fear.

Someday, my need to possess could turn violent. I could need it so badly I put my hands on someone. I've seen it before, after all. I grew up with it.

"Samuel did that to me at work once," she says, still in that same matter-of-fact tone, still looking straight ahead. My thoughts are abruptly jerked off course by that name. *Samuel.* I never even met him, but I've hated him since the day Emma told me he existed. "I had to go in for an in-person client meeting. And I was nervous because I knew it was a big deal. Samuel showed up before the meeting ended, looking for *his* omega, since I wasn't at home where he expected me. It was embarrassing."

My blood boils. I might be a possessive asshole, but at least I work on it. At least I temper my alpha instincts. There are some people out there who should be locked up until they learn some damn manners.

I could explain to Paige that Samuel wanted to possess her like a pretty trophy, and that he'd made her uncomfortable for good reason. I could explain that the idea of being possessed by her was different for me, and I'd more than welcome it. I don't.

Because that right there are the mixed signals Emma warned me away from.

"You were trying to protect me," I tell her instead. "And I appreciate that." She frowns, but at least doesn't try to argue it.

"How're you feeling, anyway?" I ask her, because that's much more interesting than what happened.

"Alright. Better than last night. Thank you for the ice cream—I ate it for breakfast."

"Did you sleep from when I left to breakfast?"

"No, I was up a few hours later. I felt better after a nap, enough to get some stuff done. Rest is really the only almost guaranteed way to adjust my pain levels."

"And they're adjusted back to normal?" I wince, because something about that sounds wrong. "I'm sorry, I don't know how to talk about it—tell me if I fuck it up."

"Normal is fine. Yeah, I'm essentially back at my baseline."

"So, quiet, cold compresses, letting you rest—anything else I should know?"

"Medication, hydration, carbs for some reason—all those can help too. Light exercise if the pain is building but hasn't crossed the threshold yet."

I don't think *light exercise* is exactly going to be something we can achieve during her heat, at least, not unless sex counts. But *carbs* is good advice, and new to me. I make a mental note to pick up bagels or something. When I drop her off tonight, I have some shopping to do.

It's been four days since she stopped taking suppressants, so her heat could technically come any minute. I need to be ready to take the best care of her.

111

My phone buzzes in my pocket, and I reluctantly pull it out to see a text from Andre. *Girlfriend???*

Another text comes through immediately after, because Andre has never met a situation where he won't double text. *Did you finally get your shit together and ask her??*

Then, *Good for you. Proud of you.*

I roll my eyes and slide my phone away. Let him—and everyone else—think what they want.

We walk for the better part of an hour, and I'm sweating buckets through my clothes. I couldn't give less of a fuck, determined to watch Paige be her contented self, somehow seeming lighter out here.

When we return to the library parking lot, Paige gives me a smile so dazzling that I lose all power of speech for a solid minute. "Thanks for doing that with me. I like spending time with you," she admits.

And I absolutely *adore* every second of spending time with her. It's the sweetest torture, and I need to get my shit together.

"Want to go out again tomorrow?" I ask her. So much for getting my shit together.

Her nose wrinkles. "You'll make the rumors spread more. People will think what I said today is true."

"I don't care about what people think, Paige. This is about us. I want to spend time together. But if you don't—"

"No," she interrupts hastily. "Let's do it. Maybe we can actually go out tomorrow? Depending how I'm feeling?"

"I'd like that." I'd like that way too much. "Can I drive you home for now?"

"Sure. Thank you."

When I get to my apartment, Andre is waiting in his car in my driveway.

I slow down. Andre and I hang out outside of work sometimes, but he's never shown up at my house before. This is new.

He opens his door as soon as I put my car in park. "Alright, spill," he says without any sort of greeting. "When'd you finally get your shit together and ask her out for real?"

Ah, so that's what this is about. I ignored his texts, and he had to come here to interrogate me in person.

"Paige wanted that mother to shut up and said what she did to make her," I tell him. "That's all."

He blinks at me. "You're telling me you have a pretty, brilliant girl who not only wants to defend you, but is willing to fake date you to do it—and you won't lock that down?"

"I'm no good for her." I walk over to my front door.

"What's that supposed to mean?" Andre demands while following me.

Andre is a friend, but there's a limit to conversations I have, even with my friends. How do I explain that I look in the mirror every day and see a man I hate, and I look at Paige and I see a

113

target for all my worst impulses, and I worry that I could fuck this up so easily?

The answer is I don't. I can't have people in my life knowing how delicate the balancing act is.

I unlock my front door and Andre follows me inside. "You know her ex is a hotshot lawyer?" I ask him instead of telling him what I'm thinking.

"Okay," he says slowly. "But he's her *ex*, right? So, she's moved on and presumably doesn't want him anymore."

No, I don't think Paige wants Samuel. I never met him, but from what I understand, I highly doubt Paige ever wanted Samuel. "My point is, that's the kind of person she deserves."

"She deserves her ex? Where I come from, some people might consider that a curse."

I refrain from mentioning that Andre comes from two towns over, born and raised. "I mean she deserves a lawyer. Someone who can move in those circles with her." Not Samuel, because he sucks. But someone like that. I'm sure Paige will eventually find someone.

"We're talking Paige, who comes to her public library, doesn't make eye contact, doesn't like loud noises, carries that worn-out old department store bag, reads like thirty fantasy books a week or something, looks at you like you hung the moon? That Paige?"

I shrug. "I've known her since she was eight. I just want the best for her." There. Let him think there are some brotherly feelings in there. It's way better than the alternatives.

Andre doesn't believe me for a second, though. He flops onto my couch like I actually invited him in. "Saying this with love, but I'm here instead of home with my people because I think you and Paige deserve to figure this out. If she's claiming she's your girlfriend, it's because she's thought of it." He puts his feet up on my coffee table. "And burying your head in the sand is a bad look. There's nothing big-brother about how you feel about her and we both know it. Everyone and their mother knows it. Mickey, you want her. So what's the issue?"

I hesitate a second. I want this world he's envisioning. I want to let go of my worries, to take what's being offered.

But I can't. Because if I don't look after Paige, then I'm not worthy of her. Even if the thing I need to worry about is myself.

"When I was seventeen, I had a girlfriend," I tell Andre.

"Alright. That's not shocking, you know?" He looks me up and down. "Given the things I've heard, I kinda assumed you had a few."

No, just the one girlfriend. Everything else had been temporary after that. I'd learned my lesson. "Her name was Katy. I asked her out, we dated for like six months. We dated all the way until her prom. She was a year older than me, so I got invited as a junior."

"Okay." He doesn't get it. The look is obvious on his face, so I keep explaining.

"At her prom, there were a bunch of drunk assholes—you know how people get. How entitled, privileged alphas get, especially. They made an inappropriate pass at her, made a few comments about the way she looked in her dress, stupid, inappropriate, definitely sexual harassment stuff—I freaked the fuck out, Andre. I punched one of them. I got thrown out of the dance and banned from going to my own prom next year too."

"So you looked after your date. What's this have to do with Paige?"

"Because I might have told the guy she was *mine* when I did it. Something like *no one hurts my girl*, punched him in the nose, and then tried to physically drag Katy away, blocking her with my body. Even kept her friends from her for a minute there until I calmed down."

"Still not seeing the issue."

"It was violent. It was inappropriate. It was an overreaction. Katy read me the riot act, and told me I was a possessive, controlling bastard, and I never saw her again after that night. She went home without me, graduated without inviting me, and left for college and doesn't come back here much."

Andre blinks at me slowly. "You're not trying to tell me you're still in love with this woman, are you?"

That manages to surprise a snort out of me. "Fuck no." Seventeen-year-old me had been obsessed, but it had faded easily

116

with her out of my life. And isn't that worse? I know for a fact that what I feel for Paige won't fade. It hasn't in nine years. So how much worse can I get when the feelings are *real*, and not just some teenage infatuation?

"Then I don't get your point."

"My point is when I say Paige deserves someone better, someone respectable and in her circles, there's a reason for it."

He looks at me for a long moment. "But what if what she wants is you?"

I don't have an answer to that question.

CHAPTER 15

Paige

M ickey takes me to Charred Oak, the family-owned restaurant that's been in town for almost a hundred years.

I like the food here. I don't go out to eat often, but I've done takeout from here more than I care to admit, and their spaghetti and meatballs is a classic. Even so, as soon as we walk in, my nose immediately crinkles against the assault of scents.

Mickey must have a sixth sense for my discomfort, because he immediately turns to me. "You okay? Something wrong?"

"There's a lot of scents," I mutter. When he doesn't stop looking at me, I explain, "I think it's going off my suppressants. Everything smells stronger." *Stronger* is an incredibly weak word. When I was in my own home earlier, it had been noticeable but not too bad. I had rearranged my bedding in my nest once more, because this time I had to get the scents to perfectly match what my omega instincts wanted. But it had been manageable.

Here, in a busy restaurant with a full kitchen and a crowd of diners, the scents are powerful. I've been on suppressants for so long that I almost don't know what to do without them.

Mickey ducks us into a booth at the end. "That must be incredibly overwhelming. I didn't even think about that."

"This is what it's like all the time for you, isn't it?" I ask. I've been thinking about that all day. I can't believe he sees the world like this, so full of so much stimuli. How does he get anything done?

"There's some studies debating the similarities and differences between alpha and omega sensory perceptions, but that's not important right now. You're not used to it at all. And I almost hesitate to ask—does it hurt?"

Leave it to Mickey to get to the heart of the matter. "Not too badly." Not yet, at least. We'll see how I do later. Like he said, this is a lot of sensory input.

"Alright, well. Let me know if you want to leave, alright?"

"We came here for dinner," I say, because a little pain is *not* going to stop me from being here with Mickey. Work was long today, and now it's the weekend, and I could go into heat at literally any moment. The increased sense of smell is a good indicator that the suppressants are completely out of my system, which means the heat probably isn't that far behind. I need this tonight.

"We'll stay. But I won't be upset if you need us to leave. Just say the word." I lean a little closer across the table. Mickey is so calm, exuding a sense of ease that I need. And if I lean in, I can pick out his scent from everything else. Pine and peppermint, it somehow matches his relaxed energy, and I want to inhale it until it's all I can smell.

"Did they say anything to you at work today?" I ask, more than ready to change the subject.

"They say a lot of things, Paige. More specific?" He picks up the paper menu on the table, despite probably having eaten here a hundred times. The menu hasn't changed in our lifetimes.

"About yesterday. Us?"

"Oh. that." He clears his throat. "She called the director's office. I had to have that awkward conversation. It isn't the first time and it isn't the last."

"You're not in any trouble, are you?" Employment law absolutely isn't my speciality, but I will tear the library to pieces if Mickey is in trouble just because that woman was an asshole.

"Nope. The director is a good person, Paige. She looks out for me, for all of us. You don't have anything to worry about."

"Good. That's good," I mutter.

"But still, thank you. It's nice to have someone in my corner."

"I'm always in your corner, Mickey." It might not look like what he does for me, or what Emma or his parents could give him, but I am. I always will be.

"I know."

"Hi, Mickey," a chipper voice says. We both look over at the waitress.

"Hey, Sarah," he says before looking back at me. "You know what you want?"

"Yeah." Sarah is still staring at Mickey. They must have been in school together, because I know she's a few years older than me. She looks at him like he's a snack who walked into her section.

I can't blame her. With his beard neatly groomed and his hair a little disheveled, and wearing another checked shirt over dark wash jeans, Mickey looks good. Mickey looks like the kind of alpha people dream about. Mickey looks like the safe, dependable guy who gives great hugs. He looks like a fantasy alpha.

But right now, he's my fantasy, not hers.

I need to talk to someone about this. I've never felt this much for someone before, never cared this much. I could barely muster up the energy to care what Samuel did day-to-day, and he and I were ostensibly supposed to get married. Mickey isn't even in a relationship with me, and here I am, possessive.

"I'll have a lemonade and the spaghetti and meatballs," I tell her.

"Those sound good. I'll take some too."

Sarah walks away, and I hope that the restaurant is busy enough tonight that she'll be kept away from our table most of the night. I don't know what this feeling inside me is, but I know she's causing it and I know I don't like it.

"You have any plans for the weekend?" Mickey asks me as soon as she's gone.

121

"Read some books, I guess. Unless my heat comes." I immediately flush after I say it. Talk about too much information.

Mickey doesn't even flinch. "Yeah, that. Would you be willing to interrupt your reading to see me again? If being out with all the scents is too much, I can cook at my place."

That sounds both delightful and terrifying, but that's not my main concern right now. "Mickey, why do you keep doing this?"

"Doing what?"

"Inviting me out. Trying to spend time together. The heat will happen when it happens. You don't need to be right here when it does; I'll call you." I'll be absolutely desperate by then, and the truth is I probably couldn't resist calling him even if I wanted to.

"It's not about that."

"Then what's it about?" I grab my bag and run my thumb over the strap, up and down. The rough texture it had when I first bought it has been worn almost smooth, but the repetitive motion I've done ten thousand times before helps a bit.

"I don't know. But I know this thing we're doing, it's going to take a lot of trust, and we don't know each other as well as we used to. It's been a long time. So, I thought I'd fix that. And the best way to do that is spend some time together."

Just like that, I think I give him another little piece of my heart. I've been handing more and more of them to him, and soon he's going to have the whole thing. And that'll hurt when I'm forced to let him go after, but I can't change it.

"You talk to my sister recently?" he asks.

"A few days ago. Why?" Why are we talking about Emma? Does he know what I talked to her about?

No, Emma wouldn't do that. She loves him, but she wouldn't tell him things about me that she didn't have to. I make myself take another deep breath.

"Just wondering. She knows you're doing all this, right?"

"She knows." Emma is certainly the person I'm most comfortable spilling all my most private moments too, although Mickey is somehow becoming a close second.

"Good. I'm glad you have someone to talk to, Paige."

Sarah drops the free bread on the table and moves on. I almost interrupt her to say we don't even have drinks yet. But I think twice about it and bite my tongue. I don't need a drink, and no drink is a fair price to pay for her not being here, staring at Mickey.

It's irrational. Mickey is objectively attractive and not actually mine. I don't get to be jealous of that. I don't get to want to tell her to back off.

Is it bad that I'm half-thinking of another situation where I might be justified in calling him *mine* in front of everyone?

Before I can come up with a stupid plan that will likely ruin everything, Mickey smiles, temporarily distracting me, and asks, "So. Tell me about the book you picked up yesterday."

Finally, something I understand. "I'm only halfway through," I tell him. "But so far, there's two servants who stole

123

the king's talking horse, a wizard they're determined to find, who may or may not be real, and I think they're about to meet a dragon. Oh, and there's a talking cat."

Mickey leans forward. "Tell me more."

When the food arrives, I excuse myself to go wash my hands, and Sarah finds me on my way out of the bathroom. "Listen. I don't want you to take this the wrong way."

In my experience, no one has ever started a conversation that way and not followed it by something wildly offensive. I square my shoulders, ready to take whatever it is. It's not like I haven't heard it all before.

Not recently, though. As an adult I can avoid most of the bullies of my childhood. I work from home, only meet with people I need to, and all of those people need something from me, so they don't get to treat me poorly. I go to the library where everyone seems a little weird, and I visit the Condors, who have always treated me well. I have to go to my childhood home sometimes, but other than that, I've cut the bullies out of my life.

"You're telling me you somehow got a guy like Mickey Condor interested in you, and all you're going to do is talk his ear off about your nerdy interests?" she asks.

The words cut like a knife, and the thing is, I genuinely think she meant what she said. She doesn't want to be mean. It hurts nonetheless.

"He asked," I tell her. I know I should walk away. I know that I can't engage with her and win. But I open my mouth, anyway.

She scoffs. "You have no idea when someone is just being polite, do you?"

Sarah didn't know me in school. Sarah probably doesn't know anything about the bullying that I went through, I remind myself. She doesn't know her advice is about to send me spiraling.

"Listen. I haven't seen Mickey with anyone he'd call a *girlfriend* since Katy. And it's not like people don't try. So if for some reason he's picked you—don't fuck it up, alright? I remember you. You're that little omega who always stared after him. If he's giving you a chance—do you want to waste it or not?"

She must see the hesitation in my eyes. "Yeah, you get it," she says. "Stop talking about your stupid books. Let him talk for a damned minute. Trust me; you need all the help you can get."

I force myself to straighten my spine. "When I want your advice, I'll ask for it. I like my books. It's really not that hard to believe that a librarian might like them too."

She scoffs. "I'm just trying to help."

"Paige?" We both jump when Mickey turns the corner down the hallway to the bathrooms. "Where'd you get to?"

"Right here." I wince. Yeah, that's obvious, and not what he was asking.

"I got nervous with you gone so long. Considering, well, everything."

Sarah's stare prickles on my skin, but I'm not going to explain what he means by that. She can figure out a guess all on her own. "I'm fine," I tell him. "I promised I'd tell you if I wasn't."

"Alright. Well, your food is getting cold. And I don't think you'll like it cold."

He's not wrong about that, so I start to walk back to the table. As soon as I walk past him, Mickey presses a hand against the small of my back. "What was that about?" he whispers, leaning down so he can get somewhere in the proximity of my ear.

I wiggle away from his hand as we reach the table. "I could ask you the same thing."

"But I asked first."

It's such a childish response, but technically true, so I say, "She wanted to give me advice."

His brow wrinkles. "About what? I didn't know you two even knew each other."

"We don't. She seems to think we're on a date and that I'm not doing a very good job."

"Well that's bullshit. Want me to go tell her it's bullshit? I can tell her to fuck off and mind her business. Or I can tell her this is the best date I've been on in a long time. Either one. Whatever you want."

"You don't have to tell her anything," I say hurriedly. "I'll tell her anything I want to say." I know omegas have a reputation for being shy and needing to hide behind a big bad protective alpha, but that's never been me. Sure, Mickey might have defended me physically as a kid, but I've grown past that. Now we're adults and the weapons are almost always words, and I always win there.

"You will," Mickey agrees automatically. "It's one of my favorite things about you."

Hell. And I just got those butterflies in my stomach to calm down.

CHAPTER 16
Mickey

I get her to agree to come to my house for dinner on Saturday before I drop her off. Judging by the fact that her senses have gone into overdrive, her heat will probably be sooner rather than later. I don't think she even realizes how obvious it was last night; she balked away from scents like they were kids with fart spray. I know strong scents can trigger her pain, but she reacted way more than usual.

And I'd bet money if I leaned over and touched her she'd be hot to the touch. Even touching her back through her shirt had felt warm.

Paige is going to go into heat at any moment, and I need to clean my house and make dinner. I need to make something she'll like.

She had pasta last night, so that's out. I'm sure she'd eat it again, but I'd feel like a chump for feeding her the same thing. You know who feeds someone the same thing two nights in a row? Guys who don't pay attention to their dates. And I damn well pay attention.

I know Paige would probably eat spaghetti and meatballs every single meal, but there are plenty of other things I know she likes. Not a ton of which I have on hand, but I do have chicken breast, and I know Paige will eat that if I grill it.

I've prepped the chicken and vegetables, and all I need to do is stick it on the grill when Paige gets here when the doorbell rings. Leaving the food on the counter, I go to let Paige in.

And immediately know that something is wrong. She looks like shit, with sunglasses and a hoodie on despite it literally being almost eighty degrees and six in the evening. "Paige?"

"Hey, Mickey." She doesn't look up.

"What's going on?"

"I don't feel great. But I'm fine."

She is not fine. I know she thinks she's fine because she's taught herself to function under terrible conditions, but Paige is *not* fine. Paige is clearly in serious pain, and I hate that she walked over here like this instead of staying home or at least texting me for a ride.

"Come sit down," I tell her instead of arguing. I'm not here to mansplain her own illness to her, and I know she takes care of herself and knows her body better than anyone else ever will. But she's made all her plans for taking care of herself on the presumption that no one else will help, and I want to change that for her.

In the back of my mind, I hear Emma's voice talking about blurring the lines. That if I can't give her my all, then I should back off. That this can only hurt Paige.

When Paige is finally on the couch and I've turned off all my lights, leaving the back window to illuminate the living room, I sit on the footstool across from her. "Any idea what triggered it?"

She shrugs, and it looks a little pitiful. "Who knows. It could be the time I spent on the computer earlier, trying to get my work all done before this"—she gestures to herself, a sweep of her hand that seems to encompass all of her—"hits. Or it could be going off my suppressants. Changing medications and dosages and hormones is not recommended without careful medical intervention for me."

I blink. "So you're telling me they're forcing you to have a heat because it might magically cure you, but actually it's making you sicker?"

"Welcome to my life, Mickey. But that reminds me." She grabs her purse and empties it on my couch, pill bottles spilling around.

"Do you usually carry all of those?"

She laughs a little. "Just this one," she says, holding up one of the essentially identical orange pill bottles. There are three, and then the sleeve of pills that are pretty universally recognized as birth control. "I wrote up my medication stuff for you, and I

130

thought I'd bring it all over—I have a feeling we're running low on time."

So she knows it too. I nod. "Yes, please. Teach me."

"It's not hard." She hands me a piece of paper. "I wrote down their names and what the dose is and when I should take it. This one is as-needed. I doubt I'll need it during heat; probably won't be lucid enough to process the pain." She shakes the pill bottle in her hand as she says that so matter-of-factly. I hate that she believes that. "These two in the morning, and this one," she says, pointing, "again at night. I take the birth control at night, too." She looks at me and must see that this is a lot for me. "I wrote it all down. If you're still comfortable doing this, of course."

"Of course I'll do it," I say immediately, because that was never in doubt. "I've never had to manage more than allergy pills in the springtime. And sometimes an antibiotic or something, I guess. But I'll do my absolute best. I promise."

She's already said messing with her medication without a doctor's intervention can make her even sicker, so it's imperative I don't fuck this up. Paige is trusting me with so much: with her body, with her safety, with her health. And I can't let her down.

"What will the new pill do?" I ask. "Will it replace these?"

"Probably. These aren't as effective as they should be, which isn't surprising. They're meant for traditional migraines, not a persistent headache, so they help me manage the migraine spikes but not the day-to-day. And Nalcodin is an injectable.

131

It'll only need to be done once a month, which would be great. Way less effort to manage that."

"That sounds nice."

"It will be if it works." I hear her trying not to get her hopes up, but I don't say anything. What would I say; that it'll work? I can't promise that. I can't even promise that I'll be right here at her side if it doesn't. That I'll love her either way, support her either way, care for her either way. I'll learn her medication routine and go with her to doctor's appointments and learn everything that makes her feel better on bad days. I almost say it, but I can't. That's too far. That's leading her on.

But I remember that Paige said carbs are the way to go when she's sick like this, so I abandon my plan of chicken and start again. Grilled cheese sandwiches it is, just like I used to make when she was younger. It was the only thing I knew how to cook for years, and I'd made plenty for the three of us while Mom was working.

"Have you taken that yet?" I ask her.

"Not yet."

"I'll get you water."

"I don't need water; I can swallow them dry."

"That sounds disgusting. Give me a minute. You should drink water anyways."

She huffs, but she doesn't protest because she knows I'm right.

So once I hand her a drink of water, I go and make us a stack of grilled cheese. I still bring out the veggies I made, because she should probably have some of those, too. And the two of us eat right there on the couch, demolishing the plate of sandwiches.

I bring the plates to the kitchen and leave them in the sink, and when I come back, Paige is asleep on my couch, bottles of medication still beside her.

I watch her for a moment, fondness spearing my heart. The wrinkle of pain on her brow has finally eased, and she has one hand curled up by her face.

I could watch her sleep all night. I could watch her sleep forever, and that's fucking creepy. I need to stop.

I kneel down on the ground next to the couch, because she doesn't need to wake up with me looming over her. Then I touch her shoulder. "Paige? Paige?"

She wakes with a start, but settles quickly as soon as her eyes lock onto me. "Sorry," she murmurs, her voice already raspy with sleep.

Paige is always sorry, and she never should be. "You're fine," I murmur. "Do you want me to drive you home, or would you rather stay here?"

She tries to push herself up to sitting. "I guess I should get out of your hair."

I put a firm hand on her back, helping her sit up even if I think she should stay lying down. "Let me rephrase. Do you want to stay here, or do you want me to come to your house and stay with you?"

"You don't need to babysit me; this isn't that bad."

This is *miserable*, and I'm not even the one in pain. I don't say that, though. I don't tell her how she should feel. "You don't have to do it alone, Paige," I tell her, voice barely more than a whisper. "You have people."

"It's inconvenient if I bother you for every little thing."

Then inconvenience me, I want to shout. I want to drive that point home, say it over and over until she gets it. I'm desperate to be inconvenienced by her.

Then I remember the line Emma told me not to cross and bite my tongue.

"I'm here," I tell her quietly. "And I'm sorry, but I don't have it in me to leave when you're sick right in front of me."

She looks up at me, opens her mouth, and then shoves me out of the way with weak arms, scrambling off the couch to run for my bathroom.

I'm stunned for half a second before chasing after her. She's already on her knees, puking up all the dinner I managed to get in her. I bend down behind her, helplessly hovering. Her hair is already held back with a hairband, so she doesn't need me to hold it. I don't know if rubbing her back will make it worse.

"Fuck," Paige mumbles, echoing my thinking. "That doesn't happen that often."

It could be a product of the oncoming heat then, or she could just be unlucky today. I stand up and grab a paper cup from by the sink, filling it and handing it to her. "Try this?" She flushes the toilet and then swishes the water, grimacing.

"I have an extra toothbrush I can open for you. Give me two seconds."

I dig it out of the closet, then open it for her. She's standing by then, her legs shaky, and I worry for a second she'll fall over.

I hand over the toothbrush and awkwardly watch her clean up, taking it as an opportunity to study her. She looks clammy and pale, and any chance I would drive her home and leave her there is long gone.

"Come on," I coax when it looks like she's done. "Let's get you some clean clothes and get you to bed."

"I can go—"

"I'd rather you stayed. I won't cross any lines, I swear."

She manages to snort, and it sounds so dismissive that my heart lightens. That's Paige; even this sick, nothing can dim her. "I'm not worried about that. I just don't want to be an inconvenience."

Inconvenience me. The urge to say it gets even stronger.

"It's fine, Paige. I promise. I'll feel better having you here."

She closes her eyes and nods. It looks like even that move pains her. "Let's get you fresh clothes and into bed."

Paige follows me almost docilely, which is such an aberration of what I'm used to that it scares me a bit. Paige isn't herself like this, and she's trusting me to get her where she needs to go. It's only now that I realize the truth; this takes as much trust as her heat will. Paige is giving me so much by being here right now, by showing me these parts of her, and my heart hurts.

My sweats are going to dwarf her, but I hand them to her, anyway. "I'll go get you some water," I tell her. "You should probably try to drink a glass before bed. Replenish some of the fluids you lost."

She nods tiredly again, and I leave before she starts changing.

I get two glasses, on the off-chance I can manage to get her to finish an entire glass. Then I wait a moment, wanting to give her time to get settled without me interrupting.

When I return to the bedroom, I knock with my elbow, and Paige calls a weak "come in" before I enter.

She's in my bed, under my blankets, and I have to tell my dick to stand the fuck down. She's sick, not inviting us to join her.

I see my sweatpants folded on my dresser and raise an eyebrow. Paige flushes. "I hate when pants are super baggy—and your shirt is basically a dress anyways."

Paige is in my bed in just my shirt and presumably her panties. If I had any hope of convincing my dick to chill, that's long gone now. He thinks this is a damn party.

My whole bed will smell like her for days. Weeks maybe, if I'm lucky, of that potent lavender-woody scent surrounding me whenever I sleep. It'll be the sweetest torture imaginable.

That bed currently smells like *me,* and while that'd usually be noticeable but not bothersome to an omega on suppressants, I hope it isn't overwhelming for her in her current condition. "I can go change the sheets."

"No." She says it so fast that I think I imagined it for a second, but then I watch her snuggle deeper into my duvet. "It's calming."

It's *calming?* Paige seems determined to make my heart explode today.

"Alright then," I croak out. "Will you be able to get to sleep? Should I get you a trash can?" It's only then that I remember the water glasses in my hands. I shove one toward her. "You should drink this."

She takes it and sips daintily. "I can probably sleep, and I doubt I'll throw up again. I think I'm good; sorry."

She keeps apologizing, and we're going to have a conversation about that, but it'll have to wait until she's feeling better. "You're fine, Paige. Get some rest, alright?"

Her eyes are already drooping when I leave the room. I know I'll be back to check on her before long; every instinct in me is fighting leaving the room. I'm rational enough to know staying is creepy as fuck, but I want to sit and ensure she gets better, and hold her if it helps, and be there for her. I hate the idea of her being alone for even a second.

I flop onto the couch, pulling the throw blanket over me, not even bothering to change. It's too early to go to bed, but there doesn't seem to be anything else to do except watch the bedroom door and hope Paige is okay, and eventually I must fall asleep doing just that.

CHAPTER 17
Paige

I wake up surrounded by the most calming, soothing scent I can imagine. It's like it tickles something in my brain, like it makes something click in place.

Pine and peppermint. A walking advertisement for Christmas, except it's June. And this bedding is soft enough, but it isn't right—

Mickey's bed. *This is Mickey's bed.* The thought comes to me slowly, but when it does, my eyes spring open, taking in the room around me.

I'm in Mickey's bed. Mickey's bed in his one-bedroom apartment. I collapsed into Mickey's bed, wearing Mickey's shirt, after sleeping on his couch when we were supposed to have dinner, and then I puked and he helped me get myself cleaned up. *Fuck.*

I fucking hate this. I know I should have accepted it by now, considering I've been like this most of my life, but I am so furious at my own body that I'm shaking. I have one chance with Mickey, and it's not even real. It's going to get taken away from me, and I couldn't even have one normal night without my body reminding both of us that it just fails to function properly sometimes.

He made me dinner, and I puked it up. That has to be the worst date ever.

No, the worst date ever is one of the few I went on with Samuel, back when he thought we were engaged and I thought he was the best I could do, and he berated me in a restaurant because I can't stand the texture and smell of fish and he brought me to a seafood restaurant. He'd called me a spoiled brat loud enough for half the people there to hear, and I'd fled the restaurant. That has to be worse.

But last night was probably a close second.

Well, I need to face the music. I'd hide in here a bit longer, but I definitely need my morning meds, and my pills are still in the living room. So I throw back the blankets, only to then learn that I fell asleep in Mickey's shirt and my panties and nothing else.

Great. I suppose I shouldn't be too surprised; I hate getting baggy pants wrapped around me in my sleep. But the fact that sick-me was so comfortable taking my pants off in someone else's bed is a bad sign.

Is this the heat? Am I starting to lose control and do things that I'd never normally do? I don't think my skin is hot, but then again, can people with a fever even feel their own fever?

I scramble around to find my own clothes, which I apparently left on the floor under Mickey's dresser. Once I'm dressed, I emerge from the bedroom only to find Mickey, bare-chested and sleep-ruffled, cooking breakfast. I freeze, watching him for a moment.

Fuck me. Mickey's back muscles look delicious, flexing as he moves around the kitchen. I don't usually notice things like that, but I sure as fuck do today.

He must hear me, because he turns, giving me a great view of the light coating of hair on his chest that trails down his stomach and thickens before it disappears in his pants and his soft smile that always melts me. I bet I could sleep on that stomach. I bet he'd be comfortable. "You're up. How're you feeling today?"

I clear my throat. "Better, I think. I realized when I woke up that I stole your bed. I'm sorry."

"Come sit down," he says instead of acknowledging my apology, which makes me feel even more like shit. I bet his gorgeous back hurts now.

He puts a plate of eggs and a glass of orange juice in front of me, and my stomach swoops with a soft wave of *something* that he remembered that I don't drink coffee.

He gets his own plate, and then, to my immense surprise, he sets the correct pill bottles in front of me. "Wasn't sure if you need to take these with food or not," he says quietly. "So I thought I'd ask."

"It can help," I say. "But it's not necessary."

"You should eat anyways. I know you threw up most of dinner last night."

And I'm starving now. I grab a fork and eat a bite of fried eggs, then push some onto the toast he made. "Thank you. It's good."

"No problem." He finally picks up his own fork, like he needed to ensure I was eating first. For all I know, he did. Was that an alpha thing or a Mickey and his savior complex thing?

"Hey, your phone has been ringing all morning," he says. "I didn't pick up, but you got three or four calls."

I frown, wondering who could possibly be calling me. It's not work, and I doubt it's Emma. There's not a lot of other people who call me.

"I'll check later," I say. For all I know, it's a telemarketer calling over and over. "But seriously. I'm sorry I took your bed last night."

He's quiet again for another moment, then says, "You apologize too much, Paige. You don't owe me any apologies."

"I mean, I ruined dinner, puked up your food, stole your clothes and your bed—I think I owe you an apology."

"No. You don't apologize for any of that. None of that was something you controlled. It just was. You're sick, Paige. I want to help. It's not a bad thing to need help."

"Listen, Mickey. Even I can see that you have a *thing* about taking care of people. It's practically a compulsion. And you've taken care of me a lot in my life. The bullies, when you'd make

Emma and I dinner, or all the nights you didn't complain as I tried to worm my way into your family."

"You didn't *worm your way in.* You were invited in because we *wanted you there.*"

"Semantics," I say, even though I have to admit I'm more than a little touched by this. "You still felt like you needed to take care of me."

"I wanted to."

"You always want to. You take care of people and don't take care of yourself. It's compulsive."

His mouth twitches into a little smirk. "Talking to Emma about me?"

Yes. But not recently. This isn't a new thing. Everyone knows Mickey would do anything to help those he cares about, even at his own expense. "Mickey, I need you to know that, despite how it looks lately, I don't want you in my life just to take care of me."

"Well, I knew *that,*" he mutters. "You've never sought help in your damn life. I know you can take care of yourself, Paige. But you don't actually have to do it all by yourself. You do know that, right?"

Even I can see that he's trying to distract from himself by bringing up me. "Mickey—"

"Taking care of you is important to me," he interrupts. "Not because I have a *thing* for it or whatever, Paige. I'd help anyone. But I want to help you more. I'm thrilled you were here last night when you weren't feeling good, because I like to think that I could give you some measure of comfort, and that's what I want. That's all I want. I spent this morning thinking of all the nights you must have spent on your own, in pain, with no one to even get you a glass of water. And I hated that so much."

I can get my own glass of water, but I know that's not what he wants me to say. And I can't always be here when I'm sick. To tell the truth, I'd much rather be in my own nest, in my own house, tucked away and safe. Mickey *was* nice to have around though, even if admitting that to him would be like enabling bad behavior.

"Eat your eggs," he says quietly. "Please. Protein is supposed to be good for you."

He'd know all about that. He's still not wearing a shirt, and his shoulder muscles are distracting. Who possibly needs shoulders that big?

Still, I eat my eggs. I don't want to disappoint him more.

Mickey doesn't start eating, though. "I know I'm a lot," he says. "Emma's told me off a million times. And she's not the only one—I've heard it from Mom, and my friends, and a former girlfriend. And for the most part, I've tried to back off. But I'm having a real hard time with this, Paige."

"I'm sorry—" I begin.

He holds up a hand. "Listen. Not with *you*. Not with this agreement between us. With *this*. With knowing you're in pain and you'll just keep living your life, ignoring it and not telling anyone because you've been told to solve it on your own for so long. I don't like that. I don't like that you're on your own. I'm not built that way Paige, especially when it's you. I want to be a person you rely on."

I gape like a fish, completely unsure what to do with that. Mickey wants to, what, save me? Take care of me? Is this flattering or concerning? He must misread my silence as something else, because he hurries to say, "But I know I'm overbearing. So tell me to back off when I cross a line. Tell me what the limits are and I'll stick to them."

He's so serious right now. Those big brown eyes, practically pleading with me to answer him, draw me right in. I hope he never finds that out, because I am a goner for that face.

Then again, if he found out, he'd never make that face again, too afraid of taking advantage of me.

"Have I already crossed the line?" he asks softly.

"No." My voice is as quiet as his. "You and your family have always been the only ones who care. And I appreciate it. I love you all for it. But Mickey—I need you to know you don't have to prove anything to me. I already know you care about me."

"Damned right I do," he says firmly. "And that means being there when you're not feeling great. And it's not a burden, Paige. It's an honor to take care of people you love."

An honor. I mouth the words to myself like they'll suddenly start making more sense.

But before I can parse through it, my phone rings again from my purse. I twitch, but it's the perfect excuse to end this conversation, so I go and grab it, determined to figure out who's been calling me all morning.

And then I lose my nerve, and this suddenly doesn't seem like such a great distraction, because the caller ID says *Mom*.

CHAPTER 18

Mickey

P aige goes pale like the life drained out of her, which pisses me off, especially since I just got her looking like she's not inches from death.

I'm about to tell her to give me the phone—as irrational and domineering as it is, I absolutely don't want her talking to anyone who makes her look like that—when she accepts the call and takes a deep breath. "Hi, Mom."

Paige's phone is relatively quiet, but my house is still, so I can hear the conversation on the other end if I strain myself.

Dinner, Friday? I pick up.

Paige bites her bottom lip and starts reaching for the strap on the bag she isn't wearing. She ends up playing with her shirt fabric, listening to the call.

"I don't know, Mom," she mutters eventually.

Honestly, Paige, I don't ask a lot of you. Your father needs you here.

"Maybe. Is Samuel going to be there?"

Probably. You know how your father adores him. You and he should try to reconcile. He's exactly the type of man you should be looking for.

"I'd rather eat glass," Paige says, causing me to snort, which is good, because hearing Samuel's name made my blood pressure jump.

I can't help myself. If Paige can defend me from jerks at the library, then I can definitely defend her from her own mother and the looming threat of her ex. I sneak over to where she is, her eyes still closed, wrap my arms around her—tight, like I know she likes—and lean in toward the phone.

"I'm done sharing you," I murmur, loud enough to be picked up by the phone. "Hang up and come back to me."

Paige's eyes shoot open, turning to stare at me. Her mouth gapes, and I take a risk, closing it with one finger on her chin. "C'mon, baby." I wince at that. Paige never seemed like a *baby* type of person.

She doesn't object, though. She relaxes slightly in my arms.

Paige? Paige? Who are you with?

"I have to go, Mom," she says, voice much higher than I expected.

Paige, bring whoever that is and be here on Friday—

Paige hangs up the phone and drops it on the table. She's shaking slightly.

"Is this a moment where I should hold you or let you go?" I ask.

"Squeeze," she says, and that's enough direction. I squeeze her harder, pulling her into me and rocking us both slightly.

After a few minutes, she relaxes, but I don't ease my grip. I won't let go until she tells me to.

"I didn't know your mom called you," I say, then wince. It sounds worse when I say it like that, but it's the truth; I didn't know Paige's parents spoke to her regularly.

"When she wants something," Paige mumbles, burying her face in my chest. "So this dinner must be for something and she needs me there to make a point."

"For Samuel?" I ask, and that's *stupid*, because Samuel doesn't matter. She already dumped him. He mattered so little to her that she never brought him around. Emma met him—and hated him—but she never even brought him to family dinner.

She shakes her head. "My father is the one who likes Samuel. I think my mom just wants to make a point."

"To who?"

"To me, probably. She doesn't think I'm spending my life wisely. I'm supposed to be married with my second kid right now and have no job other than looking pretty and popping out babies. I don't know."

That makes me see red. Paige heard every stereotype about omegas and autistic girls, said fuck it, and went to law school anyway. She killed it there, and she kills it at her job. Paige makes more money than I could ever dream of in my line of work. She makes more than Emma as a software engineer, too. She bought her own house, has a great job, and by any measure should be considered a success. But apparently, not to her parents.

"I'm going to have to go to dinner, though."

"What? Why? What about your heat?"

She freezes for a second. "Assuming I'm not in heat," she amends. "But other than that, I'll have to."

"Why?" I repeat.

"They can make things difficult for me. I don't work for my dad because he's an asshole, but he wouldn't hesitate to use his influence in the field to make things harder for me. I can't afford to piss him off. And—well, they're my parents. That has to count for something." She looks at me sideways. "You don't have to come, though. She might figure out who you are through town gossip, but I doubt it. She doesn't talk to normal people enough, and I won't tell them obviously, so you should get away without having to talk to them."

"Paige, I knew exactly what I was saying on the phone. I'll go with you on Friday. If you can be my pretend girlfriend, then I can be your pretend boyfriend."

"Why?"

"Why?" I repeat, almost incredulous, but of course Paige needs me to spell it out. "Because no one should have to handle all that alone. And you're going to pretend that it won't be that bad, because I've met you, but I've also unfortunately met your parents, and they suck, Paige."

She lets out a surprised laugh, and a soft, warm sensation encompasses me. I did that. I was here when she was feeling crappy, and I made her laugh.

"Well, at least this might finally make it clear to my father that I'll never get back with Samuel," she muses. "You'd think he'd have heard it the first hundred times I said it, but, well, he's the type of alpha who respects other alpha's claims more than my opinions."

I want to reiterate that her parents *suck*, but I know she's aware. "Why does he want you with Samuel so badly?"

She squirms slightly. I take that as a hint and let her go, and she steps away, turning her back part way. "I tried to be what he wanted. I went to law school and thought I could prove myself. But I'm still me. He refused to hire me. I was lucky that Gavin hates him so much and hired me out of spite. I can't be my father's legacy, apparently, and Mom didn't have any other kids. So, he's pinned all his hopes on Samuel, his protégé."

"You must have liked him at one point. You dated him." She won't face me, and now it seems deliberate. "Paige?" I press.

"I was told that he was the best I was going to get—and I believed my parents when they said it. It was kind of an open secret that we were going to get married, even if no one asked me first. And it took me a few months to realize that I'd actually rather be alone than put up with someone like him."

Who the *fuck* let Paige believe that she wasn't worth more than a shit stain like Samuel? I'm torn between anger and sadness, and sadness wins. I reach for her again, then drop my hands before touching her. "Did he hurt you?" I know more than I should about alphas who hurt omegas.

"No. That would look bad, wouldn't it?" she asks. "I just wasn't a person to him. I was an object. A check-box. Marry me, control me to shut me up, knock me up a few times, then inherit from my father. Simple."

"Except you weren't ever going to shut up," I murmur. "You weren't ever going to be someone he could silence."

"Samuel liked to conveniently forget that we both graduated from the same damn law school. And my class ranking was higher than his, too. For him, I was the omega he'd knock up someday. I'd give up my law career, keep his house. Nurture some babies that he'd ignore until it was convenient. And I'd rather be alone forever than have any part of that. So. I dumped him, and my father has been a nuisance ever since."

It sounds like her father basically offered his daughter to this guy, like this is two hundred years ago where rich fathers would sell off their omega children. Fuck that. But while I'm furious at him, I'm more concerned with Paige somehow thinking she's going to be alone forever.

Paige is fantastic. She's brilliant and funny and so damn beautiful. Her mind spins circles around all of us. She has great taste in books, and always tells it like it is. She's a fighter, and all she needs is a little bit of understanding. Anyone in the world would be lucky to have her. I can't let her think that Samuel was her one chance for a relationship.

"You'll find someone, Paige," I tell her, an ache in my chest developing from the thought of it not being me. That's what has to happen, and I've known that for a long time, but it doesn't make it hurt less. "You're great."

She huffs. "I'm in pain all the time and I never know what to say. I can't act like the omega people expect and I don't want to anymore, either. I've never picked up on a social cue in my life but I recognize every awkward pattern people rather ignore. I can't shut up about fantasy books and spend money on stupid shit, like replica swords and maps. I literally can't turn the lights on some days and going out to a bar is my worst nightmare. Driving a car freaks me out so I live in this tiny little town, knowing I can walk everywhere, and if I can't walk, then I don't go. I don't have a maternal bone in my body and I'm too argumentative. I'm well aware I'm not a catch to most people, Mickey. And that's *okay*; I like who I am just fine, regardless. But thanks for saying it, I guess."

"You are *great*," I tell her again, more emphatically now. "Paige, you are so bright. You got yourself through law school. You handle your own life like a boss. You're Emma's best friend in the whole world and have been for twenty years. You make our family complete. You love fantasy books and are the only person I know who can remember the names of all those characters, and you make me want to read every one you talk about.

You fight for yourself and haven't ever let life beat you down. And I can't think of anyone more amazing than you."

She's quiet for a long, long minute. I'm practically holding my breath, waiting for her to reply. At last, she mutters, "Thanks." Then, clearing her throat, she says, "You're a good fake boyfriend, you know."

Fake. It's like a knife to the heart, even if I know why I'm her fake boyfriend and not her real one. "I try," I say as lightly as I can.

If I got to be her real boyfriend, she'd never doubt how perfect she is again. I'd spend every day reminding her what I already know; she's brilliant, and amazing, and more than enough. And I'd know how to help her when she isn't feeling well. And I'd get to hold her, squeeze her like she likes, all the fucking time.

It's a fantasy that I can't have though, because that's kind of the problem. When I think about a future with Paige, I think about possessing every moment with her. I think about the obsession that I already have and know it'll only get worse. I see it every time I look in the damn mirror. I can't forget why this is a bad idea.

Paige tilts her head and looks at me. "When we were at the restaurant the other night, Sarah was saying she's never seen you date. Not for long, at least."

I snort. "Sarah doesn't actually know me."

"But is she wrong?" Paige presses. "I don't remember it either, not since high school. Maybe you're super private, but I don't think so. You seem like the type of guy who'd introduce people you care about to your mom."

Of course I am. If I had someone, they'd be at every Sunday dinner with us. And it just so happens that she has been for a long time now, but she doesn't know it.

"It is what it is, Paige."

"What does that mean?" she demands, stepping closer to me now. There's a look on her face, a look my mom called *Lawyer Paige* long before she actually went to law school, that she always gets when she's trying to figure something out. "Have you ever been in love?"

I swallow, my heart in my throat, but I won't lie to her. It's pounding in my chest, my breath coming shorter. She *asked*. I can't lie to her.

"Yeah, I have," I say shortly, and I hope that'll be it. But of course it's not, because Paige has never met a problem she doesn't want to puzzle her way through.

"Who—"

She doesn't get it. I always worried about being obvious, about having heart-eyes that would make her uncomfortable, but I should have known better.

I could lie. I could make up a name, tell her it's none of her business, say anything I want. She might be able to see the lie, she might not, but she probably wouldn't press if I did that.

But I can't lie to Paige. I can't take advantage of the fact that she can't see this obvious thing about me. Protecting her and her comfort is more important than protecting myself from embarrassment.

"It's you, Paige," I tell her, trying to keep my voice steady as my heart tries to beat out of my chest. "Emma's seen it for years, and I always worried she'd say something to you—it's you. *You're* the one I'm in love with." Then, before I can get on one knee and proclaim my dramatic love for her and turn this into a whole thing, I force myself to do the responsible thing. "But that doesn't matter. You're not obligated to handle my feelings."

"Not obligated—why didn't you ever say anything?" she demands, stepping closer to me. Her hand starts tapping against her thigh.

"Because of this," I say, gesturing between us even when I know that won't help her understand. "You looked up to me, and I wasn't going to be the alpha that chased you down and cornered you." I've fought my whole life not to be *that* alpha.

She actually rolls her eyes at me. "I've been an adult for a while now, Mickey."

"Trust me," I say, voice unintentionally lower. "I know."

And fuck, do I. I've come in my own hand too many times with all the realizations of that. Kickass Paige. Passionate bookworm Paige. The way she likes tight leggings that show off her entire shapely ass. The way she licks the spoon when having her favorite ice cream sundae. All of those versions of the very adult Paige haunt my dreams.

"Then why the fuck do you think I couldn't handle this?" she demands.

"I'm not a good choice for you."

She laughs, cold and short. "Stable Mickey who spends all his time working to promote childhood literacy is a *bad choice*? The same Mickey who calls his sister once a week and visits his mom every chance he gets? That guy?" She rubs at her temples, her brow furrowing.

I step closer to her again, a deeply unwise move on my part, but I'm blinded by her pain. "You okay? Need anything?" I ask, lowering my voice.

She drops her hand and gestures at me. "*This* is what I mean. The guy who worries about me like this? That's the guy you're saying is bad for me?"

"Yeah," I say heavily. "That guy."

"Then help me out, Mickey. I know I miss things, but I can't even begin to try to understand this."

"I first fell for you that first winter break you and Emma came home from school," I tell her, because if I'm already this far in, what's one more thing? "I picked you two up, remember?" She nods, expression tight, and I continue. "You two were in the backseat, telling me about everything that happened that semester. You were telling me about this book, and you were talking with your hands, and you were so passionate—I kept

157

looking at you in the rearview mirror as I was driving. You'd done so much growing up in those few months. I'd been away at school for three years at that point, so I only saw you two at breaks, and it was like I saw you growing up in these jumps, but that time, it was just... different," I finish lamely, unable to accurately describe what it felt to be hit by lightning like that. "You smelled different," I say.

She nods. "I'd finally had to go on suppressants that semester."

"I know," I say, because I could smell that too. "But it was more than that. Yeah, your scent was suppressed, but there was something under it. Lavender, like it always has been, but something under it—something woody. I can still smell it. Fuck, it's stronger now that you're off your suppressants. And I haven't been able to get it out of my head." The scent is so deep and layered, so sensual and fragrant, and I would drown in it if I could. I force myself to look her in the eye. "Paige, there's been no one else. I'm an obsessive alpha apparently, because I cannot let the thought of you go."

"So, what? You kept it to yourself for nine years?"

"What was I supposed to do? Pin you down and claim you? You were nineteen, Paige. Your birthday had been four days before that. I wasn't going to do that to you."

She raises an eyebrow. "I'm aware my dating experience is limited,"—and that's a whole other thing, this *Samuel* issue, and I still want to tear him limb from limb—"but I think a lot of people have success when they, you know, *ask someone out*. No pinning someone down required. No ignoring it for nearly a decade, either."

I swallow. Paige clearly isn't getting this, isn't understanding what I'm saying. "Paige, I'm not—I would love to ask you on a date. Take you out, treat you nice. But I'm worried I'd never let go. Once I got a taste, I'd never go back."

"Okay," she says.

"Not okay. Not okay at all, Paige."

"I don't believe you, though," she says, and she steps closer again, this time right into my space. She reaches up a hand and cups my face. Most people would do a gentle touch, just their fingertips probably, but not Paige. She makes the contact firm, and I half-wonder if it's her own aversion to light pressure, or if she wants to ensure she has my attention. She has it. "I don't believe that you'd ever do something I don't want. And I'm basing this on all the evidence I've already stated, and you're basing your thoughts on a hunch that hasn't ever actually played out, so, I win," she says, smiling a little mischievously at the end. Lawyer Paige is back, the same Paige who read the Monopoly instructions cover-to-cover and beat us all with obscure rules in hour four of playing every single time.

I can't help but smile back, even if she most definitely did *not* win. It's such a Paige thing to say, and fuck it, I love everything about her. Even when she's more determined to win than is good for her.

People are complicated. We don't follow rulebooks in the real world, and things can get ugly if you don't understand that. Paige isn't naive, so she gets it—to an extent. But she'll always see the world in black and white.

"You're fighting awful hard for someone who hasn't said they feel the same about me," I tell her, thinking that'll be it. She won't be able to say it. She just wanted to argue her point, a hypothetical she latched her teeth into.

She looks away from me and drops her hand from my face. I immediately miss the warmth. "Emma had to tell me what I was feeling," she admits, voice quiet. "Back when I agreed to do this. So I guess it's more recent for me. Or not, because the feelings aren't new. But I understand what they are now. That doesn't mean they've changed, or that I just feel it because of this—I felt it. I just didn't know what to call it." She taps her thigh again. "I'm not good at this Mickey, you know I'm not—that's how I end up alone and thinking *Samuel* is a good option. I can't parse through what I'm feeling half the time, and I'll probably be a shit girlfriend, but—"

"You would not be *a shit girlfriend*," I say hotly, momentarily forgetting everything else, because if there's one thing I'm not going to stand for, it's anyone talking badly about Paige. Even Paige herself. "You are kind, and brilliant, and funny, and—"

"And I can be annoying, and I'm needy, and I'm liable to come off as rude without even meaning to," she continues. "I can be both. I accepted these things about myself a long time ago, Mickey. It's okay. They don't hurt me."

The look in her eyes tells me she's lying a bit, even if she doesn't fully realize that.

I'm not surprised Emma had to gently tell Paige what she was experiencing was attraction, if that's what happened. Paige often has trouble naming her own emotions. She's better than she was—as a child, she couldn't name *mad* or *scared* or any of those things, and would shut down from how overwhelmed it all made her—but she'll never be entirely comfortable with them. And that's okay, because I can always see it on her face. Emma can too, and my mom can most of the time. We're happy to help fill in that gap for her.

Paige's thoughts must be somewhere in the same vicinity, because her whole expression goes soft, and she says, "But I know you've never made me feel like a burden. Or like I was too annoying. Or like my questions bugged you. Or any of the other things."

And we can dig into *that* later, because I need names of who made Paige think of herself like that. Names and addresses.

"You are the best man I know, Mickey Condor," she says. "And I thought you were miles out of my league, but—"

"Never," I interrupt. "You could never be—fuck, Paige, you're amazing. You have to know that."

She smiles, and I get a brief flash of the absolute *shark* of a trial lawyer Paige could have been if circumstances were different. "Then there's no reason to not do this, is there?"

I stand there, dumbfounded, so thoroughly bested that I don't know what to do next.

"Hug me, Mickey," she says, and, grateful for direction, I do.

Chapter 19

Paige

I don't think this is entirely settled. Mickey seems deeply unsure, even as he wraps me in his arms, squeezing me just right, and I bury my face into the sweet smell of his still-shirtless chest. It's even stronger today than it was yesterday, all Christmas morning and sweet candy canes. I know that means my heat is probably close now. My suppressants are definitely fully out of my system if I can scent him this clearly. This probably isn't the best time to make long-term decisions.

"I'll tell you what," I say, letting the part of my mind out that's still rational enough to think in black-and-white, clear language. I'm pressed face-first into his chest with no inclination to move, but that doesn't seem to prevent him from hearing me. "We'll discuss this again after my heat, when I'm back on my suppressants. If you want to back out, or I change my mind—then we'll talk it out then. But for now—let this happen?"

He sighs and squeezes me even tighter. "I was a goner the first time you let me hold you," he admits. "So, yeah, Paige. Whatever you want. It'll always be whatever you want."

And that's the problem with Mickey. I've told him, his sister has told him, I'm sure his mother has told him, but he doesn't hear it. He's always so worried about what those of us around him want and need that he forgets himself.

And I'll deal with that—later. Right now, my head is a little fuzzy from his scent and proximity, and I highly doubt I'd do a good job.

Fuck, he smells good. I could stay here forever, held tight in his arms. He strokes my hair, and I close my eyes, melting into him.

"I have the Sunday shift today," Mickey murmurs after a long time. "I need to get ready and head out. It's a short day, so I'll be done by two. But please—call me if you need me."

If you go into heat, he means. I nod against his chest, because he still hasn't let me go. "Okay."

"You can stay here if you want."

"No, I'm going to go home. Get my nest ready. That type of stuff."

"Alright, Paige. Sounds good. Can I see you tonight?"

Is he asking me on a date or does he want to check on the progress of my heat? Or maybe both? I don't know and I don't ask. I want to see him, so I nod, reluctantly pulling back enough so he can see it. "I don't think I can do a restaurant."

He makes a coughing sound like something's stuck in his throat. "No, I guess that'd be a bad idea. Here again? I'll cook."

"You cooked last night."

He squeezes me again before letting go. I might be projecting, but I think he's reluctant. "Trust me, Paige. Feeding you is not an imposition. Dinner will be ready at six, but feel free to come over earlier."

"Six," I agree, well aware my voice is probably coming out like I'm somehow drunk. In my defense, I'm taking in the half-dressed alpha I was just pressed all over, and it's a nice sight.

He grins, taking a step back toward his bedroom without turning away from me. "If you give me ten minutes, I'll drop you off at home on the way to work."

Usually, I'd protest that I could walk. Usually I'd *want* to walk. But the idea of even the five extra minutes with him is too tempting to pass up.

Mickey drops me off at my house, and I do spend a few hours getting my nest ready. I've ordered a waterproof mattress cover. I'm not a huge fan of the sound the mattress cover makes even if the ad promised it'd be quiet, but I don't want to ruin everything in my nest with how messy my heat will be. Blankets and sheets are replaceable, even though I know it'll be a pain in the ass to find ones I'll accept into my nest. A mattress is expensive.

But once I've rearranged my nest and my bedroom twice, I have to concede that it's as good as it's going to get, and my brain drifts to thinking about other things. Namely, Mickey.

I suppose the thoughts are related, because I haven't been able to *stop* thinking about Mickey. I carefully placed sheets and thought about him. I wondered if he'd like them, if the blanket was big enough for his frame. I added a second sleeping pillow to my nest, fluffed it up carefully just for him, although I highly doubt we'll get much sleep.

But now I'm thinking of our conversation from this morning, and how Mickey apparently believes that he's somehow *bad for me*, and before I know what I'm doing, I've grabbed my bag and started walking to the Condor's house.

It's *hot* today. I know it's almost summer, but I'm sweating buckets. I keep wiping sweat off the back of my neck, annoyed with it dripping down my back.

Sherry is home when I arrive, which is good because I realize belatedly I forgot to call ahead. She opens the door and ushers me inside, sitting me down on the couch while talking faster than I can keep up with.

"Paige, what's wrong? Do you need a doctor?" she asks, and I get the feeling it isn't the first time she's said it. She's crouching in front of me, hovering so she doesn't touch me.

"I'm fine," I mumble. Not very convincing, probably. "I will be fine. Do you know that Mickey doesn't think he'd be a good boyfriend?"

She blinks at me, then moves to sit on the couch next to me.

She smells good. I've never smelled her like this before, as a full grown omega off my suppressants. It's not that the scent is different from it was when I was a kid, or on my suppressants, but now, it's *more.*

Her son must take after her, because she smells like Christmas too, but like those simmer pots, all cranberries and oranges and cinnamon, homey and warm.

Her daughter didn't take after her. Emma smells like spring after the rain. I wonder where that comes from. How do we get our scents?

Sherry is staring at me, wide-eyed and panicked. I think she's been talking, and I didn't hear her again. What's with me? What's going on?

"Paige?" she asks again. "Paige, are you sure you're alright?"

"Alright," I agree. "But Mickey." That's right. I came here to talk about Mickey.

"Yes, Mickey," she says in that tone that people use when they're humoring me. "Paige, are you dating my son?"

"Ehhhh," I mumble, shaking my hand in that sign for "sort of." "It was fake, but I want to, and he said he wants to, but then he said he'd be a bad boyfriend."

She sighs. "Mickey has some complicated things going on. He'll figure it out, Paige. Especially if you help him." She smiles. "And I'm glad you two are figuring this out. I thought it'd happen years ago."

"But I don't know how to help him!" I protest. "I'm here because you know these things and I don't." I'm whining, I register in the back of my mind. Why am I whining?

"Paige, hon, are you sure you're alright? You didn't take anything new, did you?"

"Took less," I mumble. "Not on my suppressants."

She leans forward, getting right in my space, and then her hand is on my forehead, ice cold but at least firm enough to not be irritating. "You're going into heat. Why are you going into heat, Paige?"

"Need to," I tell her. "Insurance..." I sigh, the concept suddenly too complicated. "Is it happening?"

"Yeah, sweetheart, it's happening. I'll drive you home. Or am I driving you to the heat clinic? Which one?"

"Mickey." That's the only thought I can formulate.

"We can talk about him later—"

I shake my head. "No, Mickey. He's supposed to help me. Where is he?"

"Mickey is going to see you through your heat?"

"Mhm."

She leans away, fishing for something on the end table, mumbling to herself. I catch a "*apparently need family dinners more often, if all this can happen,*" and then she's calling someone.

I hear her say Mickey's name, firm and insistent, and I protest. "He's at work."

"And he needs to come here," she says. "Paige, hon, I got this. Don't you worry."

"Mmkay." Something about this feels weird, but I trust Sherry more than just about anyone else in the world. If she says I don't need to worry, then I don't need to worry.

I drift for a moment, and then the front door slams open. I wince back into the couch. Too loud.

But then the best scent I've ever experienced fills the room. Christmas. Pine and peppermint. I take a big draw of air, and then Mickey is in front of me, crouching down and grasping my knees.

Even through my leggings, his touch is electric. I push up against his hands, a whimper sliding out of me against my will.

"Hey, Paige," he says, voice soft enough to wrap me up and keep me warm. "I thought you were going to call me, huh?"

"I'm fine," I mumble. "Not in heat yet."

He grins, but it doesn't look right. "Oh yeah you are, honey. Trust me; I've never smelled anything this strong."

"I am?"

"Mhm. Let's get you to your nest, alright?" He looks over at his mom, says, "I'll call you when this is done." She says something back, but I don't hear it, too busy contemplating that this is *heat*.

This isn't so bad. I'm floating, fuzzy and slow, but it's not so bad yet. And Mickey's here. He'll keep me from floating away.

Then I'm moving, scooped up into Mickey's arms. He cradles me like a child. I squirm, but he tightens his grip. "I can walk," I protest.

"Maybe," Mickey says, but then he's walking toward the door without letting me down. Sherry opens it, and then we're outside, and then we're in his car.

Mickey rolls the windows down immediately. "Hey," I protest, because I don't like the wind in my hair.

"Sorry, honey. But your scent is *strong*."

"Bad?" I ask, trying to sniff myself. I can't really get a whiff, but Mickey is acting like it's overpowering.

He squeezes the wheel. "No. Not bad. Very much not bad."

The drive isn't too long, and Mickey parks haphazardly in front of my house, then turns to me and unbuckles the seatbelt I didn't even realize he'd buckled for me earlier. "Alright, you said you could walk a few minutes ago. Think that's still true?"

"Uh-huh."

"We'll see. I can carry you if you need me to. Just need to make two trips then."

"I can walk," I insist. I've been walking for twenty-seven years. I can walk up some stairs, dammit.

"Alright, honey. Give me a minute." And then he leaves the car, walking around and opening my door for me.

This is weird. Is this the dating thing we were talking about earlier? I try to cling to the memory of this morning, but it slips away, as insubstantial as smoke.

What is *not* insubstantial is the man in front of me. I want to crowd into him, hold him, bury myself in him. I want him to surround me, make me safe. But before I can grab him, he steps back, leaving me pouting.

"I know," he says. "Give me two minutes. After that, I'm yours."

Yours. That sounds nice. A shiver wracks down my spine, a pleasant fuzziness blooming in my brain, and I wait.

Mickey steps back in front of me with his arms filled, carrying a mini-fridge. "What's that?" I ask.

"Fridge," he says, looking like the fridge isn't even straining him at all. "Your kitchen is downstairs, and you need to stay hydrated. There's a Brita and water bottles already in here. Some snacks, too."

That thing must weigh a ton. "Let's get it inside then," I mumble. It takes me a few tries to fish my keys out of my pocket, and a few more to successfully unlock my door.

Upstairs. I need to get upstairs. Mickey and Sherry both said it, but it hits me that I'm in *heat*, and all I want is my nest.

Mickey follows me, still lugging that stupid mini-fridge, but then freezes halfway up the stairs. "What's wrong?" I ask, impatiently turning around once I get to the top. Doesn't he know that I need to be in my nest *now*? That it's the only place I'll be safe?

He shifts the weight of the fridge in his arms. "Paige, honey, we should have talked about this—what are the rules for entering your nest?"

"Rules?"

"Rules. It's your nest. You make the rules. Tell me how this works."

I look down. "No shoes," I tell him, then realize I'm still wearing mine. I frown and toe them off. I never wear shoes in the house.

"Alright. I'll kick them off outside the door. What else?"

I try to think, even though it's like swimming through jello. "I don't know," I tell him. "Just—if you hate it, don't tell me that."

Has Mickey ever been in some other omega's nest? Obviously he's seen his mother's and sister's, but he's never been *in* them. But that doesn't mean he hasn't been in a dozen omegas' nests. He's nice, and he smells so good, and he's strong but somehow soft at the same time. He gives good hugs. Surely omegas line up to invite him into their nests. And they probably have nice nests, with a million pillows and those fuzzy blankets that are always so popular.

My nest is sad by comparison. I know it is; I can see magazines and online ads. I know what the standard is, but I can't live up to it. Fuzzy blankets make me want to rip my skin off, and the pillows in my nest are deliberately chosen and limited; any more and then they won't sit right, and then my nest won't be safe.

"And the big light stays off," I add, because that's important too.

Mickey's face is soft, but his eyes are staring into me in a way I can't quite understand. "Of course, Paige," he says. "And if you think of any more, you'll tell me, right?"

I don't know how long I'll be able to tell him things. This heat is making me slow, making my mind not work as well as it should. But I trust Mickey. Among all the noise and distractions, I can hold onto that. I trust Mickey. He'll make sure I'm safe.

And speaking of safe, I want to be in my nest. It's the most secure place I know. So I stumble my way into my bedroom, then climb into my nest, immediately seeking out my pillow. I rub my face against it, but somehow, even that's not enough.

It doesn't smell right. I raise my head, searching for that pine and peppermint combination, only to find him messing around with the mini-fridge.

He plugs it in at the closest outlet to my nest, then sets up the contents inside. Then he turns to me. "Can I have your bag, pretty girl? I want to set your meds out."

I didn't even realize I was still wearing my bag. I take it off and drop it into his waiting hands, watching him pull out the instructions I wrote for him and each bottle of pills, setting them up on top of the fridge.

"Give me your shirt."

He looks up at that, stopping fiddling with all the bottles. "What?"

"Shirt. Please." It'll smell like him. I *need* it.

He doesn't take it off, instead staring at me for a moment, face doing something interesting I can't hope to understand right now. "Oh, pretty girl, I'm taking too long, huh? You need something?"

He knows I do. He's... *teasing* me? I think that's it. And if I was in better shape, I might even come up with a response. As it is, the best I can do is pout, but that seems to do the trick. He stops fiddling with the fridge and my meds and comes over to the edge of the nest.

Then he stops. "Do I have your permission to come into your nest?"

I want to tell him that he knows he does. That we literally planned this, that the whole purpose of him being here is to help me with my heat. But he's so serious, so sincere when he asks, and I'm forced to take it seriously too.

I want him in my nest. Not because I'm in heat and I know he'll help me. Not for my medication or any other reason. Not even because he smells so good and I want to crawl inside him.

I want Mickey. No, I *need* Mickey. So I nod, extend my hand to him, and welcome him into my nest.

CHAPTER 20
Mickey

M y body is thrumming with a nervous energy, fully aware of how big this moment is.

Paige looks at me with wide, glassy eyes, one shaking hand reaching for me. I grasp it firmly, then step into the nest.

I get a little choked up being here, looking at Paige under the soft glow of the fairy lights she's used to illuminate every room in her house. Her hair that she took down on the car ride over hangs in loose waves around her head, some sort of beautiful halo. I so rarely see her hair down, and somehow it makes this even more real. Paige is completely undone, vulnerable and un-buttoned and waiting for me. There's such deep trust in her eyes, in the way she arches toward me.

Under any other circumstances, I'd question that, worry about her putting too much trust in me. But right now, I have to accept it. Right now, doubt is the enemy; I have to be the man Paige thinks I can be while she needs me.

I take one more quick glance around the room, making sure everything is set. The fridge is humming, her meds are set on top of it, the overhead lights are off as requested, and my shoes are in a pile with hers at the top of the stairs that we'll surely trip over later.

The only thing left is her nest, and only Paige can decide if that's set up correctly.

Paige has a nest that's smaller than the one she and Emma used to share. It's still probably about the same size as my bed at home, so it's not *small* or anything. But it's tighter, because while most omegas want to sprawl out and feather a soft, plush nest, Paige clearly likes the tight, almost enclosed space.

She has a circular nest laid directly on the floor, and it's the kind with little walls around it. The side closest to the wall has a three-foot high padded back, somewhere to rest against, and I can picture Paige sitting there reading her fantasy books. The rest has a smaller barrier, about a foot high, that can be easily stepped over, but no doubt feels more secure and protected to Paige's omega instincts. I'll have to remind myself of that when one of us needs the bathroom or water or her medication, because I can see myself tripping over the walls that surround and protect her little nest. Inside the nest is a plush mattress, sheets that are luxurious to the touch, a few soft blankets, and two regular pillows and a body pillow.

It's a lot simpler than most nests. I expected a mountain of pillows, favorite stuffed animals, fuzzy blankets, and more. That's what Emma's nest had always been like, and Paige had spent plenty of time there.

But that's not Paige. Paige would be driven crazy by all that. Paige's nest is her—controlled, comfortable but understated, and no doubt carefully, meticulously thought out.

She's still looking at me with those glassy eyes, so I kneel down on the mattress with her, taking her hands in mine. "Your nest is so pretty, Paige," I tell her, and her eyelashes flutter as her cheeks flush impossibly more. "You did such a good job," I continue. She needs to hear it. She starts leaning toward me, mouth parted slightly, and I *want her*. I want her somehow more than I ever have before, more than I want to breathe.

I know it's the heat. I know it's pheromones and instincts, and that neither of us is in control right now. Her scent has taken over the entire room, seeping into my pores in a way I'll never forget. Lavender and that sweet, woody scent, but also a deep, aching need.

Arousal. My pretty Paige is aroused, turned on and hungry for me.

Saliva pools in my mouth, and I have to fight the urge to bite her. It's beyond inappropriate, beyond invasive—it would be domineering and disrespectful and I can't become that alpha now. I need to be who she needs me to be.

"It's okay?" she asks, her voice soft and needy, and it calls to something inside me I didn't even know was there. I fight back my own urges so I can focus on that soft little uncertainty in her eyes.

"It's perfect," I assure her. "You built the perfect nest for us, so soft, so safe. Thank you, honey."

Her eyes flutter shut completely, and she leans forward so far I worry she's going to fall into me. I release her hands so I can steady her shoulders, rubbing gently while I keep her upright.

She's burning to the touch even through her clothes, and it's only going to get worse if I don't do something about it. My own head is getting foggy now, needing Paige, soaked in her pheromones, but I try to hold onto the last remnant of rationality.

"Paige, hon, I need one more thing from you." After this last thing, I can take care of everything else. I can get her undressed, find out how she likes to be fucked, keep her full and satiated and happy, keep her hydrated and medicated. I can handle all of that with just one last thing from her.

"Mhm," she agrees.

"You have any sex toys, Paige? A vibrator? A dildo?"

Her brow furrows, an adorable wrinkle appearing between her eyes. "You," she says in protest, shaking her head.

I *think* she's saying she wants my cock, although she might be calling me a dildo. But she's honestly so adorable right now that I'd forgive her even if she was calling me a dildo.

This heat hit her fast. This morning I genuinely thought she'd be coming over for another date tonight. I'd spent my ride to work wondering if the proper thing to do was create a list of all the reasons she shouldn't want to be with me to give to her tonight. But instead my mom called me, and Paige slipped right into heat.

"I know, honey," I tell her. "But consider it help. The more the merrier, right?"

Her frown deepens, but she reaches outside the nest to the low end table beside it, opens the drawer, and pulls out a small bullet vibrator and a truly enormous knotting dildo.

Holy shit. Has that been *inside* her? It looks fucking huge, even bigger than I am, and I'm not small.

"You like that one?" I ask, proud that my voice comes out clear.

"Never used it. Bought it for... for... heat," she finishes, after struggling to find the word. Then she wiggles her hips. "These clothes are uncomfortable."

My mouth goes dry. "Let's get them off you, then," I say, and suddenly this is all real. I don't know why Paige wanting to take her clothes off is what makes it real and not the giant dildo between us, or any of the other things that have happened in the last few days, but it is. Paige is about to get naked. My Paige is about to be naked in front of me, and then I'm going to fuck her like she wants.

She has her top off before I even process what she's doing. She whips the t-shirt off, and then she's left wearing a soft bra, cream-colored and immensely practical, and I'm frozen in place.

She lies down and pushes herself into bridge pose, hips in the air, thrusting lewdly while she works her leggings down her thighs. When she gets them almost to her knees, they get stuck, and she drops her hips to lift her head and pout.

I briefly remember when we first talked about this, Paige kept saying it's like she wouldn't be her when she's in heat. And it's true that I've never seen Paige pout, or strip with such single-minded determination, and watch me with such a soft, fuzzy expression. But I still see her underneath it all, just a much less inhibited version of her. It's up to me to ensure that she's taken care of when she's like this.

And that reminds me of the pile of condoms I have in my pocket. I started carrying them right after Paige went off her suppressants in case I needed to get to her fast, a fear that clearly paid out. I was terrified I'd drop one out of my pocket at work and give the complaining parents real grounds to get me fired, but I'm so glad I have them now.

Everything I've read says condoms aren't the most practical during a heat. Most people seem to wonder why you'd even try, considering the most common reason to have a heat these days is to conceive. But I'm going to be as careful as I can between the condoms and making sure Paige takes her pill every day. I even picked up some Plan B to be double sure. Paige should get to have a heat with as few worries and consequences as possible.

Paige is still struggling with her pants, so I leave the pile of condoms on the bed and reach for her, using firm pressure to trace my hands from her ankles to her thighs, itching to keep going, to find skin. I stop myself, pinching the edge of the fabric, and wait. "Can I, honey?" I ask her. My voice is lower than I've ever heard it before. She shivers and nods, and I waste no more time, ripping her leggings off her legs and throwing them out of her nest.

I throw the shirt she took off out too, leaving her in her bra and panties. The panties are as practical as the bra, cotton and cream and already wet, nearly transparent with the moisture between her pretty thighs. *Fuck me*. Paige is dripping for me, soaking her underwear, and I haven't even touched her yet.

"So fucking pretty," I tell her, sounding like I've swallowed gravel, and she shivers, looking up at me with lust-blown, trusting eyes. I want to make her moan. I want to make her scream. I want to make such an impression on her that this will never end.

That's the pheromones talking and I know it, but the logical part of me is drowning, and I have no interest in rescuing him, not when this gorgeous omega is laid out before me, her thighs sliding further open like she's welcoming me inside.

I need to get my own clothes off before my dick tears through my khakis. I reach back and rip my shirt over my head, and I go to toss it out of the nest, but Paige is faster, grabbing my wrist to stop me.

It takes me a second to process it. "You still want my shirt?" I check, and she nods, a rapid bob that looks like it would hurt her neck in any other circumstances. "Alright, honey. You can have whatever you want." I let her take it from my hand, and watch her busy herself tucking it into the nest materials while I open my belt.

She presses it into the space between the cushioned wall and the mattress, and I have no idea *why* she'd want my shirt there, but I'm not going to ask, because my omega can have whatever the fuck she wants, especially when she's in heat.

I've pulled off my belt but haven't managed to open my fly yet, but that seems to go completely over Paige's head. She crawls into my lap, almost knocking me backward until I fall into a seat, securing one arm around her to steady her.

Her knees fall to either side of my thighs, her cloth-covered pussy right over my engorged cock, and I already know these khakis are going to be ruined forever and couldn't give less of a damn. She ruts experimentally, rocking her hips slightly, and moans.

I don't know if it's the friction or the moan that gets me, but my cock is now straining like it's going to break straight through the fabric, and my heart is beating faster than is probably healthy.

"Pretty girl," I grunt, trying to reduce the friction directly on my cock before I embarrass myself. "You going to let me get naked for you?"

She ignores me, continuing to rock against me. Her voice comes out in breathy little moans, her hot breath on my neck, and I groan, closing my eyes and just feeling her. *Paige.* Beautiful, perfect Paige.

"Tighter," she murmurs, and it takes me a moment to figure out what she means. Oh. My grip on her loosened, my touch not firm enough for her. Against her bare skin, I can't imagine how much that light little grip must be irritating her.

Fixing that means either pushing her away or pulling her tight to me, and giving up any sense of control I have.

It's no choice at all. I pull her close, sitting her fully on top of my cock, and let her rock against me, driving us both higher and higher.

I mouth at her neck, letting my teeth drag teasingly over her pulse. I don't bite, barely resisting the urge and swallowing a hot pang of humiliation that I'd even be tempted while my dick simultaneously jumps in my pants. Apparently, she likes it too, throwing her head back as her nails dig into my shoulders.

Her hair is everywhere, moving around us as I continue to lick and suck her skin. She smells so goddamn good. I need her. I *need* her more than I've ever needed anything else, more than I've ever needed air—

"Does that feel good, honey?" I ask, desperate to know she feels as good as I do. Judging by the sticky wetness seeping into my pants, I guess she does. Her fingers tighten even further on my shoulders. "Alright, Paige," I murmur. "Make yourself feel good. What do you need from me?"

She doesn't answer. She doesn't seem to need anything from me other than me being here, so I keep kissing her neck. When she throws her head back and pulls her neck away from my mouth, I kiss down to her breasts, pressing kisses and teasing licks to the skin spilling out of that bra.

The pheromones are drugging. My brain is foggy, leaving me with only thoughts of her and her pleasure.

"Need you to come, honey," I tell her, face pressed into her tits. "Need to make you come, take the edge off for you—what do you want from me?"

She grabs my wrist from where my hand still holds her waist, then drags my hand up to palm her breast. I make a mental note to ask if my kisses are the wrong pressure for her, if she can even answer me later. If I can even remember to ask.

I squeeze her breast, admiring how perfectly they fit in my palm, exactly how I always knew they would. Then she grinds down on me again, and her little gasp a second before a gush of slick soaks my pants tells me that she's found it, found her own pleasure.

I pull back so I can watch her, so I can finally see what Paige looks like when she's coming. I've dreamed of this, but reality is a thousand times better.

She keeps rocking against me. Whether she's so far in heat that she's already chasing the next orgasm or she's riding out the little aftershocks, everything between us is wet and hot and she's so fucking beautiful, and I don't stand a chance. I come in my pants.

My world rocks, despite the fact that the only thing technically touching me is my own underwear. I squeeze her closer and
groan out her name, needing her. Needing this.

I'm not even embarrassed that I came in my pants. No one in
my position would have managed to hold out. Paige is gorgeous
like this, loose-limbed and heavy-eyed and so fucking pretty in
her pleasure.

I shift her weight slightly, grimacing at the wetness in my
pants. There wasn't enough pressure for my knot to fully pop,
thank god, but there's a slight swelling at the base, paired with
the desperate need to rut something. And here Paige is, so ready
and tempting. It's a wonder I can control myself.

But I do control myself, because I need to make this good for
Paige. Her pleasure and her comfort come before anything, and
she just came and I had my hands all over her and I need to make
sure we're still okay.

"So fucking perfect, pretty girl," I murmur, because she needs
to hear it. She needs to know. "Do you feel good?"

She whimpers. "Empty."

Fuck, of course she is. I remember when April told me there's
no shame in tagging in mechanical help, and I think I'm going
to need it sooner than expected. She's going to wear me right
out.

"Alright, alright," I soothe, stroking down her sides with firm
hands. "Why don't you get undressed, pretty girl? And then I
can give you what you need."

She tilts her head, and I can see her taking a long minute to process what I'm saying, but she eventually nods and gets off my lap, tugging at her bra in a way that tells me it's going to take her a second to remember how to unclasp it.

I'd help her, but I need to get my pants off. I work them down my legs and do the awkward act of kicking them off, taking my briefs with them, leaving me bare for her. I throw them out of the nest before she can decide she wants them for their scent as well. I don't know why I'm squeamish about her having my come-soaked underwear; it's not like she's not going to see and feel plenty of my come in the next few days.

Paige manages to get her bra off and prowls back to me, looking like some kind of predatory cat, crawling across the bed, intent on only me. I freeze; I'm her prey, caught in her cross-hairs, and I wait for her to make the next move.

The distant part of me that's still in control thinks this might normally be embarrassing, to have the woman I've wanted for nearly a decade studying me like a lab specimen, but the part of me that's pure *alpha* is drowning in the lust-soaked pheromones she's releasing, and my chest starts rumbling for her, welcoming her advances.

"Pretty omega, what do you need?" I dare to slide a little closer. I wait for her to react, needing to see how she feels, but she drops to her ass and opens her thighs, spreading them wide and letting me look at the wet spot on her panties.

"It hurts," she complains, and something inside me seizes. My omega should never hurt. My omega shouldn't ever suffer, especially not when I can make it better.

"Do you need me inside you? Need me to make you feel good?"

She bites her lip and nods. "Please, alpha."

I think my heart stops. Hearing her call me *alpha*, like I'm hers, like she's mine—*fuck*.

"I'm going to make you feel so good," I promise her, prowling closer now, having the barest presence of mind to scoop up one of the condoms and ripping the packet open one-handed. "I'm going to make you see stars, honey, make you drip everywhere for me. We're going to permanently stain your nest, make it smell like us."

She nods rapidly again. "Yes, yes—*our* nest. Please."

Our nest. Paige is determined to kill me and she doesn't even realize that she's doing it.

"That's right," I tell her, my voice choked, and whether it's love or lust at this moment, I couldn't tell you. "Our nest, the perfect nest you made for us." She preens at that, and I roll the condom on, watching her watch me. She's sizing me up, and I don't miss how her thighs clench. "Is this what you want, pretty omega?" She nods, so I touch her thigh, running a hand over her skin. So fucking soft, and radiating heat. Her thighs fall further open. "Can I take these off?"

"Please," she whispers, and something about that hits too hard. I can't dig into that now, though, needing to give her whatever she's asking for.

Like she can read my mind, like she knows exactly how far gone I am and wants to push me that much further, she tilts her hips up so I can get her underwear off of her, then says, "I'm so empty."

"I know, honey. I'll fill you," I assure her, pulling off her panties and tossing them away, revealing the most gorgeous sight. Paige's pussy is so wet and open, like it's practically beckoning me inside. I've fucked my fist too many times to count picturing her like this. Ready, eager. Pink and sweet and waiting for me.

I want to eat her out, want to bury my face in her cunt, but I know Paige is getting dangerously overwhelmed with her heat, and I can give her the relief she needs. "Want to be on your back, or your hands and knees?" I ask her, stroking over her ankle bone. "Either way is fine with me." Either way is a fantasy come to life.

"On top of me," she whispers, spreading her thighs even further, and I suppose that's my answer.

"Alright, I got you," I soothe, stroking further up her leg now, tracing her soft calf. Somehow even her calves are overheated right now. "Oh, pretty girl, I'll make you feel so good." I grab the pillow nearest me and help her slide it under her hips, angling her so I can slide right into her.

I know she was worried that a heat would make her out of control, but I hope surrounded by her nest, surrounded by *me*, that she feels safe. Nothing will ever happen to her here, not when I'm around to look after her.

I press her legs back toward her chest, then slowly push into her when she whimpers for me. I don't need to go slow; she's dripping wet, hot and tight and sucking me in like I'm meant to be here.

I'm so close to embarrassing myself a second time in less than ten minutes. Only Paige could ever make me lose it like this.

"So fucking perfect, omega," I rasp, barely recognizing my voice.

"*Alpha*," Paige whines, her inner muscles clamping down on me like she's trying to force my knot to form before I'm ready, like she's begging for it.

I'll give her my knot. But first, I'm going to make her feel good. I'm going to make this something that neither of us forgets.

I put some of my weight on her, testing her reactions. She goes boneless, letting out a contented sigh. The alpha instincts in me roar to life. This is *my* omega, feeling safe and content and horny in my arms. I did that for her. She made the nest and I'm making her come in it. Nothing could be better than this.

I pull almost all the way out of her before slamming back in, and Paige mewls, eyes rolling back in her head. I dare to push her legs a little further back, pressing into her deeper.

I'm well the fuck aware that pregnancy is *not* the end goal of this heat. I have her birth control ready to go, I bought Plan B just in case, and I'm wearing a condom. But my brain doesn't process any of that. All the alpha part of my brain knows is that she's under me, hot and ready and so wet, so open. She wants me, she's in heat, and I push her into a mating press, needing to fill her, needing to fucking breed her.

"You're going to come on my cock," I tell her firmly, fucking her faster now. "You're going to squeeze me so tight that you force my knot to lock, because you want it, don't you, honey? You want me to fill you up, stuff you full. So every single inch of you is touching me." I don't even know what I'm saying, what nonsense I'm pulling out, but Paige nods rapidly, her eyes wide and desperate, so maybe I'm doing a good job.

"Okay, Paige, that's it. Take me, honey. Squeeze me, all tight and hot and *fucking perfect—*"

Paige squeaks like she's surprised, high pitched and adorable, and then she's coming around my cock, and I couldn't not knot her if I had a gun to my head. There is nothing I want more in the entire universe than having Paige's hot pussy suck my knot in.

I growl, rocking my hips into her as long as I can, and then I lock inside her, and my world whites out at the edges.

CHAPTER 21
Paige

H e's so good at this.

Everything is a hazy fuzz, comfortably blurry, be-cause none of it is important. The only important thing is us here, in the nest I made for us—the nest he said he liked, the nest he promised me was a good nest, good enough for us—with him over me and around me, keeping me safe from the rest of the world. Nothing can get to me here. Just him. Just us.

"Am I hurting you?" he rasps, voice calmer than he was a moment ago. I shake my head from side to side. Hurt? What hurts? Nothing hurts.

"It's good," I promise him, my voice slurring as I try to speak. Mickey smiles, running his knuckles affectionately along my jaw. Mickey's touching me. What could be better than that?

"I'm glad, sweet girl," he says. "Glad you feel good. Only ever want you to feel good."

I squeeze around his knot experimentally, eliciting a long groan from him. "You make me feel good."

"You make me feel so *fucking* good too, Paige," he promises fervently. "Nothing has ever been better than this."

I squeeze again, tugging experimentally. He's still locked inside me. It's not like a knotting toy. Those are always too hard or too soft, the hard ones impossible to get inside and the soft ones too delicate. He curses when I squeeze him again, and I wonder how long his knot can last.

There are commercials about that. *Stop taking if your knot lasts longer than four hours.* Am I going to be knotted for four hours?

The idea isn't unappealing. It maybe should be, but I can't imagine why. I'm full. I'm full and I'm safe and Mickey is looking at me like that, like he can't take his eyes off of me.His hands trace along my legs, moving from my ankles to my knees. He keeps his touch firm, then squeezes my knees slightly, moving them so they fall around his hips instead of pressed up into my own chest. I move where he pushes, but only because he doesn't move. He's still surrounding me. Mickey is everywhere—his body, his knot, his eyes, his scent. *Mickey, Mickey, Mickey.* It's just the two of us now.

I wiggle slightly. I'm not trying to make Mickey groan that deep, rumbling sound again, but I apparently succeed anyway.

Mickey squeezes my thigh, and I jolt. Have his hands always been that big? And they're so strong too. Is it normal to be this attracted to his hands?

"You uncomfortable, Paige?" he asks.

"No." I don't know much right now, but I know that for sure.

"Then why're you squirming?"

I shrug, unable to put it into words. Unable to put *anything* into words, to tell the truth. I don't know what I'm feeling, but I'm floating in it, letting the waves take me away.

Have I ever let this happen before? Have I ever let myself ride something out before? Fuck, why am I not like this more often?

"You already want more, pretty girl?" Mickey asks. "Is that why you're all squirmy?"

Do I? I shift again, experimentally, causing his knot to catch inside me, pushing *just right* on me, and I whimper. "Mhm."

He huffs. "Well, what my omega wants, she gets." His voice is a rough whisper, deep and abrasive in the best ways. I can't tell if it's his voice that makes the heat spread through me, or him calling me *his*.

"Kiss me?" I ask impulsively, watching his mouth, wanting it to form that shape again. *My omega*. I need him to say it again, need his mouth on mine, need him—

Something weird crosses his face, something I can't parse. I'm bad at that normally, and it's not fair to ask me right now, not when the whole world seems like it's behind a layer of cotton, not when my brain feels like molasses.

But Mickey doesn't leave me hanging. "We haven't kissed yet, have we?" he asks, seemingly rhetorically. "We need to rectify that right away. Need to know what you taste like." Then he carefully tilts forward, making sure not to tug his knot inside of me, and presses his lips to mine.

There's a little voice in the back of my head that says I shouldn't like this. That I've never liked it before. There's someone else, someone whose kisses weren't like this, who made me think I didn't like kissing—but I can't remember their name right now. It's probably not important.

Mickey's kisses are definitely something I like, I decide quickly. He's sweet about it, considering his knot is currently inside me. His kisses are little teasing pecks at first, then sucking at my bottom lip in a way that has me chasing him, trying to get more.

He pulls away and groans. "Careful, honey," he says. "If you keep squirming, my knot's never going to go down."

Am I squirming? I didn't even realize it. But I do want more, want to be full forever. "Is that bad?" I ask.

He grinds his hips into me. He can't move much, considering his knot is still swollen inside me, but I feel it nonetheless, and it makes me see stars.

"It's bad because I can't eat you out while my cock is inside you," he says, voice low. "Believe me, if I was flexible enough, I would."

I giggle at the image. Mickey is good at many things, but I highly doubt flexibility is one of them.

He gets a weird look on his face again, and then his knuckles stroke down my cheek once more. "Never heard you make a sound like that before," he murmurs. "It's sweet as hell, honey. Love that you feel good right now."

"Do you feel good?" I ask him, suddenly reminded to be worried.

He hushes me by leaning forward to kiss me again. I sink into it, my nest cradling me from below and Mickey covering me from above, and my whole body screams *safe* at me in a way I don't think I've ever felt before. I'm safe here. Mickey is here.

He grinds his knot against me again, making my toes curl and my back arch. "Does this ease your mind?" he asks, and when I don't respond—when I'm still riding the waves of pleasure—he continues, "Pretty girl, I've never felt better in my entire damn life."

I preen at that. Mickey is so good, so beautiful, and so good and perfect, and he's here with me. I've made us this nest, and he's inside me and he likes this.

He groans. "Squirming again."

"How long does your knot last?"

"Another few minutes. If someone stops squirming."

"I'm so full," I groan, and I know I'm not doing what he asks. I know I'm moving on his knot still, but I can't help it. I'm so full, so perfectly, ecstatically full. Mickey doesn't stop me and he doesn't scold me, either, just letting me move. "Toys don't feel this good."

"You're in heat, sweetheart. Everything is going to be better."

"No," I insist. "It's you."

He strokes his knuckles over my face again, and I turn into the touch this time, chasing his hand. I suddenly really, really want that in my mouth.

I catch his thumb between my lips, sucking lightly at the tip. "Pretty omega," he croons. "You need to be full?"

I do. I need him, as much of him as I can get. All over me, in me, around me—I know already that this nest will never be right again without him as a part of it. I took his shirt, but that won't ever be enough, not without him updating the scent on it. I need him here. This is where he belongs.

I nip at his thumb, because that's easier than explaining all this to him, and he swears. I worry for a split second that I bit harder than I thought and hurt him, but he groans, "You make me fucking crazy, Paige. All I can think about is you."

And all I can think about is him. Is there anything else to think about?

I suck at his thumb, swirling my tongue around the tip. He strokes over my jaw with the fingers not in my mouth, and soon enough the pressure inside me eases. I whimper, not liking that. I need him to fill me, need him in order to feel good. Mickey and his cock might be the only things tethering me to Earth, the only things making sure I don't float away.

"Oh, sweet girl," he soothes, not removing his thumb from my mouth. "I know. Give me a minute and I'll give it to you again, alright? But don't worry. I won't leave you hanging. I'm going to make you feel so good, honey. So, so good. Going to make you melt for me."

Haven't I already? Is that not what this is?

I watch him under hooded eyes as he ties off his condom, carefully depositing it in the trash can he must have moved over from the bathroom when he was setting up.

"You still comfortable, honey?" he asks, walking on his knees across the nest back to me. He gently pushes my thighs open, settling himself in the V of my legs. "Nothing hurts?"

Something should hurt, shouldn't it? Something always hurts. But right now, all I can think about is *him*. "Empty," I inform him, because that seems like the most pressing need to communicate.

His hands push into my thighs. "And burning up again already. Fuck, you're needy, aren't you?"

I bite my lip, unsure of how to respond. Is it bad? Am I too needy? Am I taking too much from him?

Maybe he can read my mind, because he immediately says, "It's so fucking hot, sweet girl. *Need* me. I love that you need me."

I know in the back of my mind that I don't need people. I love all the Condors, but I don't need people. I got myself through school. I bought this house. I hold down my job. I've built my life around not needing people, about being able to manage my life and my illness independently. I don't need people.

But right now, I need Mickey.

"Fucking wet and perfect for me, aren't you?" he murmurs, staring at me like my pussy is modern art. "I bet you taste so good."

I don't know how to respond to that, but I don't have to find out, because Mickey tugs the pillow under me to re-center me, then puts my legs on his shoulders and licks through my folds.

"*Fuck*," I gasp, the breath knocked out of me. Oh, I *like* that. And maybe it's the heat that makes it so electrical, so maybe it wouldn't be this special on a normal day, but I somehow doubt that. I want this all the time.

"Fucking perfect," Mickey mutters, the words a weird breathy flutter against my pussy that makes me buck my hips toward his face. "That's it, omega. Ride your alpha's face. Soak me in your scent. Mark me as yours."

My eyes roll back into my head. Does he know what he's saying? Does he want to be *mine*?

He is mine, my instincts shout at me. I'm sure as hell not giving him up. Mickey is mine, my alpha, here in my nest that I built for the two of us. Mine. All mine.

My cunt squeezes around nothing, hungry for more, needing to be filled. I whine, and Mickey must be able to read my mind, because he slides two fingers inside me while he sucks on my clit, crooking his fingers until I see stars.

I can't believe I'm practically ready to come again. Samuel never got me here this fast. My vibrator's never gotten me here this fast. Just Mickey; *he's the only one*, I think deliriously as I grind on his fingers and tongue, needing more, chasing the high he's giving me.

I come with a yelp that might be Mickey's name, squeezing around his fingers as my eyes roll back into my head, completely overwhelmed by what he's making me feel.

When I can open my eyes again, I look down my body to find Mickey grinning up at me, lips and beard obscenely wet. Am I dripping that much? I squirm, realizing what a mess I've made.

We probably have stained my nest forever, just like Mickey promised. I'll never get the smell out. I never want to.

Mickey presses a wet kiss to my thigh. "Feel better, pretty omega?" His voice is deeper than it's ever been, a rumble that makes something inside me shiver, and somehow I already want *more*.

I groan, grinding my hips on nothing, chasing something I can't quite define.

Mickey's eyes darken though as he watches me. I bite my lip, wondering what he could be thinking, when he leans forward again, pressing another kiss even higher up my thigh.

"I have you, Paige," he promises, low and earnest. "I'll take care of you."

And I believe him. I believe him even more when he surges up my body, grabs my hips, and slides right into me.

CHAPTER 22
Mickey

My brain won't stop echoing *mine*.

She's *mine* when I fuck her. She's *mine* when I coax her to drink some water or eat a snack or take her pills, making sure to hold her the whole time so she's never alone. She's *mine* when she whines and moans for me as I talk her through it. She's *mine* when I'm holding that vibrator to her clit, waiting for my cock to get with the program so I can fuck her again.

Mine, mine, mine. The most insidious part of my brain says I should bite her, mark her, make sure everyone knows she's *mine* now. I fight back the urge, but only barely. This needs to be all about her, and I can't give into my selfish desires like that.

I'm keeping track of the days solely by her medication. If it wasn't for that, I'm not sure I'd know how long we've been in her nest. I'm wrung dry, and so is my cock, but I don't stop. I couldn't even if I wanted to. I've somehow found a way to be both exhausted and invigorated simultaneously, and the way is Paige's sweet body needing mine.

I'll fill her up for the rest of my life. I'll keep her nice and full, knot locked inside her hot, wet cunt. Nothing has ever felt so good. Nothing has ever felt quite as much like home.

And I desperately want to knot her again, but it's not going to happen for a little bit. It's been three days. I've given her three days' worth of meds, made her drink eight bottles of water, helped her out of the nest to the bathroom and back a half a dozen times, barely getting a moment to look after myself. I've almost finished my supply of condoms and doubt I'll ever taste anything but her sweet cunt again. I can't even estimate the number of times I've made her come, and all I know is my cock is sore from use.

So instead, I content myself with watching her grind her hips against her vibrator, groaning and letting her head fall back because she trusts me to get her there.

"That good, honey?" I ask her. It's mostly rhetorical; I know full well I'm not going to get a response. Paige has gotten more and more nonverbal as the days go on, and it worries me a bit, but she's been more than enthusiastic about everything. I try to let her set the pace, and as long as she keeps reaching for me, demanding more with her body, I'll keep giving it to her.

I idly check the time on her bedside clock. I need to wrap this up, because it's about time for her morning meds, and I need her to take those on time. She'll drink some water when she takes her pills, and if I'm lucky, I can get her to sleep for a little bit after. She has to be exhausted; she hasn't slept for more than an hour or two at a time since this started. I know I'm exhausted.

I palm my cock, which is doing its valiant best to wake up again. I can't help it; I doubt anything could stop me from getting hard in Paige's presence. She's so fucking pretty, and she makes the sweetest sounds when I make her come, and her scent is heady enough to make me crazy. It's all lavender and woody and the heavy, drugging musk of sex. When I told her I'd make her stain her nest forever with her scent, I apparently meant it, because I know she'll never get it out. Maybe not even if she replaces every single sheet and blanket. When she goes back on her suppressants, she probably won't notice it anymore. But I'll never stop knowing her nest smells like us.

She makes that little sound she makes right before she comes, and I grin, leaning in to kiss her as she comes against her vibrator. She grabs at me, and her nails dig into my shoulders. Fuck, I hope she leaves marks. I hope they're somehow there forever, something for me to look at and admire for the rest of my life.

When I break the kiss, Paige looks up at me with heavy eyes, fucked-out and loose-limbed. I press a kiss to her forehead, and for once, she's not burning to my touch.

It might not last. Every time she comes should help regulate her temperature a bit, but then her hormones will drive her to that point again. But maybe we're getting there. Maybe we're getting close.

She whines and rocks her hips, looking for something that isn't there. I make a mental note to get Paige a plug, or at least a more reasonably sized dildo. Something she can keep inside her for long periods of time and squeeze around, because she so clearly needs it when she's in heat.

That's a stupid thought, and I have to shake it out of my head. The only excuse I can think of is that Paige's mouth-watering scent and powerful pheromones are literally drugging me, because I know full well that this isn't happening again.

I kiss Paige again, reveling in it as she turns her chin up, seeking more from me. A man could get addicted to these kisses.

"Alpha," she whines. That's about the only word she says anymore, and I do miss my eloquent, verbose Paige. I miss listening to her talk to me about fantasy books and her having an answer to everything.

"I know, honey," I tell her, keeping my voice gentle. "You're empty, hm? Take your meds for me and I'll fill you up." It's a shameless bribe, because the part of Paige that carefully manages her medication is deeply buried by the heat. Paige doesn't care about water or sleep or letting me clean her up or give her meds. Paige hasn't eaten more than a few crackers this whole time, and I have to bribe her to do anything and everything except get fucked.

I know why Paige was scared of this now. I can see how vulnerable she is, how easy it would be to take advantage of her if I wanted to. She doesn't have her own best interests in mind and is blindingly trusting like this. Every single minute makes me more and more nervous that she trusted me with her heat and her health. Paige looked at me and saw *safe*, and I don't know if she was right to do so, but I'd like to believe she was. I can't fuck it up.

I stand to climb over the wall of her nest and Paige whines, her fingers latching onto my ankle in a move so fast I'm honestly surprised she's currently capable of it. "I'll be right back," I tell her, looking down at her. She looks up at me, eyes sad and imploring, like she thinks I'm going to leave the nest, leave her.

"Oh, pretty omega," I croon at her, knowing what she needs to hear and wanting with my whole heart to give it to her. "It's okay, honey. I'll be right back. You made the perfect nest for us; why would I ever want to leave it?"

She blinks slowly at that, and her eyes get a little wet even as she smiles softly. Her grip on my ankle loosens, and I step out of the nest to get her water and her medication.

When I find out who the fuck made her think that her nest isn't good enough, I'm going to fight them. I don't know who, although I have some likely suspects, but it's obvious someone told her that. Even when Paige can't remember her own medication or basic self-care, she knows to be self-conscious about her nest. And that is beyond unforgivable.

I climb back into the nest as quickly as possible, sitting against the taller portion of the wall that basically works like a headboard. Paige settles into my lap without me even having to ask, which makes me feel like the hero defending her from a damned dragon. I wrap one arm around her, scratch up and down her back, and hand her the little cup of pills with the other. She throws them back, not even checking the contents, trusting me enough to know I'm taking care of her. I uncap the water and hand that to her, and she obediently drinks about half a bottle. I'll take that as a win.

I re-cap the bottle and press it to the wall of the nest, hoping it'll be out of our way, but maybe close enough that she'll drink more if I leave it nearby. Then I use that hand to tilt her chin, giving me access to kiss her forehead once more.

She's warm but not burning. That's progress, although she's already squirming for more.

I pull back enough to look her over, needing to take inventory. Is she alright to keep going? Is there something she needs, something I need to make sure she has?

She could use a bath, but that's not a medical emergency. Her eyes are starting to droop, an effect that only gets more pronounced as I continue to rub her back. Maybe I can get her to sleep a bit if I'm clever about it.

"You need me to fill you up?" I ask when she starts to grind her hips again. She doesn't answer me, and I didn't expect her to, but she does look at me with those doe eyes, wide and trusting and somehow hypnotizing to me. "I'll keep you nice and full, honey. A little different this time, though—look." I grab her around the waist and lift her off my lap, then lie her down with her head on the pillow.

She whines when I'm not holding her anymore, but that's something I plan to fix quickly, so I force myself to ignore it and reach for the blanket that's been pressed to the farthest edge of the nest the entire time. It doesn't move easily.

"Fucking hell, why is your blanket *heavy*?" I ask. Paige doesn't answer, but she does giggle a bit, no doubt amused watching me struggle, and that definitely makes it worth it.

It's some sort of weighted blanket. I have a couple smaller, lap-sized ones in the library, but they also only weigh maybe ten pounds, considering they're for little kids to use. This thing must weigh forty pounds.

Well, Paige did tell me she finds pressure soothing. And if this blanket is what helps her sleep, then I'm going to learn to sleep under a heavy-ass blanket.

I pull it up in her general direction, but don't bother to tuck her in yet. I don't want to imagine maneuvering under this heavy blanket, so I leave it easily reachable and then lie down behind her.

I take a second to slip another condom on. I'm running low, and I have to hope this heat ends soon, or else I'm going to have to call someone to bring me more, and that's something I don't want to ever think about doing.

"Hi, honey," I whisper in her ear. She shivers, and I wrap my arms around her, tugging her fully against me. "I'm gonna hold you just like this, alright?" She whines, and I smile, pressing a kiss to her neck. "I know you need more. I'm going to give it to you."

I release her waist so I can take her thigh in one hand, squeezing the soft skin lightly as I position her so I can slide right inside her. She's still so damn wet, dripping everywhere, her scent filling the entire nest in the most delicious, agonizing way.

She doesn't need to leave a physical mark on me; I doubt I'll ever get her scent off my skin. I don't fucking want to.

"Alright, sweet girl, just like that," I murmur to her, and then I slide inside her.

She groans in relief, rocking to get me all the way into her. I let her, but don't push for more myself. I let her have me for as long as she wants, as long as she needs something inside of her.

She fucks herself shallowly with my cock for a few minutes, and I let my eyes slide closed, her hair in my face, the sweet scent of her my entire world. I could stay like this forever, but my dick has other ideas.

My knot begins forming, which isn't a surprise. Paige's hot, tight pussy is around me; how could I *not* be desperate? I'm not even surprised that I'm managing to pop another knot. When they say that omega's pheromones during heat drive an alpha crazy with the need to care for them, they're not kidding.

"Paige, honey," I groan, pressing my lips to whatever part of her I can reach. "I'm going to knot you. You want that? You want my knot inside you?"

"Alpha," she whimpers, and I have to take that as a yes.

"Fuck yourself all the way back," I tell her. "Let me lock you nice and deep, keep you full."

I reach down to find her clit, because there's no way in hell I'm going to come when she hasn't. I rub gentle little circles, and she tenses and squeezes around me as she pushes our hips flush, taking me as deep as she can.

She comes again, but it's softer this time, especially in comparison to the last few days. She squeaks and squeezes around me, and I can't help it, coming inside her as my knot locks.

My eyes roll back at the perfect, tight heat of her. "That's it, honey," I groan. "Oh, Paige, you're fucking *perfect*." I don't know if she can understand me right now, but I couldn't care less. I need her to know it, and I need to say it. I *need* to say it because it's the truest thing I know.

We're knotted together for the next little bit, and Paige makes a contented little sigh. "Is this good, omega?" I ask her. "This what you wanted?"

She sighs again, and I assume it means *yes*.

It takes a minute to be able to pull that ridiculously heavy blanket up without moving too much, and Paige is no help whatsoever, but that's okay. I eventually get us covered, and it doesn't feel quite as heavy when it's over the both of us.

I kiss her neck again. "Go to sleep, honey," I tell her. "You're nice and full now; you're perfect. Rest."

I wake up abruptly. The sun coming through the blinds has moved, and without turning my head to see the clock, I'd guess it's about mid-day. It's the longest either of us has slept in days.

At some point while we slept, my knot went down, and I slipped out of her. The condom, stretched from my knot, slipped off at some point too. That made a huge mess, and I'm sure it'll be a pain in the ass to clean later, but I can't find it in me to regret it. I've never slept better than the last few hours.

I glance at Paige; she's still asleep. I'm risking her waking up in distress if I leave the nest, but I have a suspicion her heat's almost over, and I don't want her to become lucid again just to see what a mess we made of the place.

I dispose of the condom, clean myself up the best I can with a washcloth, and bring a fresh washcloth back in to wipe her up the best I can. I think we have to write the sheets off as a loss, and I probably need to buy her a new weighted blanket, but I dab at those stains anyway, hoping I can mitigate some of the damage. I'd change her sheets, but even if I could do that without waking her up, messing with an omega's nest during their heat sounds like a recipe for disaster.

She doesn't wake up. That has to be a good sign, right? Her body is finally letting her rest. Hopefully, her hormones are evening back out, and the heat will end soon.

I discard the washcloth, then cuddle back in behind her. I hope it's almost over, but even if she wakes up fully lucid again, no way in hell am I letting her wake up alone.

CHAPTER 23

Paige

I wake up with my brain trying to leave my skull, pulsing and pounding and giving every impression that it's swollen to the point where it doesn't fit in my head anymore.

Despite the pain, though, everything else feels normal. My body aches, but it's not painful. It's like a layer of cotton wool has been pulled away, and I can sense the world clearly again. I'm more aware of my body than I have been in what I can only guess is a while.

Or, well—there's been one part of my body I've been more than aware of. My pussy has been hungry, demanding, driving my every thought. I stretch a bit, and I'm definitely sore, but not in any serious pain. Mickey was shockingly careful, especially considering how needy I was during my heat.

I flush. *Needy.* I was so damn needy, demanding all of his attention. Did he even eat or sleep the entire time I was in my heat?

"You're awake," Mickey murmurs, interrupting my mental inventory which is being interrupted by my worry. "How're you feeling?"

That is a good question. I know my head is pounding, and I know my body aches but doesn't hurt. I know I'm a little embarrassed and not sure where I stand with Mickey yet. I also know that the arm he has wrapped tight around me is incredibly comforting, although I don't know if I'm supposed to feel that or not.

"Fine," I tell him, because I know that's what I'm supposed to say.

"If you were fine, you'd open your eyes," he argues.

Well, he's got me there. "Lights out?" I check.

He hesitates. "Yeah, but it's mid-afternoon, honey. There's a lot of sun. What do you need?" It takes me a second to answer that question because I'm stuck on him calling me *honey*. He's still calling me that. It wasn't just when I was in heat and needed him to be nice to me.

I don't know what that means yet, and I'm too slow to parse through it all right now.

"Can I have the Imitrex?" I ask, and I can hear how pathetic my voice sounds.

"Mhm. Two seconds."

He moves away from me, and I want to protest. I'm almost unable to stop myself when he physically leaves the nest, the space I made for us that's *safe* and ours. My instincts think letting him leave means the bubble of this is over, that all of the real-world things will come back now.

He's back as quickly as he promised, handing me the Imitrex and a bottle of water. I pop it without even opening my eyes, swallowing the pill and half the bottle of water. I'm definitely dehydrated, which is probably part of why my head hurts so bad. I know better than to let myself get dehydrated.

I'm sure Mickey did his best during the heat. The man showed up with a damn mini-fridge full of water when absolutely no one asked him to do that. I'm sure I was a nuisance who didn't think of things like water or my own health.

I let my head fall back to the pillow, keeping my eyes closed as I try to breathe through it. I've finally hit the type of deep breathing I need—steady, almost meditative, taking enough of my attention that it distracts slightly from the pain—when Mickey's hand starts stroking through my hair, scratching at my scalp, and I lose track of my deep breaths. I might stop breathing entirely for a second.

"Is this okay?" he checks. "Or is this type of touch annoying?"

He calls *annoying* what I call *makes me want to pull my skin off*, but it doesn't matter either way, because this isn't that. His touch is firm enough, the gesture steady and soothing. "'S good," I manage to mumble, eyes still closed. Imitrex takes about thirty minutes to start working. I can bear thirty minutes. I can...

Mickey keeps scratching at my scalp. He stays completely silent, and the only time he moves is when I fish around for the water bottle again. He presses it into my hand, and I finish the thing, tossing it aside even as something inside me cringes to know there's an empty plastic water bottle cluttering up my nest.

Finally, I can think through the pounding again. It's not gone, of course it's not; it never is. But it is more manageable, and the deep breaths are starting to actually feel effective.

"Okay," I murmur, and force myself to open my eyes.

Mickey is sitting cross-legged next to me, hand still in my hair. He's blocking the window with his body, which I appreciate, but it also makes him look like he's crowned in a halo of golden sun. Fuck, he looks good.

He's naked, I realize quickly. I'm naked. We're both naked, because we've been fucking for days.

I remember it in bits and flashes, more emotions than moments. I know it was good. I know Mickey was kind. And I know he made my body feel things I've never felt before.

Before this heat, I'd had sex four times. I've probably more than tripled that number now, and Mickey's shown me that what came before isn't even worth thinking about.

"Hi, honey," he says, voice barely over a whisper. He waits a moment, then says, "So, I'm guessing we can tell your insurance company to eat shit, because a heat didn't miraculously cure you, huh?"

I laugh, which hurts a bit but feels good at the same time. We can laugh at this. This didn't ruin us.

"What can I do to help, Paige?" he asks.

"This is good." This is *great*. This is more than anyone's ever done before except Emma, and Emma certainly wouldn't fuck me for the greater good.

"Mhm. You need to lay here for a while longer? Or you ready for a bath?"

"You saying I smell?"

"We both smell like sex, Paige. Your pheromones are saturating everything."

From someone else, that might be a humiliating statement. But Mickey says it with something close to wonder, and my chest fills with pride. Pride is a stupid feeling to have—I'm, what, proud of my biology making me sex-starved for a few days?—but I have it nonetheless.

"Bath," I agree. And after that, I can handle changing the sheets in my nest, and making sure everything is where it's supposed to be.

Mickey actually leans down and presses a kiss to my forehead, and I tilt my chin up, trying to get closer like a moth to a flame. His lips are dry and a little chapped. He doesn't usually have chapped lips.

You've been kissing for days, my brain supplies. *You haven't let him take care of himself.*

215

Mickey's standing now. "I'll be right back; let me get it started for you," he says, and this time, it's a little easier to let him step out of the nest.

I can hear the water turning on and let my eyes slide closed. "Do you like bubbles?" he calls from the other room. There's a pause, then, "Do you have bubble bath? Guess I should have led with that."

"No bubbles," I tell him. "Just need to be clean." Honestly, I'd take a shower and get it over with if I thought I could stand for that long.

He doesn't respond, so I listen to the sound of the tub filling. I have a deep tub, so it's going to take a minute. I thought I'd use that tub more often than I do when I moved in, but I can't remember the last time I used it at all.

"Hey, Mickey?" I ask.

I hear his footsteps getting closer, and open my eyes to see him standing in the bathroom door. "Yeah, honey?"

"How long has it been?" I ask him. "Since... you know. Since it started."

"Three days," he says. "Do you remember much of it?"

"Bits and pieces. Thank you."

"Don't have to thank me for any of that, Paige," he says shortly, stepping closer to the nest. I hold my breath, waiting for him to come back inside. He doesn't, though, stopping at the edge. He looks down at the little barrier and I flush.

When I bought this nest, I'd had to have it customized. The little wall is often called a *baby bumper*, and not a lot of omegas past puberty apparently want them. But I did. It makes the nest safe and enclosed, like nothing can get to me while I'm in here.

"Sorry if that was inconvenient," I mumble, because I'm sure it was. If he was stepping out for my meds and water and snacks, and I was probably grabbing at him, then it must have been so annoying.

"Again, you don't need to be sorry. This is your *nest*, Paige. I'm not an omega, but I'm the son and brother of omegas, and I know a nest is sacred. It's meant to be a place you feel safe, just for you. Do you feel safe here?"

I always have. When the rest of the world was too much, when light and sound and moving hurt me, when social expectations were too high, when I couldn't handle it all anymore, this is where I'd retreat, and I would always know that nothing could touch me here.

And now it smells like peppermint and pine, and it's somehow even safer.

"Yeah," I tell him.

"Yeah, I figured. You told me you like small, tight spaces; your nest is perfect for you." He looks up toward the ceiling. "Surprised you don't have one of those canopies, honestly."

I wrinkle my nose. "Like Emma had when she was younger?" He nods. "Those gauzy things? You have any idea how *awful* those things feel when they touch you?"

217

His mouth quirks up in the corner. "I'm sure you're right. Have you considered heavier curtains? Like a four-poster? Would those be less irritating?" When I shrug, he shrugs back. "Well, let me know. I'd be happy to hang them for you."

Does he know what he offered? Is he aware how intimate it would be to help an omega with their nest? To help *me* with my nest especially? My nest is sacred to me. Letting him in would be...

Well, it would be exactly as intimate as trusting him when I was in heat. I'd do it, and it would be easy, I realize. I trust him.

"Time for a bath," he says. "Can you walk?"

I'm sure as fuck going to try. I need to stretch out my body, anyway.

Only when I get to the bumper on my nest, I can't quite lift my leg high enough to get it over. It's not that high and I've never had an issue before, but suddenly this little obstacle is insurmountable. I'm trapped in my own nest.

Mickey swoops me up in a movement so quick I honestly didn't see it coming. He's still naked, his bare chest pressing into my shoulder. I turn my head toward him almost instinctively. He smells like pine and peppermint and sex, and I barely resist burying my face in his shoulder.

And then he's setting me into the bath, leaving me to soak in the steaming hot water. I close my eyes again, letting the water soothe my sore muscles.

I'm probably covered in absolute filth. I have vague memories of Mickey trying to clean us up in spare moments, and he wore condoms, so at least I'm not covered in his come. But I am coated in sweat. Having a fever that's only treatable through sex is no joke.

Mickey walks softly as he re-enters, and I leave my eyes closed. I'm never this relaxed around people. I remember redressing almost immediately after Samuel and I finished. But here with Mickey, it's different. It's not like he hasn't seen it all now, and he's been looking for days. And he's never made me feel bad about anything.

I also don't think he's leering, although I don't think I'd mind it if he leered a little bit.

"Hey, can you look at me?" he asks, and I do, cracking my eyes open. He's holding an armful of eclectic things, a medication pack I don't recognize, a bottle of water, and a library book. "You should hydrate more," he says. "Let me know if you want something besides water."

"Water is fine," I say, shaking out my hand to get some of the water off it before I reach for the bottle.

Mickey sets his other items on my bathroom counter so he can crack the bottle open for me before handing it over. Something in my chest goes light and fluttery.

I know we need to talk. I also know that we're probably too tired and emotional to have the conversation right now. But it needs to happen.

He picks up the medication. "It is totally your choice if you take this," he says. "But I picked up Plan B, just in case. You took your pills the whole time, and I did wear condoms, but we all know that condoms and knots aren't the most compatible, even the condoms meant for knots, and with your heat and supposedly being so fertile..." He's turning red. He's embarrassed.

I'm not. It's sweet that he planned ahead like this, and I probably should have thought of it. I know most alphas wouldn't have bothered. They'd have probably considered it a generous gift that they wore condoms in the first place.

"I'll take it," I say, switching the water bottle to my other hand so I can hold out my closer hand for the meds. He gives it to me.

"Thank you," I tell him once I've taken it. "I appreciate you thinking about it. And not—most alphas would assume nature takes its course during a heat, you know? And thanks for not being like that. I can't—*won't*—get pregnant." That is one thing I know for sure.

"I'm not saying all alphas are good, because I know there are real problems," he says slowly. "But I think you know more assholes than statistically average."

Probably.

"I also brought your book," he says, holding it up to show me the cover. "Your bookmark is still at the beginning, so I figured you hadn't started yet. I could read to you?"

And *that* is the sweetest thing I ever heard. Sweeter than the sex. Equally but differently sweet to him making sure I took my meds when I wasn't able to do it myself. This might be the sweetest gesture I've ever seen.

"I'd love that," I say quietly, and so Mickey sits on the floor, back against the wall as he rests next to the tub, and begins to read.

CHAPTER 24
Mickey

I need her to eat something. After her bath she tells me she's tired, and I know her head is still pounding despite the medication. I set her up with another bottle of water—I'm going to get her to replenish her fluids if it kills me, dammit—get her back in her nest, and leave her the fuck alone.

Paige has always needed time alone, and she hasn't had a moment to herself in days. She spent the night at my place, then had maybe a few hours before she went to see my mom, and then she and I have been together for three days. She deserves a chance to be alone.

So I steal her bathrobe, a floor-length robe on her that looks ridiculous on me, and go downstairs to check out her kitchen. There's not a lot, and the one container of leftovers looks like a health risk. I don't want to leave her house and leave her here, but I need to get something into her system that's not the granola bars she keeps in the pantry.

There's only one person to call, who I will always call at times like this. She picks up on the second ring. "Mickey?"

"Hey, Ma."

"Are you both alright?" she demands. "Everything is okay, right?"

"We're fine. She came out of it in the last few hours. Got her a bath and some water and now she's sleeping again. She's in a lot of pain, though."

She sucks in a sharp breath. "I worried about that."

"I made sure she took her meds, but she didn't sleep much and she was definitely dehydrated and—" I make myself take a deep breath. I don't need to defend myself; it is what it is. "Now I'm hoping to feed her when she wakes up, but there's not much here."

"Say no more; I'll be there in thirty minutes."

I hesitate, because I don't want her to take this the wrong way. "Can you leave the food on the step? I know Paige's nest is technically only upstairs, but—"

"But you're an alpha protecting your omega," she says, and she sounds fond. "I'm glad you're making sure she has her space. I know Paige needs it more than most."

"I'm not her alpha, and she's not my omega," I correct quickly.

"Does Paige know that?" she asks. "I know she was slipping into her heat, but she seemed pretty convinced when she was talking to me."

"Paige and I need to talk," I admit. The *last* thing I need is my mother involved in my love life.

223

She's quiet for a second, but I can still hear her breathing over the line. "It's not that you don't love her," she says. "I know you do."

Well, if even my own *mother* could see it, then I was probably way less subtle than I thought. Paige might have legitimately been the last person to know how I feel about her.

"It's more complicated than that," I tell her evasively.

She sighs. "Mickey, you and I have delayed having this conversation for way too long," she says, voice heavy. "I think neither of us wanted to talk about him. But we need to."

I tense, muscles locked as I grip the phone so tight I'm worried about damaging it. "Ma—"

"Listen to me," she interrupts firmly. "Your father was a terrible human being and that has *nothing to do with you.* It never did. It never will."

"I look in the mirror and I see him," I tell her. "I'm a fucking alpha just like he is, and I know that he used that against you, I know—"

"You know way more than you should and yet not enough. Mickey, I know you saw so many things you shouldn't have. That, as your mother, I didn't protect you like I should have. Your sister doesn't remember much of it, but I know you were old enough that it's all there. You saw terrible things and you felt like you had to shoulder the burdens. I'm sorry."

"It's not your fault," I say, alarmed to hear that my voice is slightly choked up. We've never talked about this. Emma and I

224

did therapy when Mom had money and insurance to afford it, but by then it'd been long enough that I could pretend nothing bothered me. I'd gone to three sessions before I told Mom to stop wasting her money. I couldn't have her think any of that hurt me. I couldn't be one more problem for her to deal with.

"It's his fault," she agrees. "But a little bit of it's mine, because I never made you talk about this with me. And I should have. Mickey, listen to me; you are not your father. You don't have to worry about becoming him."

"I want Paige," I tell her. "I want her so bad, have for years. I want her more than is reasonable. I would have probably hurt someone if she had her heat with someone else. Even if it was a heat clinic. When she dated that guy, I wanted to kill him. I almost bit her a half a dozen times over the last few days, even though that's insane and we never talked about that. If Paige told me she was more interested in a pack than a monogamous relationship, I wouldn't be able to handle that. I can't share her, Ma. I want her and I saw how he wanted you, how he hurt you because of it. I can't, I won't—" My words are falling in a rush, spilling over each other like rapids. I doubt she can even understand everything I'm saying.

She must understand enough, because she says, "Have you talked to her about this?"

"Of course not." Tell her I'm a possessive, obsessive asshole? I'd rather do anything than have her find that out.

"Would you hurt *Paige?*"

"I wouldn't ever mean to." That I know. But I also know a lot of harm can come without meaning to.

"Do you want her to give up her job?"

"No." As long as she's happy with it then I want her to have it.

"You offended she makes more money than you?"

"I didn't go into this field ever thinking I'd make good money."

She chuckles for a second. "Oh, I know. Emma is the one who will take care of me in my old age. Does she want a pack, Mickey?"

"She's never said." A pack wouldn't fit in her little nest. And while that's not an indication either way, I cling to it.

"You going to try to change her? Make her into some cookie cutter omega?"

Paige is perfect *because* she's Paige, not in spite of it. "Never."

"Okay, Mickey, this one is the most important—would you stop if she said *stop*? Would you listen to her when she says something doesn't feel right? If she makes a choice you don't agree with, would you talk it out with her?"

"Fuck, I hope so." I think I would. The me of *now* would. But what if getting what I want, having my obsession in my hands and my life, makes me slip into the bad habits that linger genetically inside me, like a ticking time-bomb?

"You would," she says confidently. "I know you would, because I've watched you for years."

"When I was seventeen, with Katy…"

"When you were seventeen, you were a kid who wanted someone. You didn't hurt her. She told you she didn't like how you loved and you respected that, Mickey. That's enough. You've always treated me and your sister and Paige and every other omega you meet with the utmost respect. Every kid in this county looks at you, as big as a tree, and thinks *this man is safe.* You are a good man, Mickey Condor."

I'm choked up again. "What if all that is just hiding something?"

She's silent for a long second. "Your father could hide it from the rest of the world," she acknowledges. "At least until the end, when he stopped caring about where the bruises ended up. But that didn't mean he was safe. People thought your father was cold and distant because that's the only way he could hide it. And when we were at home—it was different. I don't know what you remember. It started before you were even born. Looking back now, it was textbook. He'd exert control. I'd go against it. He'd over-react to maintain control. And then he'd be soft and sweet so I'd forgive him. He'd never apologize though, because he thought alphas don't apologize to anyone beneath them, and he thought being alpha made him head of the household and all of us were beneath him. And that's not you, Mickey. That has never been you. That never will be you."

I hear her, but it's like it's through a fog, blurry and distant. I know what she's saying, but I can't make my mind process it. "I'd die before I hurt her," I tell her shakily.

"And that's what's different between you and him, Mickey. But let's not be idealists. You'll hurt her. She'll hurt you—and if you think she won't, then you're guilty of buying into the same bullshit of dominant alphas and submissive omegas, thinking she's too innocent and pure, that she's incapable of doing harm. She's human, you're human. You'll both do it, and it'll be an accident, and then you'll talk. It's what happens."

Not for the first time, I marvel at how my mom, a teenage bride to an abusive alpha, has turned into this wise woman who can speak like she's the expert on healthy relationships. I probably owe Bill more credit than I give them, but this is all her. My mom saw the future she wanted, and she made the world give it to her.

"I..." but I don't know what to say.

"I'm going to get you two a few days' worth of food," she says quietly. "When she wakes up, if she's feeling well enough, you two should talk. Really talk, Mickey. Listen to her. Let her tell you what she wants. And then tell her what you want. All cards on the table; that's the only way this works."

I don't think she's ever asked anything harder of me. But she's right. I have to do this. I have to lay it all out and let Paige decide. It's the only way.

"Thanks, Ma."

"Anytime, sweetie. But whatever happens, I need you to remember this—I'm proud of you, alright?"

I swallow around the lump in my throat. "I love you," I manage to say, words coming out in a rush, and then I hang up the call.

I stand there, holding my phone, staring off into nothing, until there's a scuffing sound behind me. "Is this one of those things I'm supposed to pretend I didn't hear?"

I whirl around, only to find Paige standing in the kitchen archway, clutching a blanket I've never seen before around her shoulders. "How long have you been there?" There's nowhere to hide in this house; the stairs are barely ten feet from where she's standing now. I should have heard her.

"I could pretend I just got here, if it makes you feel better?"

Only Paige would come out and say that. I take a deep breath. "Paige..."

"I don't want a pack," she tells me. "That many people—no. Way too much stimulation."

"Philip's in Emma's pack and he does fine," I point out, even though it's against my best interests. Apparently, I'm incapable of not looking after her. I think too many people have made her think she's a burden, and I need her to know that she's a joy, and that she has options. Even if those options aren't me.

"Yeah well, I'm not Philip," she says, a little agitated now, clutching that blanket tighter. I squint at it. It wasn't in her nest these past few days. I didn't notice it on the couch either. Where the hell did it come from? "I don't want what he wants. I'm glad the four of them found each other, but I don't want that." She starts to look more worked up, shifting from foot to foot, not looking directly at me. "I want the one person who I trust to understand what I need. And if the last few days made it seem like that's too much for you, I'd understand. You've seen me with two migraines, seen the amount of drugs it takes to get me through the day, and seen me absolutely mindless with heat. I'd understand if that was a turn-off. But from what I heard, I don't think that's the issue."

"It's not," I say firmly. "The issue has always been with me, and never with you."

"You're a good guy, Mickey," she says resolutely.

I think she's damn trusting. I think I'm torn between explaining why she should want nothing to do with me and carrying her back to her nest to make this permanent. It's completely irrational to put a mating claim on her, but I'm barely resisting.

But she's still fiddling with that damned blanket. "What's up with that?" I ask, gesturing to it.

"My nest was gross. So I tried to re-make it, but then I pulled out this blanket and it didn't smell like you, and turns out it's hard to sleep when it doesn't smell like you. I don't know if that's an after effect of the heat or if that's a more permanent thing."

She needs her nest to smell like me? My heart swells. "Let's fix your blanket," I say, my voice huskier. "And then food will be here, and we need to get some food in you."

"And then we'll talk," she challenges, eyes defiant and firm. I get a sudden image of her pinning me down and *making* me talk. Why do I like that so much?

"And then we'll talk," I agree, and I step forward, scooping her up under her knees and spine, blanket still clutched around her, and carry her over to the couch.

Chapter 25
Paige

M ickey holds me like he's never going to let me go, and I can forget entirely about this stupid blanket; everything now smells enough like him that I can finally relax.

I can restart my suppressant in a week, and that will dull my sense of smell. It won't go away entirely, but I won't smell Mickey quite so acutely. It's the one downside of being on a suppressant, and I actually think I might miss the scent of him now. The way it wraps around me, warmer than any blanket, is a balm.

But I'll still have his arms and his broad chest and the way he smiles. I'll still have the slightly scratchy sensation of his beard against my skin, and the way he holds me, and the way he looks at me. Probably, if he doesn't decide to end this before it even starts.

"You okay?" he asks after a minute.

"I'm fine." As fine as I get, anyway. Yes, my head hurts, but I can manage it. And right now, held by him, at least the rest of me is at peace in a way I so rarely get.

"You want to go back upstairs and try to sleep?"

"No." I know I should. I know I'm sleep deprived. But I also have a suspicion that he won't come with me, and the last thing I'm going to do is give him more time alone.

I literally told him that my nest didn't smell enough like him so I couldn't sleep, but Mickey is still going to act like it's inappropriate for him to be there.

"Alright then. Can I get you more water?"

I move so, instead of having my legs across his lap, I'm properly straddling him. The blanket slips down my shoulders, but I couldn't care less about that right now. I need to know he's not going anywhere.

Could Mickey pick me up and throw me off of him? Undoubtedly. He's built like he splits logs with his bare hands, not like he does hand puppets and story time, and my primary exercise is long walks. My legs are strong, but not strong enough to pin him.

But I know he won't move me. Once I'm here, he'll let me stay until I move myself, and that's what I need right now.

Mickey seems to already be well trained on how I like being held, because his arms come around me with firm pressure, holding me to him. I close my eyes, breathing him in for a long moment, and then let myself bury my head in his neck. He tilts his head, resting his cheek in my hair, and I feel the scratch of his beard and smell the scent of his skin and everything else goes still.

I meant to talk to him, meant to make him talk to me. But I can't summon the energy to break this little spell.

"So, no on the water?" Mickey eventually asks.

I lean more of my weight on him to make it clear. "You can stop for a few minutes. You don't always have to be doing something for others. You're worth more than that."

He doesn't say anything to that, but after a moment, his arms squeeze me a little tighter.

We stay like that until the doorbell rings, and Mickey stirs under me. "Can I get that, honey?"

Honey. I'm *honey* still, and that's almost as good as his hands on me. He knows this isn't over. He knows we're going to do this.

"Mhm," I say, but it takes me another second to let go of him. I slide off his lap, finding my blanket again. It smells like us now, and I close my eyes, wrapping myself up tight.

I wish eating in my nest didn't sound like one of the most disgusting things I could think of, because I want us to be back there, making the whole place smell like us. Not like sex, just us.

Mickey comes back with three bags, and of course Sherry went overboard. "She left a note saying she'll come back with more if we need it," Mickey says. "These two are groceries. This one is Morello's."

"She picked that up fast."

"Yeah, I'm not shocked. She charms people."

She does. He sets the bag on my coffee table, then goes to put the groceries away. I dig into the bag, finding flimsy plastic ware and two takeout containers.

One is the spaghetti and meatballs, and the other is a chicken parm. The meatballs are mine, and it's always been my favorite at Morello's. Mickey likes the parm. And Sherry knows us both inside and out without even asking.

I set them out on the coffee table, stabbing a flimsy plastic fork into each. Mickey walks back in with two glasses of water and real silverware.

"Sorry I went through your kitchen," he says.

"I don't think I care about my kitchen after, you know, everything."

He sits down next to me, sliding closer than he needs to. Maybe I'm reading into it, but it feels like he wants to be touching me.

Then again, from what I heard him tell his mom, *wanting* to touch me isn't his issue.

He picks up his takeout container and shakes his head. "She really knows us, huh?"

"We used to go to Morello's for birthdays," I remember. It's not that Morello's is particularly pricey, and every one of us now can afford to consider it a casual night out. But back then, when Sherry was trucking three kids around, one of them not even hers, it was a rare, special treat.

"And you always got the spaghetti and meatballs. Have you ever had anything else?"

"Sometimes." Emma and I had once split plates there, but I'd ended up eating most of the meatballs we ordered and leaving the other dishes to her.

"Well, can't mess with a good thing, I guess."

I take a bite. It's a little soggy from being in a takeout container, but it's obviously still fresh and hot and delicious, and I haven't eaten a real meal in days. I need these calories, and badly.

I'm done with half my plate before I even look up, only to see that Mickey must have been even hungrier than I was. He's inhaled his, his styrofoam container scraped clean. He looks at it, then looks at me, shifting guiltily. "Sorry."

"I think I probably should be sorry to *you*," I point out. "Considering I'm the reason you haven't eaten in three days."

"I ate."

"I checked that fridge. It's basically cheese and crackers, Mickey. You're over six feet tall. You didn't eat enough."

"Fuck, I meant to get that out of your space. Sorry I left it."

I'm not. It had felt like his little mark on the nest, like an indication he was going to come back to it. "Whose is it?"

"Bought it for this. A friend recommended it for us. So, mine if you want it gone. Yours if you want it here."

He's so sweet without even meaning to be. He thinks this is how people are, but they aren't. He knows that I'm probably even more picky about my nest than most omegas, and he's acting like accommodating for that is no big deal. No one's ever done that. Samuel was never willing.

I'd bought a new mattress and spent a painstaking month buying new bedding after the one and only time I'd let Samuel fuck me in my nest. That had been the end for us. Now I know how selfish he was, but back then, all I knew was that my skin crawled when he was in my nest. He didn't belong there.

Mickey, though? If we didn't need to have the conversation we needed to have, I'd probably have already dragged him back upstairs.

Not for sex. Although the heat is all a fuzzy, lust-soaked haze in my mind, being with Mickey convinced me that sex is perhaps all it's cracked up to be. But I'm too sore for that, and right now, I just want to hold him. I want him to hold me.

I want my nest to smell like us even when it's not soaked in sex pheromones.

"We need to talk," I tell him, because if we put it off any longer, then we'll never make any progress.

"Let me clean up."

"No. We'll do it later." That's something I never thought I'd say, but this is more important.

"Alright, Paige. Whatever you want."

I debate climbing into his lap again, needing to keep him from trying to leave this conversation. But I do believe that he'll stay because I asked, and maybe a little distance would be more helpful.

"I want you to explain," I tell him. "Tell me why you're so sure that this is some awful idea."

"I almost bit you during your heat a half dozen times."

I raise an eyebrow. That would have been inconvenient, and probably not my favorite thing, but there's one important distinction. "But you didn't."

"Barely. I will someday."

"And I'll probably want you to someday." I've never actually thought of it. I thought about it with Samuel, but it was entirely foreign, just something I might have to put up with. With Mickey, though? I want that eventually. He'd make it so good. I'd be his, and he'd be mine, and that sends a tingle through my belly.

"I kept thinking about knocking you up," he admits, and for once, it's not me who's avoiding eye contact.

It's probably not shocking. Everyone says alphas are obsessed with breeding their omegas, especially in heat. "But you didn't," I point out. "You ensured we used *three* methods of birth control the entire time. I think we can safely say you controlled the urge."

"I'm practically obsessive when it comes to you, Paige."

"And I know nothing about having an obsessive personality or anything." I roll my eyes.

"You're not taking this seriously." His voice is getting louder, but he hasn't moved toward me. If anything, he's cringing away like he's afraid of me.

"No, you're taking this too seriously. You're too hard on yourself."

He's quiet for a minute, then says, voice quiet now, "You have any idea why I go by Mickey?"

"It's your name. It's always been your name."

He shakes his head. "My legal name is Michael. You know that."

Of course I know that. But we've never called him that. "You've always gone by Mickey."

"Sure, and that was cute for a little kid, but I'm thirty-one, Paige. Most people would have started going by Michael or Mick or Mike or something." I frown. I know Bill calls him *Mick* sometimes, but all of those names sound so incredibly foreign for Mickey.

"So why do you go by Mickey, then?" I ask, assuming the answer has something to do with his mom always calling him that and not seeing any way at all it connects to the current conversation.

"Because every day I look in the mirror, I see my father," he says tightly. "He was about five years older than me the last time I saw him, so I probably still have a while to go for that. I inherited every-fucking-thing from him, and apparently that includes his obsessive tendencies. His need to *own*. And I see that, and I needed a name that people aren't scared of. I want the kids at work to look at me and think of their favorite little cartoon character, not a big scary alpha."

I get a little choked up. "While that's admirable," I manage to say, "I think you're wrong."

He raises an eyebrow. He's still pushed all the way back into the arm of my couch, but I can see I've caught his interest. "Oh? Tell me more, Paige." That tone might be a little mocking, I'm honestly not sure; but even if it is, I know Mickey would never mean it in a hurtful way.

"You might look like your father, you might have inherited the alpha genes, but the rest of you was *learned*, and it certainly wasn't learned from him," I say resolutely. "Mickey, you worship your mother. You think—correctly, might I add—that she's the best person to ever exist. You've spent your entire life trying to make her proud and be more like her. When you spent Emma's and my childhood making us grilled cheeses and playing board games with us even though Emma cheated shamelessly and I enforced the rule book like a cop, it's all because you watched your mom do the same thing. I don't give a fuck what you inherited; if all we are is what we inherit, then I inherited some real asshole genes too. But I do know what you learned, Mickey. And that matters more. Look, your mother, your sister, me—we're all jaded. Weary. We see how people treat omegas, and we're careful. So doesn't it say something that not one of us has ever been concerned about you being in our lives?"

He looks at me, mouth hanging open slightly. "And if you're wrong?" he eventually asks quietly. "If I became like him?"

"I don't think you would. And I think you're too scared of your mother to even contemplate it."

He stares at me for a minute, but I know he can't argue with that. He and I both know he would never do anything to upset his mother.

Not that I think Sherry is what stops her son from being a monster; Mickey is the type of good guy who gives people the shirt off his back, who cares about childhood literacy and picks up cardboard on a Sunday so the kids can do a fun craft. But if this is what convinces him to believe me, then I have no problem using Sherry's name. I'm pretty confident she'd want me to do it.

Mickey keeps staring at me, and then eventually says, "I am *obsessed* with you, Paige. And staying away was the best way I knew how to control it. But if I'm here, you have to know I'm going to be clingy as hell. You okay with that?"

"Alright." He doesn't get it. What he considers a personality flaw, I consider ideal. Someone obsessed with *me*? *Me*? Not what I can do for them, not the babies I could have or the status symbol my last name would be, but me?

Emma was right: it has only ever been Mickey for me.

"I'm tired. But I need my nest to smell like both of us again. Please come help me make my nest perfect."

He swallows, his throat bobbing, and then nods, picking me up to carry me back up the stairs.

CHAPTER 26
Mickey

P aige has never lost an argument in her life, and I didn't exactly expect today to be the day that changes, but I'm still a little blown away by whatever happened.

Paige lets me hold her when I carry her up the stairs, mine to hold and protect and treasure. She looks at me with doe eyes when I place her in her nest, then get her medication from the top of the mini-fridge and hand her the right pills. She cuddles up to me immediately when I slip into her nest next to her, holding my breath until she seems to accept me into the space. She apparently wasn't kidding about wanting my scent.

"I shouldn't have put all that on you when you weren't feeling well," I mutter, scratching my nails through her hair.

"First of all, I asked," she says, voice a little sleepy now. "Secondly, if this is going to work, you have to accept that I'll be doing a lot of things when I don't feel well. It's just the way it is."

I frown. "I don't like that."

"Well, it's non-negotiable, considering," she tells me. "Is that a deal-breaker for you?"

I hate it, but nothing is a deal-breaker when it comes to Paige. "No, honey. Not a deal-breaker."

She shivers. "Like when you call me that."

"Oh yeah?" *Honey, pretty girl, sweet girl, my omega*—all things I've been calling her for the past few days. And apparently she likes it.

"Means you want me."

"Wasn't aware that was in doubt."

"People don't want me," she mutters, turning her head further into my chest. Then she hitches one leg over mine, lays an arm across me, and giggles slightly. She sounds more like she did during her heat than her normal self. "Guess I won't need that body pillow anymore."

I keep stroking through her hair. "Consider me happy to fill the job, honey."

"'M tired," she says. "Gonna sleep."

"You do that. I'll be right here," I promise her, and when she falls asleep half on top of me, I don't move an inch.

Paige wakes up groaning the next morning, hiding her face from the light coming through the gap in her curtains.

"Hurts?" I ask softly. She nods against my chest. "Alright, honey, let me get your meds. Imitrex?" She nods again, so I carefully slide out from under her, giving her the pillow to hide her face in, while I grab one of the remaining water bottles and the medication she'll need. She lifts her head enough to take it when I slip back into the nest, and then promptly rests her forehead against my thigh.

"What else can I do?"

"This is good."

This *isn't* good, though, because she's hurting and I can't do a damn thing. I open my mouth to say something, although I have no idea what. What could I possibly say that would make this better?

"Breakfast?" I eventually think to ask. My mom had included pancake mix in her groceries yesterday, and I know that Paige craves carbs when she's in pain.

"Mhm." She's face-down, so her bed swallows the words until they're more vibration than actual sound. "Please."

"Give me fifteen minutes." That should give enough time for the Imitrex to start doing something for her.

I pull her bathrobe back on. At least it's not fuzzy, but it's still way too small for me. I feel like a flasher. I need to get my own clothes soon, and wonder if it's worth calling my mom to ask her to pack me up a bag.

Paige must smell the food cooking, because she arrives down-stairs just after I plate the first stack of pancakes. I put the syrup out for her and a big glass of water, watching her out of the corner of my eye as I go back to the fry pan. She's properly dressed, wearing a t-shirt and leggings like she usually does, and she slouches at the table as soon as she sits down, turning her head away from the window over the sink.

"What can I get you to help you feel better?" I ask, stacking more pancakes on a plate.

"Nothing. This is what it is sometimes." When I don't say anything, she picks her head up to look at me, her eyes narrowed. "I'm serious, Mickey. This is my reality. I've had a lot of bad days in a relatively short time lately, and I think I can safely say that the disruption of the heat triggered them, but that doesn't mean it'll ever go away. If I get this new medication, it won't go away. You can't make me better, and if you can't accept that, then we can't work."

"Is it so wrong that I want to help?" I challenge. She's so bad at accepting help, but if we're going to do this, then she's going to have to learn, at least sometimes. She's not doing this alone anymore.

She's quiet for a minute. "Don't make me feel guilty for being sick," she whispers.

My heart clenches and I rethink everything. Paige *is* bad at accepting help, but I also need to get a whole lot better at listening to when she does and doesn't want it. "No, honey. No. Never."

"That's what it sounds like. You don't mean it but it does. I can't control it. You can't control it. Acting like there should be some way to *fix* me when there isn't makes me think the way I am is just an inconvenience to you. I'm sick, I'll always be sick, but I'll decide how big a deal to make it." She shifts her weight so she's sitting upright more properly, grabbing some of the pancakes for herself. "I'm willing to hear you out about your fears about your father and I'm willing to keep assuring you forever if that's what you need. This is what I need from you."

I consider that for a second and then nod. "Fair enough. But you'll tell me when I *can* help, right? I'll get good at it; I'll start to pick up on things. But until then, I'll need some direction."

"Yeah, I'll try." She pours syrup on her pancakes in a precise criss-cross drizzle, then cuts even little bites. "These will help."

I turn the stove off and dump the mixing bowl and spatula into the sink to wash after, and we eat in silence for a few minutes. She starts to look a little better, a little more lively and engaged.

"I need to call my neurologist," she says once she clears her plate. "See how soon I can get an appointment."

"Will they make you wait?"

"I hope not," she mutters. "It would suck if we did all this and I still had to wait six months, huh?"

It would suck. It would be colossally awful for her, and I hate that there's a system that would do that to her.

"Go ahead," I tell her. "I'll clean up here."

She nods and retreats upstairs, and I clean the kitchen, taking a few extra minutes to scrub the dishes and the table and countertop, wanting to leave the place better than I found it. Then I look through the groceries my mom brought us. There's bread and cheese and turkey cold cuts, so I can make sandwiches for lunch, and there's pasta and pre-made meatballs for dinner. There's more pancake mix and more sandwich ingredients for tomorrow, but there's not another dinner, so we'll have to see if we're ready to venture out by then.

But we don't have to be. We'll take as long as Paige needs to be comfortable. I know the heat hormones are slowly leaving her body, but she's still unsettled outside of her nest, and it's my job to protect her and our nest right now.

I stop, bag of sliced turkey in my hand. *Our* nest. *Ours.* Is it too soon to want that? Is that too presumptuous?

I know it's too soon. We've barely started dating, and we're both still riding high on the effects of the heat. That's probably enough to make me feel bound to her nest.

And that all may be true, but I don't want to leave. I want her to drag me into her nest. I want her to prefer it when it smells like both of us I want her to make us a place to just be us. I want to assure my omega she's built the perfect nest for us, tell her how good and smart and giving she is while she gives me those eyes, while she shows me that softness I've only ever seen when she's in her nest.

I want that forever. She gave me the smallest taste and I can't let her go.

Eventually the kitchen is too clean to keep pretending that I need to do any more, so I go to find Paige.

To my surprise, she's not in her bedroom. Then I hear noise from across the hall, and I move to the one room in her condo I haven't been in yet. She left the door propped open, so I knock lightly and then poke my head in.

This is probably meant to be a spare bedroom, but Paige has turned it into some combination of office and obsession room. One wall is an elaborate computer set-up with a giant computer chair she's currently sitting in, legs pulled up under her. Two of the other walls are covered floor to ceiling with bookshelves. One of them looks like dusty law books, the big thick kind I assume no one enjoys reading, but the other shelves look like they're full of fantasy books.

The last wall is covered in memorabilia. There's a giant framed map I recognize as from a fantasy book both Paige and I read a few years ago. There's an actual replica sword displayed on the wall, and I bet Paige has an exact idea of which character the sword belongs to. There're a few framed pieces of character art, too.

The whole place is lit by Christmas lights, just like the rest of Paige's house. It's soft and cozy, and almost feels like an extension of Paige's nest. If she keeps her actual nest simple and uncluttered, then *this* is where she puts all the stuff.

"You're telling me you own this many books *and* manage to read as many library books as you do?" I ask her.

She spins around in her office chair. "I buy the ones I really like," she tells me after a moment. "Because I re-read them a lot."

The ones she *really likes* probably number more than a hundred. "How many books do you read a year, Paige?"

She shrugs. "About two hundred fifty to three hundred? Usually."

I wander over to the shelves. "Which one is your favorite?"

She gets out of her chair, crossing the room to me. "Favorite for what? They each do different things. This one," she says, running her finger down a crimson spine, "has excellent action, but this one here has the best characters, and this one is mind-blowing when it comes to the ending."

Her eyes are bright as she touches the books, looking over titles and darting glances back at me. I want to see this every day. I want to be the one who makes her smile like this.

"Hey, what did the doctor say?" I ask.

"Next Monday. So, a little over a week."

That's not terrible, I guess. But after watching her be in blinding pain so many times over the last few days, I can't stand the idea of her waiting another minute. I want her to get what she needs right now.

"Want to read the one we started yesterday?" I ask her. "I can keep reading, if you liked that."

She stops and stares at me for a minute, and I wish I could see inside her head. I wish I could know what she's thinking.

But then she smiles and nods. "In the nest?" she asks quietly, like she's worried I'm going to say no.

"Yeah, if you're good with that."

And when she curls up with her head in my lap as I lean against the headboard of her nest, reading her book to her, I feel like a fucking king.

CHAPTER 27

Paige

We don't leave my nest for more than the bathroom and food for thirty-six hours. On the second day, I feel good enough that I have a loose sense that I should check in with work and at least look through my emails, but Mickey keeps me distracted all day, making us both lunch and then moving back upstairs so we can finish my book together.

But unfortunately, it's now five and I can't put it off any longer. "I should start getting ready," I mutter.

"For what?" Mickey asks, setting the book aside. He still has one arm curled around me, and I wish I didn't have to leave it. Sadly, I know it's time. If I don't want a thousand angry voicemails from my mother, I better not be late.

"It's Friday, right?" I double check. I'm pretty positive it is, but I've also been a little out of it for a few days. When he nods, I remind him, "I said I'd go to my parents' house, remember? Dinner?"

"Yeah, but you just had your heat."

"Trust me when I say that doesn't matter."

"You haven't been feeling good."

"Also not a valid excuse." I shake my head, pretending it doesn't matter. And it doesn't anymore; I'm not the little kid trying to get my parents' to understand me. I found other people to do that. The Condors, and Emma's pack, and even to an extent the people I work with, who I practically never see in person but who nonetheless rely on me and my expertise. Even the people at the library are way more understanding than my parents ever were.

I won't pretend it doesn't hurt. But it's not devastating anymore. I'm not screaming into a blank, empty void, begging to be heard; I know they'll never hear me, and I can accept it and move on.

"It's just a couple hours," I tell him. "But I can't look like this." I put on leggings again, and I don't want to even think about what my hair looks like.

He's quiet for a minute. "I can't talk you out of it?"

"Sadly, no."

"Then I guess I need to go home and change. Can't go wearing your robe, as comfortable as it is." He makes a face. "That means I have to pull my gross clothes back on."

"We should have washed those yesterday," I realize. "I'm so sorry."

"Don't be. I was ignoring the real world for a while longer." He leans down and presses a firm kiss to the top of my head, as if to make it clear why he was ignoring the real world. "But it's too late now."

"Why do you have to go?" I ask. "I'll come back tonight, if you want to hang out here..." Is that presumptuous? Am I crossing some boundary I didn't know about?

"Paige, I'm going to change because I'm coming with you."

"You don't have to do that."

"I told you I would, remember? And I'm not going to change my mind."

"You hate my parents," I protest. "They're unpleasant. I wouldn't subject you to that."

"Paige." He drops his arm from around me and I almost protest, but then he turns so he's fully facing me. "If we're doing this, then we're *doing this*. If I'm your alpha, then you need to know that I won't leave you to face things alone. Especially things that suck. If there are hard things, then we do them together."

"You can't protect me from my parents," I mutter.

"I can, and I damn well will. Now, how dressed up do I need to be for this damn thing?"

Mickey drives back to my house at six-thirty, and he actually comes all the way out of his car to knock on the door, and when I open it, he hands me flowers.

"This feels like prom," I tell him, taking the flowers and stroking over one yellow petal on the daisy. "I didn't even go to prom."

"I know. I think it was the only time Emma's ever been truly mad at you."

"Probably." We'd spent months preparing, her enthusiastic, me trying to muster up the energy. We'd both bought dresses and everything. But I freaked out about how overwhelming being there would be, and I knew Emma had a date when I didn't, so I'd be left alone for a lot of the night, and I'd backed out. "Let me put these in water."

Mickey follows me inside but waits in the living room, and I go into the kitchen. I don't have a flower vase, but I figure a tall glass will work fine. I mess with the flowers for a minute, trying to get them to fluff out and fill the glass. When I'm satisfied, I step back. The vibrant daisies brighten up my kitchen, and I take an extra minute to stare at them.

Mickey is still standing by the door. He put on a button-down shirt that I've never seen before, nicer than the ones he wears to work, and a pair of crisp black slacks. He does genuinely look like he's trying to pick me up for prom.

"You didn't have to buy me flowers," I tell him, walking over to get my shoes and bag.

He catches me around the waist and pulls me into him, kissing the top of my head. "Of course I did. We did all this and I haven't even taken you on a date yet, not a real one, anyway.

And this might be the shittiest date ever, but you should still be treated like a princess. *And* I promise I'll bring you on a better date soon." He hasn't raised his head yet, his face still buried in my loose hair. I don't wear it down often, but I left it down tonight, and he seems to like it. "You look lovely, honey."

"Thanks. You look good too." I've pulled out a black dress that hopefully is neutral enough that my mother doesn't remember that I wore it the last time I visited her house too. I've only ever worn it to her house and one funeral. It fits fine, with a fitted bust and flaring out over my hips to end just over my knees, but it's not something I'd usually wear. But for my parents, leggings won't cut it. "You have to let me go so I can get my shoes."

He pulls back slightly, but instead of letting me go, he nudges me with one arm. "Sit down," he says, gently steering me toward the couch. "Which shoes?"

I have three pairs of sneakers, a pair of sandals I almost never wear, and a pair of short heels on the rack by the door. I'm pretty sure I haven't worn the heels since the last time I was at my parents' house, either. "The heels," I tell him, sighing.

He picks them up and walks over, but rather than handing them to me like I expected, he kneels in front of me, heels still in one hand. "What're you doing?"

He looks up at me, smiling slightly. "Helping you out."

"I can put on my own shoes."

"I'm aware. And yet I'm going to help."

At some point we're going to need to talk about this compulsive need to help. But if it's helping reassure him that he's a good man and not six seconds from turning into his father for some reason, then I guess I can let him have it for now. I extend my foot to him, and he grips it gently, stroking along the arch of my foot and up to my ankles.

"You have a foot thing I should know about?" I blurt out, then blush, because even I know I shouldn't have said that right now.

He laughs slightly. "What do you know about foot fetishes, huh? You have something you want to talk about?" He touches my foot again, and it tickles. My toes wiggle, and he smiles wider, then slides my foot into the shoe before picking up the other one.

Once I have my shoes on, Mickey pushes himself to stand and then extends a hand to help me up. "Shall we?" he asks grandly, sliding my arm into the crook of his elbow and escorting me to the car like this is a way fancier date than it is. It's more and more like prom every minute.

It's a feeling that is only increased when we pull up outside my parents' house. I had barely been living here when prom came around, spending most of my nights sharing a nest with Emma, but I had legally lived here at the time. I'd hated being here. I hate being here now.

Mickey tries to park on the driveway, but I shake my head, pointing around back. "They don't do cars on the front drive. Think it doesn't look classy."

Mickey nods, going around back. "And my car doesn't look the part, does it?"

Mickey's ten-year-old Toyota is *not* what my father considers a respectable car, no. He'd throw a fit if someone saw it in front of his house. "Yeah, they're... yeah. Not too late to back out, Mickey."

"Not a chance, Paige. I'm not letting you do this alone." He parks by the back door while my heart flutters uncontrollably. When I reach for my door, he reaches across to stop me. "I got it. Give me two seconds."

He gets out of the car before I can argue with him. When he makes it to the other side, I tell him, "I can open doors still, Mickey."

"Mhm. Full confidence in your abilities. Still—let me?"

What am I going to tell him, *no?* I give him my hand when he holds his out, letting him help me out of the car. "We go in this door?" he asks quietly.

"Might as well," I sigh. "I forgot—you've never been here, have you?" Emma came a few times, but neither of us exactly liked it, so we'd avoided it as much as possible.

"I drove you here a few times, before I left for college. Am I going to get a tour tonight? See your childhood bedroom and stuff? Little baby Paige's first nest?"

"I don't have a nest here," I tell him. "And my childhood bedroom got converted to a guest room ten years ago. There wasn't a lot in it."

He stops, and trying to keep walking when he's stopped moving is like trying to drag a tree while wearing heels, so I stop too. "Why not?"

"Why not what?"

"You're telling me you didn't own five thousand books and a neat little nest here?"

"Nope." When he doesn't move, I relent. "I was not the convenient omega my parents pictured. You can see my father still tried to match-make and get some value out of me, but that didn't work either. I wasn't supposed to be the lawyer; I was supposed to be the lawyer's omega wife. But long before I squashed that dream, it was obvious I'd never be what they wanted. After the complete, total, public meltdown I had when I was six over a scratchy dress that my mother *still* won't let me forget about, the writing was kind of on the wall."

"You deserved so much better."

"I was a sad kid. But if they didn't want to give me what I needed, fine. I found it with other people." I move my hand from his arm down to his hand, giving it a squeeze so it's crystal clear who I mean.

"You're making me hate these people even more," he mutters, then looks at me. "Sorry. I know I shouldn't say it. But I do. I hate them."

I don't. Not anymore. I don't think about them much, truth be told. But I've also had years to come to terms with that, and Mickey's had a few minutes. "You can feel whatever you want. But this is your last chance to back out."

"No way am I letting you go in there alone. C'mon. It's time for dinner."

I debate for half a second if I should stop him. I have a hard time reading how mad people are—it's why it's safer to usually assume people *are* mad, even when I don't know—so I have no idea if Mickey is going in there spoiling for a fight. But before I can decide if it's better for us to turn back, he knocks on the door, and Hannah Jane opens the door.

Hannah Jane has been cooking for my family for twenty-five years now. She's the consummate professional, which is why my mother always liked her. She keeps her mouth shut about anything that happens in this house. When I read fantasy stories about kind cooks looking after unwanted children, I definitely saw no connection to my real life.

"Ms. Bowers," she says, stepping aside so we can come in. "They're expecting you."

"Thank you," I tell her, then tug Mickey by the hand past her, through the kitchen, and through the pristinely set dining room to the front parlor.

This house is way too big for three people, never mind the two who live here now. The charitable view is my parents genuinely thought they'd have more kids, but it's much more likely they just like the status symbol of a big house. This place has always felt so cold.

It'd been okay when I'd had a semblance of a nest to retreat to, although it hadn't been a very good nest. My mother bought the nesting materials she saw in high end fashion magazines, the latest and greatest any omega child would be lucky to have. But they were never right, always scratchy or some weird texture, and I'd discarded way too many pieces, which had pissed her off. So this house had never been anything but intolerable.

My mother is sitting on one of the couches that cost triple one of my mortgage payments. She rises when we enter, pasting on that smile she uses when she's trying to smooth something over. I'd always wished I was able to imitate that, but I couldn't fake it quite right.

"Paige, darling, you're looking well," she says, looking me over and quirking an eyebrow as she says it.

I look a damned sight better than I did a few days ago, not that I'll bring that up to her. "Why was it so important for me to be here?" I ask.

"Can't I want to see my daughter?"

"You don't." I at least know that much for sure.

She sighs. "It's business, Paige. Surely you of all people understand how it is. You wanted to *join* the business, after all." She turns to Mickey. "Paige, introduce me to your friend."

She's met him once or twice before, but I don't bring that up. "Mom, Mickey. Mickey, this is Claire Bowers. My mother."

"Nice to meet you," Mickey says, sounding like it's anything but. Then, without waiting for permission, he sits down on the couch and tugs me after him, pulling me right into his side.

I never saw my parents sit like this. I never saw any of my mother's many guests sit this way. I have a feeling I'd be in Mickey's lap if he thought he could get away with it.

She gapes at us for a moment. "Where's Dad?" I ask, wanting to break the tension.

"On his way," she says stiffly. "Can I get you a drink? I had Hannah Jane open a bottle of red for us."

"No," Mickey says curtly. "Paige doesn't drink alcohol and I drove us here."

I don't think my mother knows what to do with someone like Mickey. Someone who's honest, defensive of me, and who she can't kick out—she did technically invite him, after all.

"I'll get a glass for myself then," my mother mutters, and disappears from the room.

Mickey squeezes my hand in his lap, stroking his thumb over my skin. "The lights here suck," he murmurs, and my heart beats faster. He noticed. Not only that, but it took him less than five minutes to notice something no one blood related to me has ever figured out.

"They do," I agree, trying to not look around at the harsh white brightness of everything. My parents apparently need visitors to see every inch of their house at all times. Can't let a single corner or shadow of darkness remain. "I'm gonna need to go straight to bed when we get home."

"Whatever you need, honey," he tells me, squeezing my hand again. "Promise. And hey—I don't mind being the rude one. I have no stake in what your parents think of me. If you need to leave early, tell me. I'll get us out of here."

"Aren't new boyfriends supposed to want to impress their girlfriends' parents?"

"If you cared one bit about what they thought and I respected them as your parents, sure. But you don't, and I don't, so I don't give a shit about impressing them. My mom apparently thinks we're good together, so I'll focus all my energy on impressing you."

"That's sweet." I dare to lean over and kiss his bearded jaw. "You're sweet. I'm impressed by you, Mickey."

Before I can pull back, he uses his free hand to tilt my jaw up, then kisses me, deep and insistent. "Sweet?" he asks when he pulls away, putting an inch of space between us.

I frown. I don't like that inch. "Still sweet," I tell him, and then kiss him again.

The front door opens and we jump apart like guilty teenagers. I never actually kissed anyone like a guilty teenager, and certainly not in this house, so I guess I'm having my teenage rebellion a decade late.

No, I'd had my teenage rebellion. It had been called "I'm going to college and then law school and I don't care if you don't pay for it; you can't stop me." It had been difficult and worthwhile. Kissing a man my parents probably wouldn't approve of is much more fun.

"Claire? We're home," my father calls, and I turn so I'm facing him fully. As reluctant as I am to pull away from Mickey, it's always best to face my father with the strongest set of armor you can, and that means not leaning on my boyfriend. "Oh, Paige. Nice of you to join us. How fortuitous."

I'm about to ask when he's *ever* considered my presence fortuitous, when my question answers itself. Samuel steps in the door behind my father, looking like he belongs here more than I do.

CHAPTER 28
Mickey

I don't even have to ask to know that's the piece of shit ex. He has a sort of slimy look, and his eyes latch onto Paige right away like they're laser sights locked onto her. I bristle and narrowly avoid the urge to wrap my arm around her.

She pulled away a moment ago. She wants to face them without me being a part of it, and I have to respect that. Do I want to jump between her and danger? Absolutely. Am I going to go against what she wants for tonight? Nope. It's her family and her choice.

And I'm not an insecure piece of shit who thinks the ex is a legitimate threat. From everything I've heard, he's an absolute tool who would be lucky to breathe the same air as Paige, but he squandered his opportunity, if he even ever had it. It sounds to me like he was never even a contender, and Paige just had to realize she was better than being guilted by someone like him.

That doesn't mean I'm going to let him say a single thing that makes her uncomfortable, though. Her father or mother, either.

Paige is here because she's doing them a favor, not the other way around, and I'm not going to let them forget it.

I haven't slept in Mom's house except for Christmas Eve since I was twenty-two. Yet I still have a bedroom there. And while I wouldn't blame Paige's parents if they needed the room for something, you're telling me they couldn't keep *one* bedroom for their kid in this giant house? This place probably has eight or nine bedrooms.

"Samuel," Paige says, voice completely flat. "What a surprise."

"Paige, baby," he says, looking her over like she's a piece of meat. "And, who's your guest?"

"Mickey," I say shortly. "Didn't know you'd be here tonight."

Samuel shrugs, a truly insufferable smile crossing his face. "I'm here all the time—like family, you know. And when I heard Paige would be here tonight, I couldn't resist."

I want to punch that smile off his face. I reach for Paige's hand instead, and she plays with my fingers.

It takes me a second to realize she's playing with my fingers the same way she plays with the strap of the purse she must have left in my car, because I don't see it anywhere. She never goes anywhere without that bag.

Well, if I can be an adequate fidget substitute for the next little while, you won't hear me complaining.

Claire Bowers comes walking back in on heels that are ludicrous to wear inside your own home, wineglass in hand. Paige looks a fair amount like her mother, although she got her father's darker hair. But the physical is where the similarities end, clearly.

I haven't said more than two sentences to these people in years, but it's so obvious why Paige fled their house whenever she could as a child.

Her father looks me over, sitting in one of the armchairs opposite the couch. Paige's mother takes the other armchair, which leaves Samuel on the couch with us. Paige scoots closer to me to put as much distance between the two of them as possible, and I debate for a second moving her onto my lap or getting up to physically switch our spots. If he bothers her at all, I will.

"I remember you," her father says. "The Condor boy."

"That's me." I feel like I should be tacking on a *sir*, but at this point I'm refusing on principle.

"You were at Paige's graduation."

"I was." I'd been at everything, all of her and Emma's big moments. She'd been at mine too. But Mr. and Mrs. Bowers had been at almost none of those events.

"What are you doing here?" he asks, and I have to wonder if he's really that dense.

Mrs. Bowers gestures with the hand holding her wineglass. "They're, you know, together," she says.

Her father's face looks like a thundercloud. "Absolutely not."

Paige squeezed my hand back. "You don't get a say in that."

"You have a duty to this family. An obligation to our legacy."

"You don't feed me, house me, or employ me," Paige points out, her voice flat. "You didn't pay for my education, either. Given that, I owe you nothing."

"You are my daughter. You have a duty—"

"Then you should have done literally anything to incentivize me to fulfill that duty," Paige says. "Laughing me out of your office when I applied for a job so I could do my duty to that family legacy wasn't a good start."

"*Omegas* don't—"

Before we can find out what omegas apparently don't do, and before I can deck her father, Mrs. Bowers speaks up. "Not the time," she says tightly, fake smile back in place. "Guests will be here any second."

"Guests?" Paige asks. "You didn't tell me there'd be guests."

"This is a dinner party, dear," her mother says. "Of course there are guests."

"Business associates," her father says. "Who you will *not* embarrass me in front of."

Like Paige is the embarrassing one here.

Samuel stretches out on the couch. I can't say he's specifically trying to get closer to Paige, so I don't jump in, but I'm so close. He gives her an oily smile. "Your father and I are making connections," he tells her. "You know, clients with deep pockets. But we can't all be making a difference for the firm, I guess."

"Remind me," Paige says without looking at him, "which one of us graduated in the top ten percent of our class, and who was middle of the pack?"

Samuel scoffs. "You're still stuck in school? What have you done since, Paige, baby?"

"I'm excellent at my job," she says primly.

"And I'm going to be partner within the next two years."

Paige's father clears his throat. "That's the goal, anyway."

There's a sharp knock on the door, and Paige's mother straightens her dress before going to answer it.

"You didn't know this was coming?" I whisper to Paige.

"Of course I didn't," she replies, then sighs. "He just wants to sell the family man image. It's not the first time I've been dragged out for that. Just need to get through tonight without being weird, then they'll leave me alone for a while."

I *hate* how she says that. *Weird*. Like there's something wrong with her, like it's somehow her problem if she doesn't meet what they expect. "I think your father doesn't like me," I tell her.

"If it helps, he doesn't like me much either."

A half-dozen people in business clothes are shown through the door. Samuel and Mr. Bowers stand to greet them, the schmoozing already starting. Paige doesn't move an inch, and I couldn't be more proud of her.

"My daughter," Mr. Bowers says, not even able to fake interest. "Paige."

"I'm Bridget," one of the two women says. "And this is...?"

"My partner," Paige says, squeezing my hand while Samuel scowls over everyone's shoulders.

Not for the first time, I have to wonder what his interest is in her. I know Paige said he was supposed to marry her so her father could have the alpha heir he dreams of, but he seems to have taken in Samuel just fine with Paige out of the picture. Samuel clearly doesn't like her much, because he obviously has terrible taste. I have no idea why he seems so invested in what she does.

Unless he's just an asshole who thinks if he can't have her, then no one should. I know all about alphas like that.

"Dinner is ready," Mrs. Bowers says, voice a high-pitched tinkling. This woman is so fake I'm surprised you can't see the seams. Everything about this place is fake. Why did Paige and I bother to come?

It's only made worse when I turn to Paige and she's squinting slightly with her head down. I'd bet money that she's starting to hurt more, and I can't believe her parents live in a giant house absolutely inhospitable to Paige. My mother turns down the lights when Paige is coming over, and Paige isn't her child.

"Let me walk you in, Paige, baby," Samuel says, reaching a hand out.

Paige leans back, revulsion obvious. "No," she says, then stands, contorting to keep her body away from Samuel. She's still holding my hand, so I step behind her, staring Samuel down.

He's not that much smaller than me. He looks like he works out, too. He's the type of alpha who thinks strength is a personality trait, I can already tell. I can't use my size to stare him down as easily as I do some idiots, but I try regardless.

Samuel doesn't even look remotely unsettled.

I let Paige go in front of me, staying behind her while we walked to the dining room. I'm sure Mrs. Bowers had a seating arrangement, but Paige doesn't ask, just sitting near one end. She'll have one of her parents beside her at the end, presumably, and I'll take the other side, effectively blocking Samuel from sitting next to her.

"You do a lot of dinners with him at this house?" I mutter to her as we sit.

"Define a lot."

"Any?"

"Like four. Maybe five? They were miserable. I felt like I was under a microscope. I hated everything."

Everyone else filters in around us, taking seats. Unfortunately, Samuel sits opposite Paige, so I vow to do my best to keep her attention on me so she doesn't need to think about him.

From there, the cook who let us in brings out plates, setting them down in front of the eleven of us. I thank her, and she doesn't even look at me. When I turn to Paige, she tilts her head. "She's like that," she whispers.

Great. Everything about this house sucks more and more every minute we spend here. I study the plates in front of us, noting the lamb we're apparently eating tonight. I'm not convinced Paige even likes lamb.

Bridget turns to Paige again. "And what do you do, Paige?"

Paige has her fork in her hand. "I'm a lawyer."

"Went into the family business, then?"

I see Paige open her mouth, no doubt to explain that her father wouldn't let her join the family business, when another voice interrupts. "Well, a different branch of the family business anyway." We all turn toward the doorway. There's a man there with the same dark hair as Paige and her father, and I've never met him before, but I think this is her Uncle Gavin. "Sorry I'm late," he says, moving to sit at the opposite end of the table.

"What are *you* doing here?" Mr. Bowers asks, doing a poor job trying to contain his anger.

Gavin smirks. "Family dinner. Where else would I be? Your assistant talks to my assistant, and things end up on my calendar. It's all very convenient." He turns to the audience watching this little tableau. "Gavin Bowers of Bowers & Weston. Paige is my niece and my employee there."

"How interesting," one of the men at the table murmurs. "So, two brothers at two different law firms?"

"Everyone needs space," Gavin says, flashing a smile. He's clearly the more charming brother. "Paige, I've missed you at work. Will you be back soon?"

Paige stiffens as everyone turns to her. "As soon as my *legally mandated* time is up," she says. She emphasizes *legally mandat-*

ed, no doubt to tell Gavin to mind his business, but all it does is pique everyone's interest.

Samuel's mouth puckers like he ate a lemon, but he rallies quickly. "Paige was never quite cut out for high stakes," he says. "She prefers filing paperwork in her quiet little office, so she was never quite right for us."

The man is a snake, and my blood starts to boil. Paige deliberately puts her hand on my thigh, distracting me long enough so she can say, "You can admit the work is too technical for you, Samuel. It's okay; we can't all be good with the details." There's a sort of choking sound around the table, and the woman who asked Paige about her career in the first place at least looks intrigued. Gavin looks damn proud, too, and it's the first time that I think he might actually like his niece as more than a bargaining chip in this proxy war with his brother. No one else looks quite as amused, though.

Mrs. Bowers jumps in, determined to save her little dinner party. She chuckles lightly, then says, "Children. Now, please—try the food before it gets cold."

Paige obediently takes a bite and doesn't manage to disguise the face she makes. I take her hand that's still on my thigh and squeeze it, trying to reassure her. She doesn't have to eat it if she doesn't like it. We can stop at Morello's on the way home, or I can make us a stack of grilled cheeses. I don't care. I just want her to be comfortable.

"Don't be a brat, Paige," Samuel says, his voice low but nonetheless carrying. "Eat what's in front of you and act like a grown up for five minutes."

That's it. I don't have any more left in me, no understanding for this fucked up family, no patience for this piece of shit. He doesn't get to talk to Paige like that. And what's worse is I can already see her shoulders curving in, see her making herself smaller, and remember back to the first time I asked her what she does and doesn't like.

Don't call me a brat.

"Wanna try that again?" I offer through gritted teeth, one last attempt to keep the peace, one last attempt at the rationality I pretend I have in me.

Samuel's eyes barely flick my way, like I'm something negligible. And I know I am to him; he thinks of people like me like the dirt beneath his shoes. He doesn't see me as a threat, because he thinks he holds all the power. He sees people like me as things to be ignored and people like Paige to be bullied and conquered.

"Try. Again," I tell him, this time an order, because he's not going to get away with treating Paige like that.

"Just because *you* can't keep your omega in check doesn't mean the rest of us are okay with her running wild like a spoiled little brat."

I'm out of my chair before I even know what's happening. I have his shirt in one fist as my other tries to knock his teeth out, the crack of his face splitting my knuckles, but the pain is distant because all I care about is *killing* this useless, chauvinistic piece of shit. There's screaming, I hear distantly, and then someone is trying to rip me off of him. I get in another punch, then two, then a third before whoever it is succeeds.

"That's enough!" someone roars, hauling me back. They wrap both arms around me, holding me back even as I struggle.

"Fucking animal," Samuel snarls, but with a busted face, the word comes out slurred and my adrenaline spikes with a sharp surge of pride. Fucking right I am. Defending Paige? I'll be a fucking animal if that's what it takes. Absolutely no one gets to make her feel small.

"Mickey." That's Paige's voice, and I turn, no longer fighting whoever's holding me. I take a ragged breath, looking her over on the other side of the table.

She's not hurt, but she's breathing as hard as I am. Her eyes are a little wild, and I can already see that the hand she's reaching toward me is trembling. I try to go to her, but the hold on me doesn't loosen. "Let me go," I snarl.

"Not until you're in control." I recognize the voice now. That's Gavin, Paige's fucking uncle. He's the one holding me back? "You're not getting *near* my niece like this."

"I'm *fine*," I snarl, no doubt showing how not fine I am. "I'm not the one implying that Paige is a fucking pet to train."

Paige flinches away when I say it, and I feel like a monster. "Paige, honey..."

She straightens and looks me in the eye. "Let him go, Gavin," she says, then looks around cursorily at everyone else. "We're leaving." Her eyes land on her father. "And I think maybe this time they won't make me come back." She looks at the woman who tried to talk to her earlier. "Samuel is a terrible lawyer and my father is a self-aggrandizing idiot. You'd be better off finding literally anyone else." Then she walks around the table to me and takes my hand.

"Get out of my house," Mr. Bowers can barely manage to whisper the words, but I don't need encouragement. This man lets his protégé talk to Paige like that and doesn't say a word, and I know full well it wasn't the first time. I couldn't always be around to stop the bullies when we were kids, and I fucking hated it when I found out later what they'd put her through. Now it's a gut-punch to find out it happened all over again, only these were people she was supposed to trust.

I jerk out of Gavin's now-loosened grip, keeping my hand firmly in Paige's. She squeezes my hand, half leaning on me for strength. Bizarrely, her leaning on me is the only thing keeping me upright.

Gavin sighs behind me. "And I just wanted some fucking food," he mutters, shoving me in the back until I get the hint and start walking.

CHAPTER 29
Paige

M y mind is a mess, stuck permanently a few seconds back—or minutes, or hours, I can't tell anymore—where Mickey crossed the table to pummel the shit out of my ex for being an asshole.

It's not worse than a thousand other things Samuel said. It's not worse than the person he learned them all from, my father. I've learned to either fight back the only way I can, by being smarter than them, or to keep my mouth shut and take it. It's started to feel like maybe these moments don't even matter. Maybe I'm the one overreacting.

And then Mickey comes in and doesn't need to hear more than a couple sentences before he's ready to beat the shit out Samuel. He let me get my digs in earlier, looking more and more unsettled but holding himself back. But I hadn't been able to fight back against that. I didn't know what to say.

Mickey hadn't let my silence look like a concession. He wasn't willing to let me lose. In a few seconds of pure chaos, he reassured me that I'm not wrong to feel this way. That I shouldn't be treated this way.

I know my hand is in Mickey's. I know we're walking, and Gavin is at our back. I know I'm leaving a mess behind me and that I don't give a crap about it. It can be my father's problem; I doubt I'm invited back. Other than that, I can't sort anything out.

If I was able to think, I would assume Gavin would force us out the door, but instead he pushes us into the butler's pantry, pulling the little pocket door shut behind us.

"Goddamn shit, you have any idea what kind of mess you stepped into?" he asks, running a hand over his face as he talks. His suit is rumpled, no doubt from holding back Mickey, and I take a minute to study him.

Gavin isn't an exceptionally formal person. When he doesn't have to talk directly to clients, he wears jeans a lot of the time. But while he's not formal, he is put together. I've never seen him quite so disheveled in my life.

"I'm sorry, but did I hallucinate you sitting there and letting them talk to your niece like that?" Mickey fumes. I try to squeeze his hand, and he squeezes back, but I don't think it calms him down any.

"There are other ways to end fights than with fists, you idiot," Gavin growls, and I shrink. This room is feeling more and more like a tight space with two big alphas getting ready to go at it, and I'm trapped in the middle. And while I'd normally never think of either of these men hurting me, this isn't about *me* anymore. I'm just the pawn caught in the middle.

Except Mickey's eyes shoot to me the minute I shrink away, and he steps closer to me, softening his expression. "Paige, honey—"

"You're scaring her," Gavin retorts.

"Paige isn't scared of me," Mickey snaps, then freezes. "Are you, honey?"

I don't know a lot right now. My brain is overwhelmed, too much noise and no way to sort through it, but I do know one thing: I'm not scared of Mickey.

But maybe I don't sort through that thought fast enough, or I don't react right, because Mickey's face pinches and he turns back to Gavin, stepping away from me, and that *hurts*. It hurts like a stab wound, an ache deep in my gut, and I want to go to him even when I can't make myself move.

"If I'm going to be the fucking monster, then I should get it all out," he says, voice calmer now, but somehow scarier. "You didn't stand up for her. *You* use her like a pawn in whatever little game you play."

Gavin's eyes flick between Mickey and me. "That's what you think, Paige?" I try to talk but can't make the words come out. My mouth opens and closes, but nothing comes.

Gavin stops paying any attention to Mickey and stares directly at me. "I came here tonight to see *you*. I heard you'd be here and I decided I'd suffer through your father if I could see you. I'm worried about *you*, Paige. You're my favorite niece and I didn't even know you were seeing anyone, and now I find out you're serious enough about this guy to have a heat—are you trying to get pregnant, Paige?"

"I'm your only niece," I say at the same time Mickey snarls, "That's none of your damn business."

Gavin ignores Mickey entirely and looks only at me. "Your father sucks, Paige. I've tried to be there for you. I've done an okay job, haven't I? And now I hear—I just don't want you to get hurt."

I wrap my arm around myself. I could use one of Mickey's hugs right now, but he's standing all the way over there. "It's not your job to save me from myself."

"No, but it is my job to look after you. And what the fuck are you doing, Paige?"

I stiffen. I hate this, hate how he thinks he can question me. He employs me, and I know I could be hard to employ; I get it. My father told me all about it before he laughed me out of his office, and I'm well aware of the accommodations Gavin made. I hate how he thinks that gives him license to intrude. "I'll be at work on Monday," I tell him. "And that's all. You're not entitled to any more. You're not—this isn't—"

He steps closer, and I shrink back. I don't want him touching me. "Paige—"

"She said no," Mickey cuts in. "Take what she gives you and leave her alone."

Gavin looks back and forth between the two of us. "I'll go clean up in there," he sighs, turning away. "Paige, just—I'll see you Monday." And then he goes, leaving the two of us standing in the butler's pantry like idiots.

"Let's go home," I whisper. "I want to go."

"Alright," Mickey says, but when I reach my hand out to him, he doesn't take it.

The drive home is absolutely silent. No radio, no talking, just the sound of the light summer rain that started sometime while we were inside. Eventually Mickey clicks the windshield wipers on, and the rhythmic *swish-swish* is the only thing helping to settle my mind. I track my breaths by it, syncing my heartbeat to the wipers.

The silence hurts like it's a solid object pressing inside me. It's an ache I can't fight and have no idea how to stop. I open my mouth a dozen times, but I can't make anything come out.

What do I say? What will make him feel better? What makes up for dragging him into nonsense like that?

He parks in front of my house, but when he doesn't shut the engine, my heart sinks even further. "Come in?" I ask, my voice barely a whisper, but he shakes his head.

"I don't think that's a good idea, Paige." Paige. Not *honey.* And it's not like I don't like him saying my name, or want him to stop entirely, but I could really go for the reassurance right now. "I'll call you when I've got my head on straight, alright?"

That sounds awful. That sounds like the kiss of death, like this is over before it began, like I've somehow ruined us before we even got a chance. But what am I supposed to say? I nod, grab my bag from where I stashed it in the footwell, and get out of the car, letting the rain nearly soak me as I walk to the door. I walk slowly, hoping he'll change his mind, say something, anything.

He doesn't.

When I get inside, it's like my brain is on autopilot. I leave my bag by the door. Take my shoes off and line them up neatly. Trudge up the stairs, not bothering to turn on any lights even though the evening and the gray fog of rain has cast my whole house into darkness. I debate for a minute going online—I could really use the comfort of another person right now, even if it's just a silly debate on Discord—but that seems like it'll take too much energy.

What I need right now is my nest and all the safety it provides. I take off this stupid dress, then crawl into my nest, holding the pillow that Mickey slept on last night close, and bury my face in it.

Chapter 30
Mickey

I make it half a mile of aimless driving—I can't go home, there's nothing for me there—before I think of a logical thing to do.

I call Emma.

"About time I heard from you," she says, picking up on the third ring. "Mom's called me like seventeen times to see what I know about what the hell is going on with you and Paige, and I don't want to spill any secrets, but someone is going to need to tell her something soon before she bursts a blood vessel and—"

"Em," I interrupt firmly. "I need you to call Paige."

There's a pause, then, "Can this wait until tomorrow? We're kind of in the middle of something here, and—"

"No," I say. "I doubt she's doing great right now, and I need—please. Check on her. I don't want her hurting."

Another pause. "Why aren't *you* checking on her?"

"Because I'm the one who hurt her." And then before I can stop myself, before I can try to hide it or put a spin on it or worry about what my little sister will think of me, the whole story of what happened at dinner spills out. Samuel and Paige's father and their casual cruelty, and me flying off the handle, solving the problem with my fists. Scaring Paige, and Gavin having to tear me away from it all.

"Okay," Emma says when I finally run out of steam. "So they were assholes and someone finally did something about it. Good. I fucking hated Samuel, and honestly I hope you broke his smug face. Still not sure why you need *me* to call Paige and don't go comfort her yourself. From what Mom told me, it kind of seems like that's the way to go right now."

"Fuck, Emma, she couldn't even look at me after. She wasn't okay. I warned her this would happen. I told her, and I told Mom—that same obsessive, violent thing that was in our father, it's in me. I look in the mirror and see it. I feel it inside me every day. And tonight, Paige saw it for the first time and I need to get the fuck away from her before I end up hurting her."

She's silent for a long moment, then says, "Fuck this." I hear a muffled, "*I'll be right back, watch the oven,*" seemingly aimed at her pack and not me, and then I hear quiet footsteps as she walks away from them. "Alright, Mickey, are you ready to listen?"

"Em—"

"No, it's my turn to talk. You're usually so damn good at listening, too. Alright, here it is: there is a colossal difference between being *down bad* and just *bad*. And you are the former. You have been down bad for Paige for years. Everyone can see it except Paige, and you have to cut her a little bit of slack on

283

that, alright? You defended her tonight. Defended her honor from someone hurting her, it sounds like. And from what you said, you let her fight the fight first, and then stepped in, all chivalrous and honorable and ready to finish it so she knows she's not alone."

"I punched a guy's face in, Em. I genuinely think I might've killed him if Gavin didn't pull me off. That's not chivalry."

"Tomato, tom-ah-to," she dismisses. "Mickey, our family are the only people who ever defended Paige. Maybe Gavin, but he wasn't in that house much. So what if it's over the top? Maybe Paige needs someone willing to be over the top for her. Paige doesn't do subtle, Mickey, and if you're going to show her she's loved, you're going to have to go big or go home. And it sounds to me like you went big."

"She was *scared*."

"Did she tell you that?" Emma challenges.

I pause. She never got the words out, no. But she hadn't been able to talk, and Gavin had stepped in like her guardian angel, like she needed protecting from me.

Emma doesn't seem to actually need an answer. "Mickey, you've known Paige since she was eight. She's had meltdowns and been the most stubborn person in the world. She once gave you a thirty minute lecture on how you were playing Monopoly wrong. We've had to cancel plans because she was in pain, and she wore leggings to your graduation even though it was a formal affair because we didn't realize that her only dress was scratchy until it was too late. She once told you to your face that your haircut looked stupid because she saw it before I did so I couldn't warn her not to say anything. You've listened to her talk about a book series for hours. You are the first person to remember to dim the lights when she's around. Paige takes a lot of effort, Mickey. She's amazing, but there's no denying she's also complicated. She can be hard sometimes. Through all of that, have you ever *once* thought about hurting her?"

I swallow, my throat tight. "No. Never. Not for a single second. None of that bothers me—that's just Paige."

"Exactly. You're not a danger, Mickey. You're the exact type of protective she needs."

"*I beat a guy's face in*," I emphasize in case she didn't hear me say it the first few times.

"Oh, you mean the guy who belittled Paige repeatedly and made her feel like she's unlovable and only worthy as a trophy? That guy? Gosh, what a loss for the world." I hear a rustling, and then she sounds serious again. "Listen. I'm not going to pretend it works for everyone. I'd be weirded out if one of my alphas started beating people up. But I also don't have anyone who deserves to be beat up, and Paige does. You stood up for her when no one else did. That'll mean a shit ton to her. So, I'll just say this—I can absolutely call her, I guess. Or you can go act like you're the same brave alpha ready to punch a guy's face in for her and go have a fucking conversation. Which one are you picking?"

Leave it to my sister to tell it to me straight. My mother and sister have always seen straight through me, and I remember what Paige said about the omegas in my life, how long they've watched me, three wary omegas, and how long they've considered me safe.

"What do I say to her?"

"What we just talked about?" she huffs. "I told you before—you need to be clear with her. No beating around the bush, no assumptions. Ask questions to elicit the answers you need because she doesn't always know to give them. Have a real conversation if this is worth it to you."

"It is."

"So go, talk it out." There's another rustling noise. "Alphas. Honestly. You all are the most obtuse, clueless idiots I know."

That breaks my thoughts of Paige for a second. "Need me to come say something to your alphas?"

"Didn't I *just* say I don't need anyone to beat someone up for me? Besides, you think I put up with any nonsense? You all are obtuse, but that only means I need to be even more obvious. Now, excuse me. I have cinnamon buns in the oven I need to go take care of." She says *cinnamon buns* like it's particularly important, but I can't think of why. I don't remember her especially liking them, and anyway, Emma doesn't cook. But before I can ask, she hangs up on me, leaving me driving down an empty road in the silence.

I keep driving for another half a mile, trying to get my head on straight, wrestling with whether or not I fucked things up irrevocably by leaving, before I make a U-turn and head back.

CHAPTER 31

Paige

I'm cuddled deep in my nest and thinking of never leaving again when there's a pounding at my door.

I debate ignoring it, but the knocking continues, so I reluctantly climb out of my nest. I had already shed my rain-soaked dress and thrown it out of the nest, so I find a sweatshirt and leggings, pulling them on before I go to see who is so insistent that they want to bang down my door.

It's Mickey, soaking wet and looking like a kicked puppy. I frown, swinging the door open. "Get inside," I tell him, ushering him in. "You must be freezing."

He stares at me for a moment, but then walks in, dripping water on my floor. I step back, trying to take him all in, and he retreats until he's almost at the foot of the stairs, leaving a good couple of yards between us. "Are you okay?"

"Am *I* okay?" he asks. "Paige, you watched me beat the shit out of a guy over dinner. You were scared earlier. I scared you."

"I'm not scared of you," I tell him, and it's true. Tonight was a lot, but I know that hasn't changed.

"Maybe you should be," he says.

"I'm scared of Samuel, because he's an asshole and he doesn't like not getting his way, and I'm scared he's going to press charges. I'm a little scared of how my father will react, and I'm nervous about talking to Gavin on Monday. But you're not on that list. I'm an adult. And just because it doesn't always look like everyone else or I sometimes can't put it into words doesn't mean that I don't know what I want. And I want you."

He takes another step. I could reach out and touch him now. I don't know if that's the thing to do, if that's okay, but I take a deep breath and do it anyway, landing my hand on his arm, trying to pull him closer.

He moves easily when I tug him, getting the picture and wrapping his arms around me. I let my eyes slip closed, because he knows exactly what to do without me having to tell him. His grip is firm and comforting, allowing me to lean into him. I know he'll hold me up.

"I felt safe," I murmur, my voice half swallowed by his chest. "I know it's weird, but Samuel says stuff like that all the time. So does my father. And no one ever stops them. And I'm not saying you should always punch people in the face, because I don't want to see you charged with anything, but it's nice that you stood up for me."

His arms tighten even further around me, and he rubs his bearded jaw against my hair. "I will always stand up for you," he says, voice rough now. "That's a promise, Paige. Whether or not you want to be with me."

"So, you're saying your behavior won't fundamentally change whether we're together or not. And since I don't have a problem with your behavior, and I want to be with you, and *not* being with me wouldn't do anything but make us both upset, shouldn't we be together?" I ask.

He groans. "You have been arguing circles around me since you were eight, honey. I guess I should prepare for this for the rest of my life, huh?"

I smile. "I'll let you get your way sometimes," I offer. I like the idea of the rest of our lives.

Not that I ever pictured a future without Mickey in it somehow, but this is different. This is the Mickey who knows what I need without asking, who learned me, who makes my nest complete. This is the Mickey who tells me his fears and holds me and *wants* me. This is the man I want to spend forever with.

"How generous," he laughs, squeezing me. "Paige, honey?"

I shiver. "I like when you call me that."

"Yeah? What else do you like?"

I tilt my head against him, considering. "I like the way you hold me."

His arms flex. "My arms are always available. I like the way you feel in them. What else?"

A little more daring, I tell him, "I don't remember a lot of details of my heat, but I remember how it ended. How you stayed inside me. Kept me full. I liked that."

He groans, deep and long, sounding like it was ripped out of him. "*Fuck*. Paige, you're going to ruin me."

"Was that wrong? Should I not have said that?"

"First of all, telling me what you want and what you like is *never* wrong. Second, *fuck*, honey, that's goddamn hot. Like, so fucking hot."

"Did you like it too?"

"Did I like being locked inside your tight pussy and keeping you stuffed with me? Yeah, you could say that." He's quiet for a second, then says, "I'm going to get a vasectomy, then."

I sputter and pull back so I can see him. "*What*?"

He shrugs. "You don't want to get pregnant. Fair enough. I know you're on the pill, but I also know you, and you wouldn't risk just one method of pregnancy prevention. And they did in a pinch, but I can tell you that condoms weren't super effective during your heat. They don't play well with knots. And if you want me to stay inside you, keep you stuffed, then we need a better method. Plus..." He trails off for a second, looking away from me. "The idea of literally stuffing you with my come? If you like it too, then I *really* like that."

I like that. I didn't know if I would like that part of it, but fuck if I do. Maybe it's the way his eyes got all dark and heavy when he said it. Maybe it's the way my pussy clenches at the thought of having him inside me again.

"A vasectomy is kind of serious. I know it doesn't have to be permanent, but it's a lot more serious than most forms of birth control."

"That's kind of the point."

"What if you want kids?" I ask.

"I want *you*. And you don't want kids. And I'll have my kids at the library and get to watch them grow. I'll spoil the shit out of the kids Emma eventually has. But I don't need biological kids. I just need you." When I don't answer right away, he asks, "Paige, honey? I need to know what you're thinking."

"I want that," I say in a rush.

He takes my arms, grip firm but not squeezing. "Good. I want to give you what you like. But you'll have to tell me, alright?"

"If you tell me what you want."

"I want *you,* Paige. I want to be inside you, but I also want to hold you and be there when you don't feel well. I want to have dinner together at my mom's, and hold your hand at the table. I want you to tell me all about every book you read and I would be honored if you kept letting me into the nest you made for us." He leans in and kisses my forehead. "I want you to trust me. I want to stay. To be here, with you. I want to *want you* and have it be okay, to know you want me too."

"You have that. I want that too. Can we go to my nest?" I ask him. The world is suddenly too big, and I need it to just be us. Just us in the small, safe, comfortable place I've made for us.

"Of course, honey. Need me to carry you?"

I should say no. I should protest that it's stairs and I'm not a child. But I want his arms, his hold, the security of knowing he has me, so I nod. He scoops me up under the knees before I even know what's happened, and then I'm in his arms as he walks up the stairs.

"Shoes," I remind him when we get to the top, and he obediently stops to remove them, shifting from foot to foot, but not letting me slip in the slightest.

Then we're in my room, in my sanctuary. There are no lights on up here, so I reach for the Christmas lights and click them on. Once the room has a soft glow, Mickey walks us straight over to my nest, setting me inside like I'm made of glass.

I whimper when he doesn't join me. I can't help it; I'll blame being so close to my heat, still off my suppressants and my hormones still running high, but the idea of being separated from my alpha right now, even only a few feet, is untenable.

"It's okay," he murmurs. "Just keeping the wet clothes out of the nest." And sure enough, he starts pulling off his clothes, tossing them into the bathroom behind him so they land on the tile and not my carpet. He strips right down to his underwear, black boxer briefs that do nothing to hide his cock.

Well, damn. If he's going to undress, I should too. I arch my back, pulling my leggings down and off, and then pull off my sweatshirt. When I rip it over my head, I look up to see Mickey staring at me.

"What?"

"Paige, honey, your tits are out."

He's right. I didn't bother putting anything else on before I went downstairs. I shift. "Was that wrong?"

He's in my nest before I even process him moving, pulling me into his arms. "Let's assume that anytime you feel comfortable showing me your tits is a good time to show me them. You're very pretty, Paige." He buries his face in my neck. "And you smell so *fucking* good."

"I want you to bite me there someday," I tell him. "You said you wanted to when I was in heat—I want it too. Not today. But someday."

"God *damn*," he mumbles. "You know how to drive me crazy, Paige. Yes to all of that. You just tell me when." He falls back into my pillows, pulling me down with him so I land on his chest, running my fingers through his chest hair.

"Paige," he says after a long moment, "remember when I said earlier that you need to tell me what's on your mind? That's an ongoing thing. Be as explicit as possible. I can't mess this up."

"You won't. Are we going to sleep or are we fucking?"

"What do you want, pretty girl?"

"I'd like you to fuck me when I can remember it all," I tell him quietly. "Without the heat and the hormones. It wasn't as bad as I thought, mostly because you were there, but I still didn't feel like me. And I want this when it's *me,* you know?"

"I know," he says, stroking my hair off my face. "And I want that for you. I'll give you whatever you want."

"As long as you want it too."

"You don't have to worry about that. Not about this." He stretches under me, hands coming up to cradle my back as he guides me off of him, leaving me laying on the mattress. "Did we have any condoms left when we finished? I didn't bring any more."

"There were two left," I tell him. "I stuck them in the bedside drawer."

"Same one your vibrator's in?"

I nod, blushing. I've never talked about a sex toy with another person before. Mickey gets up on his knees, moving to the edge of the nest to dig into the drawer.

"You were fucking beautiful when I used this on you," he says, lifting my vibrator enough to see it, like I was somehow going to forget it was there. He puts it back and lifts the giant dildo I've left in there because I can't think of where else to put it. "Do you like this?"

"Never used it. They told me I'd need toys if I was going to do the heat alone, so I bought it."

"It's fucking huge. Insanely huge. Do you think you'd like it?" He lifts it so we can both look at it, like I'd forgotten how giant it actually is. "You seem to like being full, and this would make you very full."

I like being full of *Mickey*, but I don't know. The idea is kind of tempting. But not right now. Right now I know exactly what I want, and it's not made of silicone.

Like he can read my mind, Mickey drops it back into the drawer with a heavy thunk. "Something to consider for later," he says, then withdraws the two condoms and drops them into the nest.

And then he returns to my side, closing the gap between us. My whole body relaxes when he's close again. I didn't even realize I'd tensed up, but it's like my body responds to his presence. I know I'm safe when he's here. I know I can be whatever I need, even if that's sick or weak or stressed or confused or needy, and everything will be okay.

And he smells good, too. That doesn't hurt. I lean closer until I'm nestled against his chest, inhaling his scent.

He holds me, arms coming around me and closing out the world. If I thought my nest with its soft blankets and little walls was the most secure place I could be, then I was mistaken. This is clearly the safest place in the world.

"I got you," he whispers. "All good, Paige?"

"All good," I say, letting my eyes slide closed. "You smell good."

"You smell better. Your scent makes me absolutely crazy sometimes. I can't think when you're around. Or at least, I can't think of anything but you."

"Is that bad?"

"I used to think it was. I'm, you know, obsessive. But if you like it…"

"No one else has ever cared like you do," I tell him.

He kisses the top of my head, leaving his face pressed into my hair. He doesn't say anything, but the silence is nice. It's just us here, safe and secure and together.

And then I slide onto his lap, and he's hard under me. I rock against him experimentally, liking the way he feels but liking the way he groans and squeezes me even tighter more.

"Honey, you're going to make me come in my shorts again."

I stop for a moment. "When did you…" I can't make myself finish the thought. Is he talking about someone else, right now, when he's holding me like this?

He lifts his head to look at me, then bends down to kiss the corner of my mouth. "You don't remember?" he asks gently. "The start of your heat. You climbed into my lap and were so fucking pretty and smelled so good, a goddamn dream, and I'm not embarrassed you made me come before I could get undressed for you."

"Oh." The jealousy dissipates immediately and I find myself preening a bit. *I* did that. I made him come before he was ready. It doesn't matter that I don't fully remember it. That was me.

"But let me tell you, if it's all the same to you, I want to finish inside you this time," he continues.

I nod like a bobble head. "Yes. That. I want that."

He smiles. "Good. What else do you want?"

"I want to watch you come this time. I don't remember that either."

His throat bobs when he swallows. "Can pretty much guarantee you'll get that. What else?"

"I want your knot."

"Yeah, you'll get that."

"What do *you* want?"

His eyes darken, like he's already thinking through the possibilities. "I want to eat you out until you're screaming my name," he says, voice low and intense. "And then I want to find out exactly how you like to be fucked when you're not in heat. I bet you're the type who likes slow and deep, huh? But we'll find out, because you're going to tell me, right?"

I nod, breathless and unable to form words. I think I'd agree to whatever he asks when he looks at me like this, like the whole world is us here in this nest.

"Is that a yes? I can have all that?" he checks, smiling when I nod again like he's somehow won something. "Alright then. Give me a second."

I do, watching him and trying to figure out what he needs a second for. He lies back, situating one of my pillows under his head. "You going to take a nap?"

He chuckles. "No, honey. You're going to sit on my face so I can drown in your sweet scent."

I raise an eyebrow, blushing just thinking about it. "You could literally drown from that, couldn't you?"

"You wet enough to drown me, Paige? I want to see that." The lewd words are punctuated by the heavy tone of his voice, punching through me and making me squirm.

"Fuck, Mickey—I don't want to hurt you."

"You won't hurt me, honey. Have you never done this before?"

I mutely shake my head.

"We can talk about that later, when we're not in bed, if you want. Or not, if you don't. But you're telling me I was the first to do this to you during your heat, and it's going to be like the first time all over again today?" His words are practically a growl, and he uses his elbows to prop himself up, watching me intently. "Fuck, Paige. You keep feeding right into my obsession." He looks me over, eyes raking across my skin, the sensation almost physical. I've been mostly undressed in front of him for probably about twenty minutes now, but I haven't truly felt exposed until this moment.

But it doesn't feel bad. I can't quite name the feeling, but I know it's definitely not bad.

"Can you take off your panties for me?"

I don't think he blinks when I slide them down my leg, removing them and tossing them to the side. His eyes devour me, hungry and wanting.

I think I could get used to this kind of attention. Just from Mickey, though.

He drops his head back to the pillow, then pats his chest. "Come here, honey."

Hesitantly, I straddle his chest, careful of my weight. "Good girl," he rasps. "Slide a little closer now, c'mere, let me taste you."

I worry about hurting him, but Mickey apparently doesn't share the same concerns, because when I don't move fast enough for him, he grabs my thighs with his giant hands and drags me where he wants me, not letting go even when I'm literally seated on his face. I wiggle, his beard scratching at my thighs as I try to get comfortable over him.

And then his tongue is on me, and he tilts his head until he's sucking at me, wet and hot and exactly the right pressure. I groan, rocking forward on him, chasing more. My hands desperately land on the wall of my nest, needing something to keep me upright.

His hands squeeze my thighs, his tongue makes me see stars, and I whimper out his name, brain short-circuited and nothing left except *Mickey* and *more*. Fuck, is this what this is always like? Why haven't I been doing this for years?

"Mickey, I need—I need—" I have no idea what I need, just that it's *something*, and he told me to tell him what I want.

He seems to know though, because he pushes my thighs wider, making me fall even lower against his face, and spears his tongue inside me.

I think I shout his name. It's like I'm here but not here, and for a brief moment I'm thrown back to my heat, the floaty feeling where nothing mattered except Mickey and me and my pussy.

"So *fucking* pretty," Mickey mutters when I come down, voice muffled. "Can I make you come like that again, Paige?"

"Now or in general?" I manage to ask, breathless, like I ran a marathon.

"Both, either. Take your pick. I'll take what I can get," he says fervently.

"Not now," I decide. "I want you inside of me. But later—yes to later."

I try to move off his face, but his hands are still holding my thighs in place. After a moment he lets me go, and I move off of him, carefully swinging one leg over so I don't accidentally knee him in the head.

I get my first good look at him, still lying there and looking punch-drunk. His mouth and beard are soaked, absolutely dripping, and I think again of that comment about drowning him. It looks like I legitimately tried.

He's also grinning, lazy and self-satisfied, so I can't say it did him any harm. If anything, I watch him lick his lips, then look me over.

"If we're talking about things we want, I want to do that literally whenever you'll let me," he tells me. "Always feel free to sit on my face, Paige. There's no better place to be in the world, I promise you."

"You can't have liked it that much."

"I abso-fucking-lutely can," he argues immediately. "You know how your nest is like home, like somewhere safe? That's exactly how it is when I have you on me, around me—when I know exactly where you are, can smell you and touch you. When I know you're not only safe but feeling *good*. That's literally my ideal situation."

He stares at me as he says it, eyes sweeping over me and taking me in like I'll disappear if he doesn't watch. I shiver under his stare, under the intensity of what he's saying. When he thinks of safety, he thinks of *me*.

And he is that for me, too. I've always retreated into myself, into my space and my nest. Becoming an adult meant I could do that and no one could stop me. But now, I don't want to just hide up here in my nest. I want him here with me. It's not complete without him anymore.

That should scare me, but it doesn't. Maybe it's that it's so obvious he's just as obsessed. Maybe it's that it's Mickey, and he's so easy to trust.

"Hey Mickey?"

"Yeah?" His eyes are like fire on my skin.

"I think I remembered something else from my heat."

"Oh yeah?"

"You said you were going to make my nest smell like the two of us forever. We were going to soak it and I'd never get the scent out. Right?"

He groans. "Damn right."

I pretend to sniff, even though I can only smell him. "I think it's worn off already. Don't you?"

He sits up, prowling toward me like a predator stalking prey. "We should fix that, shouldn't we?"

CHAPTER 32
Mickey

I f I taste nothing else but Paige for the rest of my life, I'll die a happy man. I don't need anything else, don't want anything else.

Well, nothing except stuffing her full like she asked earlier. I need that about as much as I need oxygen right now.

I was serious about the vasectomy. I don't know if Paige will like the mess of coming inside her, but it does seem like the safest way for me to keep her full all the time. I'm scheduling that appointment as soon as physically possible.

I scoop up one of our two remaining condoms and grab her up, wrapping her legs around my hips and sitting her on my lap. Then I lean in and kiss her, needing to taste her, needing her to taste herself.

"Can you taste what I do?" I murmur against her mouth. "You're fucking delicious, Paige."

There's some sort of manic energy under my skin, an electric charge that I can't shake. It's her. It's finally having her. It's knowing that I have someone precious in my arms and I have to ensure she doesn't want to go anywhere.

Her eyes have slipped closed, and I move to kiss her nose, her cheeks, her forehead. My hands cup her shoulder blades, and she's leaning a lot of her weight on me, trusting my hands to keep her upright. It's intoxicating in a way I can't quite explain; she trusts me to have her implicitly.

"How do you want me?" I ask her, watching her face intently. I can't fuck this up.

"I want you to knot me and stay in me for a long time. What's a good position for that?" She asks it so simply. There's no guile, no attempt at seduction. But it does something to me, anyway.

I think about her question for a moment. "Couple options. I can fuck you from behind, and then we can spoon when I'm knotted. You liked me spooning you like that last time. Or you can ride me and stay on top of me after." I'm about to suggest another option, but I can see her eyes are already blown wide, and I can't help but grin. "Which one did you like, honey?"

She doesn't answer, instead leaving my lap and moves onto her hands and knees, ass in the air and so fucking tempting. I wonder if she'd like being fucked there. If she likes feeling full—

But that's not for today. This has to go well today before I can even think about that.

"Spread your knees a little wider. Yeah, like that. Good girl," I murmur, and she shivers, her chest now even lower toward the bed, her face turned so she can watch me, her eyes blown wide and wanting.

"Give me two seconds. And then I'm going to fill you up, surround you, make you feel good." Her chest heaves as her breathing gets rougher, and I force my underwear down and off, tossing them aside. I tear open the condom package, roll it on, and then I'm behind Paige, watching her present for me, and I've never been harder in my fucking life. I wasn't even this hard during her heat, because this time she's choosing me clear-headed. There's no ulterior motive; she wants me, trusts me, knows I can give her what her body is begging for.

I give her two fingers, testing to make sure I won't hurt her, and she arches back into my touch, already looking for more. "Is that good?" I ask her. "Tell me how you feel, honey."

She whines a bit, shaking her hips. "Alpha, please—"

Fuck, I can't resist that. I pull my fingers out, line up my cock, and sink inside her wet heat. My eyes fall closed for a minute, my brain short-circuited by how tight she is. But then I force them open, because there's no way I'm missing a moment of this.

"Alpha," she whines again, and I slide the rest of the way in, seating myself balls deep inside of her. I could knot her right now, probably. It wouldn't take much, just grinding my cock inside her for a second. But she deserves better than that. So I take a deep breath and center myself, thinking of doing the upcoming budget forms at the library to keep myself from immediately popping my knot.

"Pretty omega," I croon at her, moving my hands from her hip up her back, touching and stroking and making sure my pressure is even and consistent. She shivers under my touch, but it doesn't look like it's in a bad way. "Okay, Paige?"

She shivers again. "Okay," she repeats. "It's good, Mickey."

That response is lucid, and that's reassuring. She seems to think I did a good job during her heat, but I'd like to not have to play interpreter of her needs this entire time. That's a lot of pressure.

"Keep telling me," I instruct her, and I slide almost all the way out, until just the tip is in. "I need to hear it, Paige. Need to know that what I'm doing is okay."

"It's better than okay," she murmurs, and she tries to rock back against me. My hands shoot back to her hips to hold her in place. I can't let her rush me in this; it'll be over too early that way. "Mickey. You make me feel so good."

I push back into her. I can't help it; it's like my body is magnetized to hers and I can't resist being further inside her. There can be no space between us, no daylight. I need her that badly.

And then I'm fucking her, deep and steady, listening to the music of her moans. She squeezes around me, tempting me deeper and deeper, and I think hazily that I'm never fucking leaving her. She likes being filled? Good. She's going to spend a lot of time this way.

I curl a little closer to her, surrounding her more, and I worry for a second that it won't be right, that the pressure will be wrong and irritate her, but she sighs and goes boneless like that was just what she was looking for.

Safe. She's safe, and she's feeling good, and I'm going to make her feel even fucking better. I reach for her clit, her hips bucking underneath my hand. "Alright?" I check, and she nods.

"So good," she promises me, voice a little hazy. "Knot me, please, want to come on your knot."

It's like her words are connected directly to my brain, like she gave an order, and I'm absolutely hopeless to resist it. My knot inflates, and I curl around her even closer, grinding my knot deep inside her until we're tied together.

Our groans echo off her walls as we lock, my knot fully inflated, stuck inside her perfect cunt. She groans and then whines, her orgasm sweeping through her like all she needed was my knot. She milks me and I can't resist, falling over that edge with her, filling the condom and wishing with all my heart that I was filling her.

I'm a sweaty, panting mess. I feel like I worked out for six hours, like I ran a marathon. And like most exercise, I'm high on endorphins.

"Hey Paige," I murmur, "am I crushing you?" I'm resting more of my weight on her than I'm fully comfortable with. I went a little boneless there for a minute, and now that we're tied together, I don't have a lot of wiggle room.

"No," she sighs, voice barely a breath. "Feels so good. Like my weighted blanket but better." That weighted blanket is heavy as shit, but I probably have a hundred eighty pounds on it. I can't stay here long, but if she likes being squished like this, then I'll give her a minute or two of it.

She squirms on my knot, and I groan. She can't move much, pinned as she is, but even the smallest movement is liable to make me one of those alphas who need medical intervention to get their knots to go down.

"You did this last time, too," I mutter. "Couldn't stop squirming. Are you uncomfortable?"

"Feels good," she tells me. She's face first in a pillow now, so her voice is a little muffled, but I hear her nonetheless.

"You can do better than good," I tease her. "I know your vocabulary is off the charts."

"I'd win that vocab contest you ran last year," she agrees.

I snort. "Yeah, you'd dominate the field of eight year olds." Then, "You remember that?"

"I remember everything you talked about."

There's a warmth blooming in me that has nothing to do with my cock inside her. "Fuck, we wasted a lot of time, didn't we?"

She tilts her head back like she's trying to look at me. That's not happening right now, but it'd be nice if we could talk a little easier, and I'm still worried about squishing her, so I carefully roll to my side, taking her with me so she's snuggled up against me. To keep up the pressure she likes so much, I lay my leg across hers and my arm around her middle.

She snuggles in, and I grit my teeth so I don't complain about her wiggling on my knot again. It's not really a complaint, anyway. It's the sweetest torture I can possibly think of.

"I don't think so," she muses. "That's not how things work. Things happen when they happen."

"Very philosophical."

"You know I read five-ish books a week, right?"

"I have literally never seen you check out a philosophy book."

"It's all philosophy in the end. All about human nature, and how we are and how we show up for each other. Everything I learned about being a person came from books and your family." She lets that hang in the air for a second, then continues, "And that's how the books work. The stories can only happen when they're meant to. Life unfolds because of everything that came before, you know? You are who you are because of everything you've been through. I'm the same. And we're only going to work because of everything behind us now."

I kiss the crown of her head. I don't know how to get closer to her than I already am, but I'm desperate to. I need there to be no space between us, not even a molecule. I want her to consume me, to become the same being at this point. "Those books have a happy ending, Paige?"

She's silent for a second "Some of them," she says. Then, almost shy now, "I think this one will."

Yeah, I think it will, too.

CHAPTER 33
Paige

We spend the rest of the weekend together, most of that time being spent in my nest. Mickey goes out on Saturday to do some shopping, and he shows back up with food and more condoms and yet another Plan B pill for me. Considering that my heat ended a few days ago, I'm probably at an incredibly low risk of getting pregnant, but I appreciate the thought, anyway. He wasn't wrong about the condoms not working great with a knot inflating and deflating.

But on Monday at six-forty in the morning, the little bubble we've found ourselves in bursts. Mickey is still asleep in my nest, the weighted blanket half over him, when I kiss his forehead and climb out. He groans in his sleep, reaching for me, but all he manages to get is my pillow, hauling it into his chest like he refuses to let it go.

I waste time watching him. The sight of him in my nest is a good one. I spent a lot of time thinking I never wanted anyone in my nest; I thought I'd be one of those omegas that kept their own nest separate from everyone else in the pack, should I ever find someone I actually wanted to be with. But with Mickey here, I know I was just waiting for someone to *fit* my nest. Like waiting for the blanket with the right texture and not buying the first "close enough" blanket, I needed the alpha that was actually right for me.

I know he'll have to get up to go to work soon, too. He's been out of work for an entire week, and the summer reading program should be kicking off any day now. He'll be needed there.

I want to be gone before he wakes, though. Honestly, I'm worried if I don't go now we'll end up curled together in my nest longer. Emma told me right after her alphas gave her their mating marks it was a little like this, but this is crazy. He hasn't even bitten me yet, but it's like the world's axis has shifted for us both. We're orbiting each other.

I check his phone to make sure an alarm is set, then set one when it isn't. His phone passcode is still his birthday, which is terrible security, but at least made things easy today.

Then I find paper and leave him a note on the kitchen counter explaining I went into work. I debate for a long moment, but eventually add, *and I really want to see you later.* Too much? Maybe. But I'm not worried about him turning me down.

I don't usually leave my house to work, but today I pull my shit together and put on actual slacks instead of leggings, and a blouse instead of a sweatshirt. I take an extra thirty seconds to make my hair look like I didn't tie it up in the dark. It's still a bun on the top of my head, but I at least attempt to control the fly-aways.

And then I have to get in the fucking car.

I haven't driven my car since my last doctor's appointment. I hate driving, hate everything about it. There is no good reason why I should operate a piece of machinery that weighs thousands of pounds, requires you to manage moving parts and lights and make snap-second decisions, and where the machine can kill people if you mess any of that up.

Unfortunately, Gavin doesn't live in anything even close to a reasonable walking distance. He's two towns away, and if I walked I'd probably get there after dinner. So I'll drive in the early morning, hopefully before too many people are on the road.

The drive is nerve-wracking, but I pull it off, parking horrendously crooked in Gavin's driveway a little after seven-thirty.

My Aunt Lydie opens the door, still wearing her bathrobe. I can hear voices in the kitchen behind her, so I at least know part of the household is awake.

"Paige." She blinks. "This is a surprise."

I bet it is. I haven't seen my aunts and other uncle in years. We don't actually socialize, and while I'm sure they go to the office Christmas party and stuff like that with Gavin, I avoid those like the plague. Drinking, bright lights, loud music, and small talk make me want to run away screaming.

"Is Gavin here?"

"Are you okay?" she asks instead of answering.

"Is Gavin here?" I ask again, not in the mood. Lydie is a nice person, but I don't know her. I came here today for only one thing.

"I'm here, Paige," Gavin says, walking down the hall from the kitchen. He's wearing low-slung pants and nothing else, which makes this whole thing awkward. "I thought I'd see you at some point today, but I thought it'd be a meeting on my calendar. Maybe you'd show up at the office. Never thought I'd see you here."

"Didn't want to wait."

His shoulders slump, and he nods. "Have you eaten?"

No, but I also have no plans to eat here. This isn't a social visit. "I'm fine. Can we talk?"

He nods again. "Lydie, I'll be a bit, okay? Tell the others?"

She squeezes his shoulder before retreating down the hall. "C'mon," he says, not looking at me. "We can talk in my office."

I follow him up the stairs, where he grabs a shirt too big for him hanging over the banister and shrugs it on. Then he turns to the left, which leads to a minimalist home office. He must not work here often, or if he does, he must like a neutral, boring aesthetic.

He slides into the chair behind the desk, gesturing for me to sit on the other side. As soon as I'm seated, he says, "I don't accept your resignation."

"My resignation?" I repeat, trying to make sure I heard right.

"That's why you're here, right? You said you didn't even want to come into the office. I assumed..." He shakes his head. "Well. thank god, then. Far be it for me to put ideas in your head. Why are you here?" He leans forward. "You didn't answer Lydie. Are you okay? Did something happen? Did he do something?"

Was he at the same dinner I was this weekend? "I came here to tell you to go fuck yourself for what you said about Mickey," I tell him. "And then to ask if you have any ideas for how to prevent Samuel from pressing charges."

"Ah." He sits up a little straighter. "And this *go fuck yourself*, how serious is it?"

"You're my boss, and I recognize that you give me accommodations that I'll have a hard time getting other places without a protracted fight. So, not that serious, I guess. I don't have much leverage. I figure I'll say it, and then you and I will go back to only talking about work and only occasionally, because we don't talk that much."

"You can't blame me for looking out for you," he points out. "I don't mean this to be insulting, Paige, but you're not a great judge of character."

"It's harder for me than some other people," I admit. "But I'm actually not as bad as you think. I've just spent my entire fucking life being told I'm bad at it, and being told that every time I judge someone's character, it's wrong. My parents are looking out for me. Samuel is an upstanding guy and the best

316

someone like me can hope for. Mickey is one of the first people to tell me I'm not wrong. That I should trust my instincts."

There's a knock at the door. "We'll be a few minutes," Gavin says, but the door is opening before he finishes, and Wash pokes his head in.

Wash is as big as Mickey almost, incredibly unusual for an omega, and I don't think he ever leaves this home. And it's not in an *omegas love to nest* way, either, or some old-fashioned idea about an omega's place. I think there's something traumatic there, but I've never been told and I don't ask. I know I'm just Gavin's niece, and worse, his hated brother's child. I know it's not my place.

Right now, he's carrying a tray. "Lydie said you both needed to eat," he says, setting the tray on Gavin's desk. There are eggs sunny side up and home fries, a little bottle of ketchup on one side. "And Magda doesn't want her food to get cold, so. Here you go."

"I'm not hungry," I mutter, more petulant than I mean to be, but Wash levels me with a look.

"You come to my house and you're going to eat," he says sternly. "Eat up. Everything else can be solved when you have some food in you. Or do I need to sit here and watch you two eat?"

That sounds even worse, so I take one of the plates off the tray and grab one of the forks Wash brought up.

"Thank you, Wash," Gavin says, taking his hand and kissing it softly before he lets him go. "I'll see you downstairs later."

"Alright then," Wash says, looking us over once more before he leaves the room.

Gavin sighs once the door's closed. "He worries," he murmurs. "He worries about you too, you know."

"Me? He barely knows me."

"Yes, but I talk about you, and he worries. It's what Wash does; he's a worrier. And anyone who comes to his house, he's going to worry about them even more. Eat your eggs; he'll lose it if you don't."

I take a bite, but contrary to his own advice, Gavin doesn't pick up a fork. He watches me for a moment, seeming to study me eating.

"You talk about me?" I ask, needing to break the silence.

"Of course I talk about you."

Is this because we're family? Am I doing it wrong that I barely talk about him ever? I don't have a lot of thoughts or a lot to say. "Why?"

"You're my niece. And my employee, I guess, but first and foremost, you're my niece."

"We don't talk."

"You don't come to dinner," he points out. "You don't come into the office or to holiday parties, which is all fine. But you don't even come to dinner."

"Yeah, well. I know I'm lucky to have this job in some ways, but I don't actually enjoy being a pawn in the petty rivalry you and my father have."

He sits back slowly. "Is that what you think?"

"He thought I should get married and have babies. You encouraged me to go to college, then law school. He wouldn't hire me, you did. Everything you do is to needle at him."

"Have you ever considered it's because I genuinely care about you and have your best interests at heart?"

No. I hadn't considered that, because who outside of the Condors had my best interests at heart when I was growing up? I'd heard Gavin and my father arguing with each other, trading insults and barbs and one-upmanship often enough. It had been easy to see the pattern and conclude I was one more link in that chain.

"Your father is a shitty human being, and so was our father," Gavin says. "That type of behavior is learned, and he learned it like an expert. You never got to meet your grandmother, Paige, which is a shame. She was a lot like you. When you first got diagnosed with autism and I learned it was genetic, a lot of things about my mother started making sense. And my father was awful to her about it all. I couldn't watch that happen again, even as I knew I couldn't stop it."

He leans a little closer when I don't say anything. "I gave you a job because I firmly believe you deserve a job, and I haven't been proven wrong. You're not a pawn between your father and I; you're a person, Paige, and a person I respect very much."

My grandfather died when I was three. From there, my father, the oldest son, had inherited the law firm. And rather than work under his brother, Gavin struck out on his own. I re-evaluate every interaction we had since in a new light. Maybe he wasn't talking to me to make a point to his brother. Maybe he'd invited me around because he wanted to see me.

I'd been so used to being treated like an object, something for my mother to dress up and prime for a future I didn't want and complain about when I wasn't her perfect little doll, something for my father to ignore until I was useful in a business transaction. I guess I never saw that anyone in that world could ever see me as a person.

He sighs, seemingly able to discern my answer without me having to say anything. "That's on me," he admits. "I could have done better. I didn't know how, but I could have tried."

"I don't need a protector," I tell him. "I protected myself. I'm an adult."

"You weren't always an adult, and I know firsthand how hard it can be to protect yourself as a child. Children are vulnerable, Paige, and I know you don't like to hear it, but you were even more so. I was happy when you found your people—I know what a difference it can make. I wouldn't be who I am after all that without my people."

"Mickey is one of those people," I remind him.

320

"Mickey went straight from pissed off to violent last night, and I've seen first hand what the marks of that can do. Everyone in this house has. He was out of control. Has he ever done that to you before, Paige?"

He didn't do it *to* me at all. He did it *for* me, and that's a huge difference. "Mickey's father used to beat the shit out of his mother," I tell him, words coming out fast and a little angry. Angry about what happened, angry that I have to share it, angry that I have to justify myself to him. "Mickey remembers it; he saw it all. And when she took her kids and ran, Mickey learned what it meant to be brave. He's never forgotten it. He idolizes his mom and is his sister's biggest supporter. He's looked out for me for years. He won't stand for omegas being hurt. He let me handle it. He let me fight back. But my words have never been enough because *no one else will speak up for me.* So Mickey solved the problem, and I'm not going to let someone who I'm still not sure even deserves the explanation judge us for it."

He looks at me for a long, long minute. There's a ticking clock somewhere in this office, and it's starting to drive me absolutely crazy when he finally speaks. "Wash told me the same damn thing when I got back here after that. Lydie and Magda agreed. I hear you; I might not like it, but I hear you. I've been going about this wrong, and I apologize. And to prove it, I can get Samuel not to press charges."

All my breath leaves me in a rush, and my chest feels lighter. "How?"

"Your father owes me one last favor. He's been a shitty person his whole life and I bailed him out one too many times. Not in a long time, but still. He won't have forgotten. Tell the truth, he'll probably be glad it's not hanging over his head anymore. I've held onto this one for years. I'll call in my favor, and your father will pressure that little suck-up into keeping his thoughts to himself."

I swallow. "And you'd use it on me?"

If this was anyone but Mickey, I'd tell him not to bother. I'd tell him I'm sure I can solve this by myself, and I'd find a way. But it is Mickey, and even a dismissed assault charge will probably ruin his career. It'd hurt him, too, having that label applied to him, no matter how different it is from his father. I'm not going to risk not being able to get Samuel to not press charges. If Gavin has a sure-fire way, then I'm going to take it.

"I'll take care of it this afternoon," he says. "Consider it, I don't know, a gesture of goodwill? A sign I mean what I say? If we have to start again, Paige, then let's start this way. I'll put my money where my mouth is."

I nod. I don't know what else to do, what else to say. If he wants to be my uncle, then I guess I'll let him. I can try, anyway.

"I'll be back at work tomorrow," I tell him, standing up. "I guess I'm asking for PTO for the rest of the day." My heat leave has now gone a full week, and it's definitely run out.

"I'll see you then. I'll put a meeting on your calendar to get you caught up."

It could be an email, I almost say, but I manage to resist. This is one of those times where people aren't saying what they mean, and Gavin knows full well it could be an email. He wants to talk tomorrow.

If he protects Mickey, then I'll let him have it, so I nod. "See you then."

I walk out of his office and out of the house. Thankfully, no one else stops me or tries to talk to me. I maybe should get to know my aunts and uncles better, but that's not something I'm doing today.

Right now, I only want one thing, and he's at the public library setting up for summer reading.

CHAPTER 34
Mickey

I hated waking up alone this morning.

That's going to be a problem, because even my obsessive ass knows it's too early to ask to move in with Paige. It's obvious that if—*when*—we do move in together, it'll be her place, considering that's where her nest is, but inviting myself in is probably flat-out predatory at this point.

Soon, hopefully. But not yet. For now, I'm going to have to learn to suffer through sleeping alone more nights than not.

I pick up coffee on my way to work, my first cup in over a week, but I know I'm going to need it to get through today. If Paige invites me to stay over more, I'm going to have to ask if she's okay with me adding a coffee maker to her kitchen. I know she doesn't drink it, but I'm not sure if I can successfully go to work without it.

When I use my access badge to let myself into the library's side door forty-five minutes before opening, April is standing by the main circulation desk. She gives me an up-and-down look, eyebrow raised. "You survived, then."

"I like to think I more than survived."

"You finally convince her you're crazy about her?"

"Finally convince yourself she's into you too?" Andre asks from behind me. When I turn, he waves. "Heard your voice. Wanted to make sure you came through unscathed."

"It was... good." *Good* is way too mild a word to describe the last week with Paige, even through the stress of being responsible for her during heat or that clusterfuck of a family dinner. "And yes, Paige and I are dating now."

Andre claps me on the back. "Good for you. Knew you had it in you."

"You look like she put you through the wringer," April notes. "Did the heat just end?"

"We took a few days. It hit her pretty hard. Her health..." I shake my head, because they get the picture without me having to share the details. "All good now."

Probably. Paige went to work this morning, actually left her house—in a *car*—to go to work, and I'm still a little nervous that any intrusion of the real world will break the little bubble we've made for ourselves.

She told me she wants to see me later, though. That has to count for something.

Andre and April no doubt want to ask more, but I'm desperately behind on work, so I go to the children's room and look at everything my team left for me this past week. Today's going to be busy, trying to get everything set up for the upcoming summer reading programming. I can see where everyone stepped in and tried to help, but there are still plenty of gaps to fill.

So most of my morning is spent in the office, which isn't a warm welcome back to work. I much rather be out on the floor with the kids, checking in with my regulars, recommending books to families, but instead I have to contact the ice cream vendor for the kick-off party next Friday, and the petting zoo people for July, and make sure those prizes we ordered will arrive on time because they were back-ordered *again*.

I crack my neck at noon, rolling my shoulders to shake out the stiffness. I have another four hours, and if I'm lucky, I'll get out from under this paperwork hole with time to spare.

And then there's a knock at my office door. I turn around and there's Paige, smiling at me softly and holding a takeout bag in one hand.

"What're you doing here?" I ask, pushing back in my chair so I can go to her.

She frowns. "Am I not supposed to come here? I'm sorry. I should have called."

I shake my head, taking her shoulders in hand and squeezing gently. "Assume you're always welcome wherever I am," I tell her firmly. "I just didn't expect to see you. It's not your normal day. Plus, it sounded like you had a lot of work to do today, considering you went into the office. Did you drive yourself?" I can't remember the last time I saw her drive. I know she *can*, but kind of in the same way I know she knows how to do CPR or operate a fire extinguisher: something I only expect to see in emergency circumstances.

"I did. Drove here too. Which is a mistake, because that means I need to operate a vehicle *again* and I am not looking forward to it," she mutters. "And I didn't work today."

I frown. It makes sense considering she's here at noon, but she said... "You left me a note that you were going into the office."

"I went to Gavin's house," she admits. "I yelled at him a bit. And then we talked." She says *talked* like the word is toxic, and I have to pull her into a hug to hide my smile.

"What'd you two talk about?" I ask her.

"You," she says simply, then pauses. "Us? He wants me to believe that he's always been looking out for me. And I don't know what to think. And Samuel, too, I guess."

"What about Samuel?" If Gavin is telling her that Samuel is a better choice—

"He says my father owes him one last favor, and he'll use it to ensure Samuel doesn't press charges," she tells me, completely derailing my train of thought. "And that's what I wanted from him today, so that's good."

"Thank you for doing that," I tell her, kissing the top of her head. "You don't have to put yourself out to protect me."

She shoves at my chest, but when I go to back off, she grabs at my shirt and doesn't let me go, so I'm assuming the shove was more of a reaction than an actual need for me to stop holding her. "Oh, okay. In which case, you didn't need to protect me from Samuel either."

I growl. "That was absolutely non-negotiable. No one gets to talk to you like that."

She tilts her head back to look up at me and grin that shark grin, and I know I walked myself right into her trap. "Exactly. Glad you understand."

I shake my head but can't help but smile. Fuck, she loves me, doesn't she?

"We should eat before the food gets soggy," she says. "Unless you can't take a break?"

"I can always take a break for you." I wasn't planning on taking a lunch today; there's a lot to get done and not a lot of time to do it in. But Paige coming by changes things. I'll be scrambling to finish all the paperwork later, but I don't give a shit. "We can go to the break room? Or actually, it has fluorescent lights. Is outside in the garden better?"

"Anything is better than fluorescents," she says. "Maybe in the shade?"

"Sounds good. What'd you bring, anyway?"

"Just sandwiches."

"Turkey and swiss, no pickles?" I smile. My girl is nothing if not predictable.

"Yeah. That."

"Sounds perfect. Let's go eat."

There's a big tree in the garden behind the library with a few little benches under it. I love running events out here in the warm weather, and in a few weeks there'll be the absolute chaos of a petting zoo here. But today it's quiet. School has one week left to go before it ends, so there are no children running around at this time of day. It's just Paige and I.

At least, it is until Andre joins us, and then April. I raise an eyebrow, knowing how unlikely it is for us all to take lunch at the same exact time.

Andre grins like the cat who ate the canary. "Hey Paige," he says. "Nice to finally meet you."

"Uh, hi?" she asks, clearly having no idea what's going on.

I'm not surprised. I've never introduced her to these two, and while she's undoubtedly seen them around the library, that's not the type of thing that sticks in Paige's mind.

"We're the ones who've been telling this one to ask you out for ages," Andre continues.

April elbows him in the side. "We wanted to say hi," she says. "We can leave you to your lunch, though."

"No, stay," Paige says after a moment. "I'd like it if you stayed."

I'm not a hundred percent sure she means it—socializing with near strangers never seems high on Paige's priority list—but she doesn't seem put off by them. At the very least, she seems interested in them.

Andre doesn't need further prompting, sitting down on Paige's other side. He leaves a healthy distance between them, but he leans in closer. "So, has this one told you how obsessed he is with you yet?"

She raises an eyebrow and turns to me. "Yeah?"

"You know I'm obsessive," I say.

"*Obsessed*," Andre says, like if he says it slower, it'll have a whole new meaning. "Head over heels."

I think he might be trying to embarrass me, but he's not wrong. I *am* obsessed with Paige. And she seems to like that.

Case in point, she reaches over and squeezes my hand. "I'm kind of obsessed with him too," she admits.

Andre grins at me with the most obvious, shit-eating *I told you so* look I've ever seen, but I can't even say anything, because he definitely did. He's entitled to have that look for the rest of my life, probably.

"So," he says, turning back to Paige and relaxing onto the bench. "I'm going to do weekly genre displays for the teen summer reading program, generate some buzz about books they might not naturally be drawn to, and I figured I'd start with fantasy. Any thoughts on the must-read fantasy books for our teens?"

Paige's eyes light up, and she leans a little closer to him to start expounding on the virtues of probably a dozen books. She begins to talk with her hands, and her voice gets a little faster as she really hits her stride, and Andre just nods and takes notes in his phone, interjecting a comment here and there.

Andre was right. I'm fucking *obsessed* with Paige, in the best possible way, and I know I will be forever.

CHAPTER 35

Paige

I spend the next four days absolutely buried in work. I missed six whole days, so I'm not shocked exactly at how urgent the stack has gotten, but it is overwhelming. I lock myself in my home office, only emerging when Mickey shows back up after work.

He doesn't sleep here every night, but he does stop by every night. We have dinner together and talk about our days, and sometimes even talk about the future. On the nights he stays, we go up to my nest, and I've replaced the body pillow with him. I sleep better when he's here, too.

By Thursday, I've sent myself into a full-on migraine. It's a combination of staring at screens for twelve hours a day for three days straight, skipping lunch most of those days, probably not drinking enough water, and stress. At least I can say I'm sleeping well on the nights Mickey stays.

Mickey coaxes me away from the computer at nine, feeds me grilled cheese, and carries me to my nest, handing me the right pills at the right times and acting like it's nothing. I didn't even know it was possible to feel this way for another person.

On Friday, I get as caught up as possible on my work. Gavin hasn't contacted me since Tuesday, but right before five o'clock, an email from him *dings* in my mailbox that says nothing but *good work this week, as always*, and I swallow. I don't know if I quite trust the innocent, fatherly intentions he told me he has, but some part of me wants to trust it, or at least try. I star the email for later, close out, and make dinner so it's ready for Mickey and I.

On Saturday, we call Emma and let her say *I told you so* for a half hour or so before we actually get a word in edge-wise, which is nice because it's good to know that Emma will be Emma no matter what, and me dating her brother hasn't made anything weird between us.

On Sunday, we have dinner at the Condors. It's not the right weekend for it, but I definitely owe Sherry an explanation and a thank you, and I know Mickey needs to see his mother's reaction to us being together to know it's okay. Sherry gives me the longest hug of my life, and I lean into it, closing my eyes as she squeezes all her love into me.

And then on Monday, I have my neurology appointment. I took the whole day off. Doctor's appointments are always exhausting, and for some reason every doctor's office has terrible, pain-inducing fluorescent lights. I'll need the time after.

And if all goes well, I'll be giving myself a new medication this evening.

Mickey shows up at my door thirty minutes before I need to be at my appointment, just when I'm psyching myself up to drive over. "What're you doing here?"

"I'm going with you to your appointment," he says simply. "Are you ready to go?"

"Why?"

"Because you shouldn't have to be alone at something like that. And if the doc is going to say anything about how to better take care of you, I'd like to know. I need to know. I want to be able to help you, Paige."

I've been managing my own condition for decades now, but I don't say that. It's nice that he wants to help me; I like that he cares enough to want to be a part of this.

"Plus, I know you don't want to drive," he adds, smiling slightly.

"You know me so well."

"Yeah. I do. Do you need anything else before you go?"

I check my bag for the third time, but I already know I have my phone and the tiny little notebook and pen I use to take notes if something important comes up. I shake my head. "I appreciate this."

He wraps an arm around me and gives me a squeeze while I lock my door, kissing the top of my head. "Thank you for letting me come."

The drive isn't bad, and we don't even have to wait in the overly sterile waiting room that long. Dr. James' nurse calls me back quickly, and after she takes my vitals, we're left in the observation room alone.

"How're you feeling?" Mickey asks, sitting in the little chair by the desk. I usually sit there, pathologically avoiding the awkward exam table, but chair space is at a premium with an extra body in the room, so I suck it up and sit on the stupid table, swinging my legs while we wait.

"Okay. Want to get this over with. But I trust Dr. James. This should be easy. Well, as easy as these things ever are."

He opens his mouth to respond, but before he can say anything, there's a knock at the door. "Come in!" I call, and Dr. James lets herself in.

"Good morning, Paige. Oh, and guest."

"This is Mickey. My, uh, boyfriend." We haven't discussed labels. I think it's the most accurate one, but who knows what he thinks? He doesn't correct me.

"Good to meet you, Mickey." She sits at her little rolling stool by the computer. "It's okay if we talk in front of him?"

"Yeah, it's fine. Mickey's heard all this stuff. He wants to hear what we have to say because he wants to be able to take care of me when I'm not doing great."

She gives Mickey a small smile and a nod. "That's a good sign right there. Alright, with that out of the way: I see you're here to discuss the Nalcodin today?"

Dr. James is a beta in her late fifties, I'd guess. She's been doing this a long time and is no-nonsense without sacrificing warmth. She sees me and listens to me when I'm here. Considering the amount of doctors I've seen in my life, that's not that common.

"Yeah. The insurance should cover it now." I hope we don't have to discuss *why* the insurance will cover it.

Sadly, I don't get my wish. "So, I can tell them that you tried their supposed *heat cure* and nothing came of it?" she asks.

"It made her sicker," Mickey says. "She was laid out for a while after."

Dr. James nods slowly. "Sadly, going off your medication for any point of time can cause fluctuations, rebound headaches—it's not recommended. I'm sorry you went through that."

"Oh, no, I took my meds the whole time. Well, everything except the suppressant, obviously. Mickey made sure, and he was good about it."

She looks at him again, taking him in slowly. "Impressive. And a guy worth keeping around, Paige. I imagine the destabilizing hormones, paired with the inadequate sleep and hydration and nutrition, didn't do you any favors. So, we can safely say it hasn't cured you. How have you been outside of the heat?"

"Fine."

"You were feeling so crappy on Thursday that we ate dinner in the dark," Mickey retorts.

I open my mouth and close it again. Is that where the bar is? "I feel like that on a regular basis," I point out. "That's normal."

Mickey doesn't look like he likes that answer much, but before he can say anything, Dr. James interrupts and says, "Well, the goal would be for the Nalcodin to minimize how much time you spend like that. Did you take the Imitrex on Thursday, Paige?"

"Caught it too late. It wasn't helpful." I'd been so hyper-focused on work that I'd missed the ideal window, and the medicine hadn't been able to touch the pain by the time I stopped to process what my body actually needed.

I tense slightly, half expecting a scolding for that. I've definitely had doctors scold me before. Never mind that pain management isn't a precise science—as much as I'd like it to be—and it can vary from body to body, day to day. Never mind that my autism can make it hard for me to process what my body feels until it's too late. They'd like me to be a picture-perfect patient who they can just cure.

Dr. James doesn't say anything, nodding slowly. "It happens, and I'm glad you had someone there with you to help you through it. Alright, I think you're a great candidate for the Nalcodin. I know we talked about it in the last appointment, but I just have to cover my bases: it's a prefilled syringe that needs to be injected into your thigh muscle once monthly. I recommend you pick a regular day and stick with it. You can inject it at home by yourself, and it's perfectly safe to do so; however, if

337

that's a struggle, then we can schedule monthly appointments to do it here. The medication should minimize the number of migraine-level spikes you get, and paired with the Imitrex, it should hopefully make those manageable. But the biggest hope is that it will also help manage your day to day headache. The goal would be to have much milder pain, and even possibly pain-free periods. Understand that no one can guarantee this, but the research is promising."

I nod along, having heard all this before. I haven't had a pain-free period since I was a kid. The idea sounds almost unbelievable, and it's a little too much to let myself hope for just yet.

"Will the injection hurt?" Mickey asks.

Dr. James turns to him. "All injections hurt. But the syringe is actually gentler than the auto-injector some other injectable drugs come loaded in, so as long as she can handle seeing the needle, this is the less painful option. It's no worse than your flu shot."

That's not so bad. I can handle a flu shot.

"Alright, Paige, you still on board?" she asks, turning back to me.

"Yeah. Of course."

"Good. Only one last thing. You can't be on this drug if you're pregnant. In fact, if you ever plan to get pregnant, you have to come off it months before you even start trying. And, since you just had a heat and everything, I need to run a pregnancy test." She makes a face. "It kind of feels like the insurance tried to set you up for failure on this one."

"We were careful," I say. "We used three forms of birth control. Mickey made sure I took my pill every day, and we used condoms, and when they weren't super effective, he got me Plan B too." I try to say it like it's matter-of-fact, like I'm just reporting information, but my chest is getting tighter.

What if I'm pregnant? What if we beat all the odds and three forms of birth control aren't enough? They do say your heat is the most fertile time for any omega, and that getting pregnant is never easier. I can't be pregnant. I can't do it.

Mickey is out of his chair and in front of me before I can get a deep breath. He pulls me into a hug so tight it resets my brain. "Hey, you're okay," he murmurs. "It's all okay."

"Mickey, I can't—"

"If you're pregnant, we'll handle it," he says firmly.

"Mickey, I *won't* be pregnant. I know you love kids, but I can't do it. The idea of having a baby inside me and my body changing, and then the crying and the no sleep and the spit-up and sticky hands—it's a nightmare. I can't handle it."

"I know," he says, releasing one arm from around me so he can tilt my chin up. "When I said we'll handle it, we'll handle it. We'll go to a clinic, and I'll be right there. If you're pregnant, we'll end it and we'll get you your medication. And I promise, you won't have to worry about this ever again, right? I'm going to take care of it."

339

I force myself to draw deep breaths, then nod. Alright. We'll handle this. We're going to be okay.

"Whenever you're ready, Paige, I'll need a pee test," Dr. James says quietly. "It'll kill two birds with one stone; a pregnancy test, just in case, and we can test for traces of heat hormones still in your system if the insurance gets uppity about proof."

Mickey doesn't let me go right away, and I don't want to be let go. Dr. James waits patiently while my world quiets back down and comes to center.

When my brain is clear again, I take the proffered cup and follow the directions down the hall to the restroom, peeing in the cup and putting it in the little slot in the wall for testing. Then I go back to the exam room, prepared for an awkward few minutes of sitting around, waiting for the results.

When I open the door, Mickey's deep in conversation with Dr. James. I listen for a second, but apparently he's grilling her for every migraine-based tip she can give him. He's not going to be told anything new, but I appreciate that he wants to know anyway.

She's telling him about the importance of adequate protein in my diet when there's a knock at the door. Dr. James gets up to answer it, and someone hands a paper in. She reads it, and before the door is even fully closed, says, "Test is negative. No pregnancy."

A thousand pound weight has been lifted off my shoulders. "Thank god," I mutter, pressing a hand to my chest. My heart is going a thousand miles an hour.

"Hear that? You're all good, Paige. It's all good," Mickey says.

"It is," Dr. James agrees. "Do you want me to send the prescription to your usual pharmacy?"

CHAPTER 36
Mickey

I can't believe that the culmination of everything Paige has been going through is in one tiny pharmacy bag.

I can't believe we got it today. For some reason, I expected this medication to be so exotic they'd have to custom order it or something, and that we'd wait days or weeks. But the prescription was ready by the time we made it to the pharmacy, and now it's in a little bag in Paige's hand as we walk into her house.

Honestly, that makes me a little angrier. Paige jumped through hoops for this, made herself sick, put herself in a position where she felt vulnerable and out of control. Surely that should make this treatment difficult to obtain, something rare and special. But they had it in stock.

When we pull up at her house, she takes the pharmacy bag, still so small despite the fact that it contains the syringe, instructions, and a few alcohol swabs. I pick up the sharps container the doctor's office gave us and follow her inside.

Paige clutches the bag like someone's going to steal it from her. "I'm going upstairs," she tells me shortly, looking over her shoulder after she kicks off her shoes.

"Want me to join you?" I ask, wanting to make sure. Sometimes Paige needs alone time. I don't want my obsessed ass to run right over her because I didn't take a second to check in.

"Please." She clutches the bag tighter.

"Give me two seconds," I promise, taking off my own shoes.

She nods, retreating up the stairs.

When I get to her room, she's seated in her nest, the needle in her hand. She's still fully dressed, sitting and staring at the needle.

"Do needles freak you out?" I ask, putting the sharps container on her nightstand.

She shakes her head. "What if it doesn't work?" I hear what she's not saying, the little hitch in her voice. What if she jumped through all these hoops and it's for nothing?

I can't make her promises. She's done way more research about this than I have, and talked to the doctor more times. She's lived this. She knows full well that it might not work.

And if that happens, then I'll comfort her when we get there. But for now, I step into her nest, crouching down in front of her. "You won't know until you try it. Can I?" I ask, extending my hand for the syringe.

She holds it for a long second, then gives it to me. "Thanks, honey," I murmur, looking at the thin little needle in my hand.

Dr. James said this will hurt less than the auto-injector as long as we follow the instructions, but I'm wishing we had the auto injector right about now. This seems so flimsy.

"Can you take your pants off for me?" I ask, shaking my head. "How you're still wearing leggings in this weather, I have no idea."

"They're comfortable," she mutters, raising her hips as she rolls them down her legs to expose those perfect thighs to me. All that walking has given her truly fantastic legs.

I pull out the instructions from the little bag, scanning them quickly even though the doctor went over them with us not even two hours ago. I wipe down the spot on her thigh with the little alcohol pad, then line up the needle.

"Feel free to squeeze my shoulder or something if it hurts," I tell her.

"I've done like a hundred blood draws in my life. I can handle a little needle stick."

"Alright, tough guy," I smile at her snark, then use my free hand to hold her thigh steady and press the needle into her muscle with the other, depressing the plunger slowly until it's all emptied into her skin.

I pull out the needle, being careful not to wiggle it around any. That's what Dr. James said would leave a bruise if we weren't careful, and Paige doesn't need any more pain. "There," I murmur, looking up at her. "All done. Your first dose."

She bites her lip and looks down at me. "All that for that, huh?"

I carefully reach out of the nest to deposit the empty needle in the sharps container. We'll have to find a better place to store it later, but for now, I want to get back to Paige as quickly as possible. "All of that for that," I agree.

She's still staring at the injection site, her leggings around her knees. She looks lost now, and I know how she feels. She worked so hard for this, and now it's done, and she doesn't even know if it worked.

I kneel back in front of her and run one hand down the outside of her thigh, careful not to touch the injection site. There's a single drop of blood on her skin, but it seems to have stopped. I did a halfway decent job with the injection, then, and I'm grateful. "Does it hurt?"

"No."

"Need a bandaid?" She shakes her head, so I gently lift her leg, bending down at the same time so I can press a kiss to the spot.

Her breath hitches. "What're you doing?"

I kiss the spot again, firmer this time. "I don't know," I tell her. "I'm so fucking in love with everything about you, Paige. You're brave and strong and determined, and I'm proud of you for fighting for yourself. And I don't want you to hurt ever, but I promise I'll be here when you do hurt, and I'll be here to help with your injections if you want that." I kiss her thigh again. "Mostly I just love you. That okay?"

"More than okay," she whispers.

"Good." I kiss her knee this time, still looking at her, watching her face. Her eyes slide closed. "Still okay?"

The doctor did say the meds could possibly make her feel crappy this first time. She read off the whole list of side effects, and they seem to have freaked me out far more than they did Paige.

"I'm fine."

"Let me know if that changes, alright?"

"You'll know, considering it's most likely going to make me puke if it does anything. It's been, what, a week and a half since I last puked on you?"

"One, it wasn't on me. And two, I am more than ready to hold your hair whenever you puke for the rest of your life."

She tilts her head. "That's actually really romantic."

I grin, pressing it into her thigh so she doesn't see it. Of course it is. "I know. Can I take these leggings off, Paige?"

"Mhm." I roll them the rest of the way off, discarding them outside her nest. She's already tugging her shirt off, and I let her, but I take it from her when it's off, tossing it with one hand while running the other over her stomach, watching her head tilt back, exposing the long, lean line of her throat.

I'm going to bite her there one day, putting my mark in the crook of her neck. Honestly, it's a fight not to do it right this moment; I already know I'm going to spend eternity with her.

I'm not going to change my mind. I'd be fucking honored to have her tell the rest of the world that I'm her alpha.

But no, not tonight. When we do that, she'll be ready, and it'll be special.

"Can you get the condoms?" I ask lowly, watching her open her eyes and take a second to sort through what I asked. "I'll schedule that doctor's appointment as soon as possible, Paige." After watching her freak out at the idea that there was a remote possibility that she might be pregnant, it's increasingly obvious that I need to take care of this. I want to be able to fill her up like she wants, but for now, I watch her reach for the condoms while I shed my clothes, because protecting her comes before everything else.

She picks up my discarded shirt absently, shoving it into the edge of her nest. What she wants with it, I can't say, but she can have whatever of mine she wants. I kiss her, because I can, because I want to, because I need to prove to her exactly how much I want her. I'm seconds away from bending her backward and pressing her into the mattress when I remind myself to slow down.

I gentle the kiss and unhook her bra, dropping it to the side. Then I take her hair out of its bun, doing my best not to tug, and watch it cascade around her, a perfect halo of dark waves. "Lay back, honey," I tell her, and she does, eyes wide and trusting as she looks up at me, head resting on her pillow and hair spilling everywhere.

I work her panties down her hips, then shed the last of my clothes and fish around for the condom, opening it quickly and putting it on. I fucked her like this during her heat, but I need us both to remember this one. I need this to be special.

"So fucking pretty for me," I tell her. "Can you put your legs around my hips, pretty girl?" She does, holding me like a vise. I reach over and stroke along her calf, just enough to get her to relax slightly, then line myself up and push into her.

Her eyes roll back. "Fucking perfect," I groan, hands gripping the sheets by her head tighter to gain some modicum of control. "So goddamn good."

"Mickey—"

"Yeah, pretty girl? You feel good?"

"Feel full."

"Good full?"

"Always with you."

I can't help it, leaning down to kiss her tenderly, needing to show her how absolutely full of love for her I am. I hope she understands. I hope she feels it.

I thrust into her tight heat, letting her feel every inch of me, swallowing her groans and whimpers until she starts to squeeze around me, the little pulses of her pussy nearly driving me over the edge early.

"That's it, honey," I tell her, pulling back enough so I can see her. She's holding my biceps now, nails digging in enough to leave marks that I'll probably spend too long looking at tomorrow. "Fuck, you're perfect, aren't you, Paige? So damned perfect, I love you, I need you to know that, need to make you feel good—" I'm babbling, saying whatever thought comes to mind first, but Paige continues to spiral higher, her moans breathy, her nails digging in deeper, her pussy drenched around me. "Come for me, honey. Milk me dry so I can fill you like you want. Let me fill you up."

That sends her over the edge, and I kiss her again, swallowing her cries as her pussy strangles my cock, pulling my orgasm out of me in a way I have no hope of resisting, even if I wanted to.

I press kisses to every inch of her face, then her neck and the top of her chest. I'm putting too much of my weight on her again, but she doesn't ask me to move. If anything, she makes a happy little contented sigh, and settles deeper into the mattress under me.

"You doing okay?" I ask. I mean about me on top of her. But I also mean the meds, and her head in general. And hell, I mean us too. I know this has been a lot.

"So good," she agrees, eyes slipping closed as she relaxes, completely boneless, under me.

Epilogue: Paige
Seven months later

Today is a bad day.

I have them sometimes. Nalcodin has been a viable treatment for me, thankfully. It helps manage the worst of the pain, and it makes most days more bearable, but no drug is perfect. I'll never be cured.

There's been a lot of big changes going on lately. Between preparing for Emma's babies' imminent arrival and Mickey and I talking about moving in together and Gavin wanting to talk to me every single day about taking on more responsibility at the firm—"Because I value your input, Paige, and you're a highly qualified part of my team"—there's been a lot to adjust to. I know that having to make adjustments like that sends my mind into overdrive, and the stress can trigger a nasty flare up, which explains exactly where I am now.

What hasn't changed in my life is Mickey. Yes, we've been talking about him moving in here, and that'll be a change, but not a big one. He spends most nights here already, and my nest is complete only when he's in it. I found a person who doesn't feel like work and who only makes my life better.

Mickey's there whenever I have flare-ups. He's also there to drive to the pharmacy and inject my meds for me. I could do it, but it's always this quiet, peaceful moment between us.

He's there when I want to go to Molly's for ice cream and knows without asking what I want for dinner. He'll read his own book while I read mine, but now I usually do so with my legs thrown over his lap, and sometimes he'll squeeze my ankle in this comforting way I like. He's there when we go to his mom's for dinner and when Gavin is stressing me out and when I have a bad day at work and when I'm lying around in my nest.

And he's here today, when I feel like shit.

"Alright, I got a drink for you," he says, voice quiet as he walks into the bedroom. The lights are out entirely, but he navigates his way around deftly. "I have the water, but if you're up for it, you should try the Gatorade. I think you could use the electrolytes."

I hate Gatorade, and he knows it. "Noოo."

"It's the red one." The only semi-tolerable one. I pause, considering. The electrolytes might actually make me feel a little better, and I should start replacing what I already threw up earlier.

"Give it to me." I force myself to sit up, and Mickey hands it over along with an Imitrex pill. I haven't looked at the clock once, but I trust him to have timed my doses correctly. Mickey knows all my medications inside out at this point.

I swallow the pill, forcing myself to down some of the Gatorade. "Water now," I say, and he hands it over, allowing me to wash down the gross aftertaste of Gatorade.

"Thank you, honey," he murmurs, like I've done him a favor. "Better or worse than earlier?"

"About the same."

"Alright then. Think you can sleep for a bit?"

"No, we're supposed to go shopping. Emma's baby shower is *Saturday*. We need to get stuff. The twins deserve presents."

There's a depression in the nest as he enters, and I feel the warmth of his hands on me through the blanket, tugging me slightly so I'm laying next to him, sheltered into his side. "Let's be real. We're going to go to a bookstore and clear out the picture book section. And then we'll add in a gift card for a baby store or something so Emma, the picky princess, can get whatever she wants. It's not going to take long, and it's no reason for you to go to a mall today."

"Hate this," I mutter, because he's right and a mall would make me a thousand times worse right now.

His hand strokes through my hair. "I know, honey. But you'll probably feel better tomorrow, and we can make new plans then."

"Sorry," I mumble, even though I know he doesn't want to hear it. Some habits die hard.

"No sorries. It is what it is. Now, you didn't answer; think you can sleep for a bit?"

"Will you lie down with me?"

"Of course. Don't even have to ask," he says, and then he moves so he's laying down too. I reach over, touching him, feeling the soft clothes he's wearing. He's not dressed to go out. He'd already known I wasn't going to be up for our plans.

"C'mere, honey," he mutters, moving us so I'm lying on my side and he has an arm and a leg over me, squishing me like I like and holding me close like he needs. He buries his face in my neck, his warm breath fanning over the place where I'm probably going to let him bite me soon, making my whole body go soft and liquid.

We haven't had that conversation yet, but I want it. I've dreamed about it a few times. I'm going to tell him soon.

We both work to pull the weighted blanket over us, and then I let my eyes slide closed, relaxing entirely into his embrace.

I've learned to accept that there's no miracle cure. I'm never going to be healthy, and I'll always have days like today. But they don't seem so unmanageable anymore. Maybe it's that they're few and far between now, or maybe it's Mickey and his patience and the way he holds me.

He kisses the back of my head. "Sleep, Paige. I got you." I know he does, and I let myself slip into the blissful relief of sleep in his embrace.

Looking for more?

Get an exclusive Paige and Mickey bonus scene by subscribing to my newsletter!

A Final Note

If you never heard of NDPH before this book, you're not alone. It's a rare condition that causes constant pain and is notoriously difficult to treat. Some people find success with certain migraine medications, but many do not, leaving them with pain that is essentially untreatable. NDPH can resolve, but for most people, it never does. Having chronic pain means adjusting to a new normal and re-building your world around what your body will tolerate.

If you see yourself in Paige, or just want to learn more, I encourage you to do some research. A good place to start is the Cleveland Clinic or the American Migraine Foundation.

Having chronic pain of any type can often be lonely and isolating. If any part of Paige's experience resonates with you, I see you. Your experience is valid, and you deserve the same compassion, love, and support Paige finds.

Thank you for reading.

Also by Addison James

The Crae Romance Series

Callum

Bryce

Heath

Celia

Silas

Estrid

The Supernatural Christmas Series

A Werewolf for Christmas

A Recipe for Love

Standalones

Dragon's Treasure

About the author

Addison James is a romance book author from New England. They are obsessed with all things mythical, mystical, and magical. A lifelong fantasy reader, that evolved to fantasy romance as they grew up. Addison always has a story to tell and is excited to introduce you to their world of fantasy romance.